TRINITY BOOKS

TWELVE DOORS

TWELVE DOORS

In as one person and out as another, twelve brave people looking out for each other.

LES JONES

with MICHAEL POWELL and STEVE EGGLESTON

Copyright © 2023 Les Jones

All rights reserved. No part of this book may be reproduced, stored in any retrieval system, or transmitted in any form or by any means, electronic, mechanical, photocopying, recording, or otherwise, without express written permission of the author or publisher.

The moral right of the author has been asserted.

This is a work of fiction. Names, characters, businesses, events and incidents are the products of the author's imagination. Any resemblance to actual persons, living or dead, or actual events is purely coincidental.

First published in 2023

ISBN: 9798851336997

For the 19,000 on-call firefighters here in the UK, and their on-call firefighter colleagues worldwide.

Preface

12 Doors is a fictitious novel with more than a hint of factualisation and is dedicated to the 19,000 or so, on-call or retained firefighters who serve here in the UK. These brave men and women are part of a special family of emergency service staff who give up so much of their free time to respond to an alerter system activated by fire service control room staff up and down the UK, 24/7/365.

My local fire station is around 70 years old and during this time many things have changed within the on-call fire service here in the UK. New equipment, risk assessments, health and safety to name a few, but some things remain the same, such as bravery, commitment and responding to help those in need within the local community, at any time during the day or night.

Many on-call firefighters have normal jobs, some are self-employed, some are stay-at-home parents, some are unemployed, and they come from all walks of life and in all shapes and sizes. Fire, risks and danger doesn't discriminate. These brave men and women volunteers are a vital part of the emergency services family, both here in the UK but also globally, as many countries have on-call or volunteer firefighters.

Some get injured whilst on duty and some have sadly died at incidents. Their training is very realistic and professional and when called to serve they simply get the job done with great personal risk to themselves with dignity, courage, dedication and determination to win the fight. They are all part of a noble profession. They often become close friends on and off duty. Crews are paid for the hours they work when called out, and often miss out on family and social events, due to being on call. Crews carry a pager and have 5 minutes to get to their fire station when called out or mobilised by their fire control room colleagues.

To the general public, in areas where these fire stations are located (and that's about 60% of the UK), they are the fire service. During research into *12 Doors*, many members of the public who I spoke with about the retained on-call fire service, had no idea or knowledge that only 5 or 10 minutes prior to the fire appliance attending an incident – and it could be anything – the crews were doing normal everyday life things either at home, in work, or even out shopping with their partners and children. One retained firefighter told me that he even had to leave his haircut mid-cut at the barbers to attend a fire call out.

The crews must never lose their cool and remain calm and in control when faced with chaos and dealing with incidents ranging from life threatening to the comical.

Most retained fire stations are in rural areas or small to medium urbanised areas and towns. Some work alongside and support whole-time or full-time fire station crews, as the training is the same whether you are a full-time or an on-call firefighter. Some on-call fire stations answer 50 or so incidents a year, others can attend over 800 incidents a year.

My journey to become a published author with *12 Doors* started many years ago and was an itch that I simply needed to scratch. I attended many incidents as a police officer with the Fire Service. It wouldn't have been possible without the help and support of many other people. Firstly, to my wife and children who suffered the pains of me constantly going on about this book project I had, called *12 Doors*. They listened and nodded frequently in support. Later they would encourage me to take it further as the narrative and incidents progressed on my project wall in my daughter's old bedroom.

Thank you to the many others who assisted, such as Mr Colin Cross who I met whilst he worked in a support role at a local major hospital. Colin was a retired on-call firefighter with whom I shared my ideas, and he produced all the technical fire operations information surrounding the incidents.

Sadly, Colin suddenly took ill in December of 2021 and passed away. I was devastated when I found out over the Christmas period and I attended Colin's funeral in early 2022, and it was a fitting tribute to Colin that members of the North Wales Fire and Rescue Service, NWFRS, were present and paying their respects to him. It is with the consent of Mrs Cross and her family that Colin's valuable input into *12 Doors* has been recognised. RIP Colin.

Others involved in the support and development of *12 Doors* are Ruth Bateman from my local Fire and Rescue Service, for her support in allowing me to attend on-call drill nights, fire station visits, breathing apparatus drills within the BA training building, crew interviews and generally accommodating all my requests. This support and that of senior management at North Wales is an endorsement of the valuable work the on-call firefighters play in society.

Many others have chipped in with help and support, such as Qasim and Dave from HA Creations in Rhyl, who took some great *12 Doors* fire images one night in the Autumn of 2022, raising so much interest that night that even the Police and Coast Guard were called to see what we were up to. Thanks also to them for the great cover photograph.

Also, my friends Wyn and Richard for the photography session at a fire station and the support and interest from the many Facebook friends.

Someone recently asked me 'Where exactly is Stockwood on Sea?', I replied, 'It's everywhere and all around us and in every seaside town, city and resort in the UK.'

Read more about *Twelve Doors* on its dedicated website, https://www.12doors.info.

Les Jones

Fire Crew

WM   Leah Walsh (Watch Manager)
CM   John Turnbull (Crew Manager)
FF   Lee Stones
FF   Chelsea Schofield
FF   Matt Dolan
FF   Alan Morgan
FF   Jordan Powell
FF   Steven Jones
FF   Ricky Worthington
FF   Raj Hussain
FF   Mike Williams
FF   Sandi Weston

Fire engine call signs: Sierra Whiskey- SW01. SW02.

Prologue

05:40 Friday 6 December 1991

When Leah Walsh was 14 years old, she delivered newspapers in the dark. During the winter, she loved being woken early by her alarm clock and wiping her finger through the condensation on the inside of her metal-framed bedroom window. After splashing her face with cold water, she would quickly dress and stroke the dog to stop her from barking with excitement. Then she stepped outside, where she could imagine she was the only person awake in the whole world.

She enjoyed cycling from house to house, puffing small clouds of breath into the cold air, challenging herself to improve on her time, while everyone around her slept. Every morning felt like a tiny adventure. A few early risers would have their bathroom lights on, but other than that she was completely alone. She even got a kick out of battling the elements – the rain, wind and cold. She knew she wasn't a normal child!

One typical December morning, she was pedalling hard up a farm track, well away from the streetlights on the main road. It was pitch black, so she used her purple LED torch to illuminate the road ahead. As she rode further upwards, she became aware of an orange glow coming from the other side of the field, but the curvature of the landscape prevented her from seeing its cause.

After another minute of climbing, she was able to see over the brow of the hillock. A huge barn was on fire. The entire roof was ablaze. Bright orange flames shot out of the gable window and clawed a path ever upwards, as if trying to reach the stars. Flames were escaping through every horizontal slat below the gable window and the dazzling glow inside shone behind the vertical slats on the other side, so that the entire skeletal structure of the building appeared in sharp silhouette.

It was as beautiful as it was terrifying. There must have been two hundred tonnes of hay inside the barn and she guessed the flames were at least ten metres high. Even though she was a safe distance away, she could feel waves of heat, she could hear the crackling of the flames and smell the thick acrid smoke that was billowing into the air and being blown in her direction.

She counted three fire engines, two police cars and an ambulance. Two hoses were trained on the barn and another on nearby outbuildings and trees, but it was obvious that this was a matter of extinguishing the fire and preventing it from spreading further, rather than trying to save the structure, which was beyond help.

Leah stared at the conflagration in awe. There was so much human activity going on, of which moments ago she had been completely unaware. She felt like crying, not in fear but in wonder at the sheer magnitude of the scene she was privileged to be witnessing, with all these grown-ups busy doing their serious and dangerous jobs, completely unnoticed while the town slept.

Later that year, three firefighters visited her school to

give a demonstration about fire safety. She stayed behind and spoke to them. She asked them about the barn fire and they said it had been caused by a chainsaw throwing out sparks, but she had been surprised to learn that the most common cause of hay fires was too much moisture. That was weird, but it piqued her interest. Clearly, there was a lot more to firefighting than she had imagined. She signed up for a guided school tour of the station and its equipment and met some more of the retained crew.

Even then, she had a sense that the barn fire and those three firefighters had ignited a spark inside her. But she couldn't have predicted, that over the next thirty years, that tiny glint could grow hot enough to cast her future and temper her destiny.

Chapter One

13:00 Sunday 17 March 2019

Leah Walsh closed her eyes and tried to suppress the nausea that was threatening to rise again in her chest. She breathed in and out deeply whilst gently moving her head in small circles – first clockwise, then anticlockwise. As she exhaled for the fifth time, noisily through her dry mouth, she opened her eyes and looked around the now over-familiar A&E waiting room. There was nothing new to see: the same custard yellow walls, pistachio green linoleum, rows of tubular steel chairs and at the far end, a semi-circular reception office painted electric blue.

It was too hot. Dry air. Prickly heat. She could smell disinfectant mixed with the sweet hospital odour of unwellness. She shared the space with eighteen people she hoped were less sick than her. She knew there were eighteen because she had counted them. Several times. The word *triage* kept popping unbidden into her head. *Triage. Triage.* Earworm. And now her ears felt wrong. *Triage.* Bloody air conditioning. She swallowed hard to try to equalize the air pressure but that just made things worse. Eventually, her right ear became completely blocked. *This is ridiculous*, she thought. *This isn't an aeroplane. I hope it's not another symptom.* Two brusque clicks of her jaw and . . . momentary relief. The air bubble dissipated with a satisfying pop, and things felt relatively normal again, apart from the pulsing headache that had dogged her on and off for a week. It felt as if a small child was hammering at the base of her skull with a steak tenderiser. She'd maxed out on over-the-counter painkillers and hadn't slept properly for 72 hours, which was why she had finally dragged herself into A&E . . . *yesterday morning.*

A rangy youth in his early twenties carefully manoeuvred himself onto the seat at the end of her empty row, slid his aluminium crutches carelessly underneath and then immediately busied himself with his mobile phone. He was wearing shiny white joggers, with one leg cut short to accommodate a plaster cast that swathed his entire leg from ankle to crotch. He was fizzing with nervous energy. His good leg bobbed up and down as the ball of his foot stimmed against the floor whilst his plastered leg, in total contrast, rested stolidly like a fallen Roman pillar. Five mottled sausages brazenly poked out of the end.

She quickly decided that Number Nineteen wasn't a threat, at least not in the sense of being ahead of her in the queue. He was a sorry sight for sure, but he didn't appear to be racked with pain or need urgent medical attention. His now complete absorption in the seven-inch screen in his left hand indicated a tacit familiarity with his restricted mobility, whilst his constant sniffing and the relentless jouncing of his other leg – as if operating a demented potter's wheel – told a different story. He could have powered his phone all day long with a fraction of the nervous energy expended by that wayward limb.

Maybe he was having his plaster removed today. She imagined him staring gormlessly at his phone while a nurse diligently got busy with an angle grinder.

Gormlessly. Without gorm. Triage. Her daughter had broken her arm when she was four years old. Leah remembered how scared little Katie had been when the nurse had produced what looked like a circular saw and how she had demonstrated that it couldn't cut skin because it only used vibrations. Ultrasonic. Leah had asked the nurse to press it against her own arm to show how harmless it was. It was very clever, like a magic trick – nibbling through the hard plaster like it was melba toast but incapable of harming human flesh. Little Katie's tears had turned to giggles when the nurse finally removed her plaster, because her 'saw' was so ticklish. Ten years on, she could still recall with gratitude how gentle and patient that nurse had been.

Right now, if someone held a gun to her head and made her guess what the young man did for a living, she would have to say either unemployed or drug dealer – not just by his appearance but it was a safe bet given the area and his demographic. Neither had he broken his leg playing doubles at the tennis club. It was either a football injury, or most likely his reward for escaping from the police or landing badly after spraying his tag on the roof of the underground car park on West Parade.

Then she noticed a tattoo on his neck – a black line drawing of a frog made of two hexagons. Except, she knew it wasn't a frog. The rest of the tattoo disappeared beneath his shirt. She recognised it, only because it was a common sight around these parts, not because of a deep knowledge of psychoactive chemicals: it was half of the structural formula of MDMA. Ecstasy. *Molly.* Even if this young man didn't sell drugs, he was self-evidently one of their biggest fans.

His plaster cast was dappled with the obligatory scribbled messages from friends and family, but she couldn't help noticing that the entire front of his thigh was covered with Chinese hanzi – six rows of three. They looked rather beautiful. Someone had applied them with a fresh green sharpie. She wondered who had written this, and what it said. Was it a poem, a positive affirmation or a dirty joke? Or a restaurant menu? Maybe it was just a mundane message: *Hope you get well soon.* No, it was more substantial than that and, given its prominence, the author clearly knew him. She looked away. Best not be caught staring at this twitchy, volatile youth.

Chapter Two

'Hey, Father. What's the wevver lake up dair?'

Retired priest, Philip Jones blinked slowly in the early-afternoon sun and took a deep breath. *Sweet Jesus, not now.* He didn't think he had it in him to smile politely and pretend he hadn't heard that joke more times than he'd administered the seven sacraments.

'Well, hello down there.' He aimed a weak smile at the three hoody-clad teens standing astride their bicycles, a gob's distance from him across the ALDI car park in the West End. Black scarves hid the bottom half of their faces. They were probably fifteen years old, but they looked small for their age, their growth stunted by traumatic domestic circumstances, drink and drug abuse and a lifetime of junk food and sugary drinks.

His light-hearted reply was intended to be self-deprecating, continuing the joke about his height, but he could see by their clenching fists, that he had badly misjudged the situation.

'Fuck off, yoo Slender Man.'

'I'm sorry. Do I know you?'

'No, but we know everyfing a bow yoo.'

'I . . . I think you've got the wrong person.'

'Don't fink so. My dad says you're a fucking nonce.'

'Look, I don't want any trouble, son. So, I'm going to

take my shopping home—'

'Don't call me dat. I'm not your son. Eugh paedo, you *are* a paedo. Stay away from me. I'll fucking shank yoo.' The lad lowered his arm to reveal a glint of heavily etched metal, partially obscured by a grubby sleeve.

Philip shuffled in a wide arc past the unholy triune, affording them plenty of space. He hoped the matter was settled and that they wouldn't follow him. The other two youths hadn't said a word, but suddenly they burst out laughing. That was a good sign. He hoped it meant that this unpleasant exchange had reached its natural conclusion. *Better take the long way home. In case they follow me.* When he was thirty yards away, one of the two previously silent lads shouted, 'Nonce'. And that, it would appear, was the end of that.

Under normal circumstances, Philip would have taken the quickest route home, but today he hurried along the West Parade. He felt safer on the wide promenade, where the sight lines were better. Also, there were more CCTV cameras along this route.

He passed The Range and then walked for another ten minutes past a dozen yellow brick seafront hotels. He kept up the brisk pace and enjoyed filling his lungs with the salty sea air, even though he couldn't see the sea or the beach from the road. He passed a couple of near-deserted amusement arcades, with their forlorn blinking and plinking, followed by the Casino Lounge, Harkers Arcade and Lazer Zone and then when he reached the new Sun Centre building, he turned off and circled back over the Vale Road bridge towards Princess Street heading for his social housing estate.

As Philip walked, his mind insisted on drifting back to

the worst moment of his life. It had happened nearly two years ago on Saturday, 6 May 2017 at San Giovanni metro station in Rome. He was on secondment to a diocese just outside the city, but he'd made a special trip because he was something of an armchair archaeologist. He was very excited to have acquired one of 500 coveted tickets for a special viewing day ahead of the opening of the new Line C. It was the opportunity not only to see the hundreds of artefacts that were on display in the metro station, but he had heard that he would be able to view almost 30 metres of stratigraphy, perfectly preserved behind tempered, extra-clear glass.

He had just stepped off the rammed carriage into which it seemed that he and half the citizens of Rome had been decanted. For twenty minutes he had stood with his head and shoulders pressed uncomfortably against the roof of the carriage. It had him in mind of the throngs of people who pressed around Jesus when he was preaching on the shore of the Sea of Galilee; not that he was comparing himself to Jesus. A sudden wave of guilt at this blasphemy flared up his back, so he had rattled off two Hail Marys as he stood regaining his equilibrium.

Suddenly something stabbed aggressively into his back. He turned and looked down at the blue peaked cap of an officer of the Polizia di Stato; it was his gloved index finger that had been drilling so urgently into his right kidney.

'Voi. Stronzo. Vieni con noi.'

'Excuse me?'

'Pezzo di merda. Ho detto vieni con noi.'

'I'm sorry, *Non parlo Italiano.*'

'You piece of shit, you must please come with us.'

'Why? What? Is something wrong?

'Sì. Qualcuno ha fatto un reclamo su di te.'

'I'm sorry, I—'

'Someone complaint about you. You come now *stazione di polizia.*'

The policeman grabbed him by the arm and with a single flick, locked a handcuff around his wrist. Then he pulled the padre's other wrist roughly across his stomach and clamped that too. Ten minutes later he was sitting in a windowless room with a table, three chairs and a one-way mirror wall, just like he'd seen in countless procedural police dramas. Then a female police officer walked past the 'mirror wall' and he realised it was just a glass partition. *Stupido.*

Then the same officer returned, accompanied by two women, whom he guessed were in their late forties. They stopped outside the window and held an animated conversation with much gesticulation. They were clearly discussing him. Every so often, they stopped talking and just stared at him, with their arms on their hips and their heads cocked.

The identity parade – or whatever it was – ended as quickly as it had begun, and he was alone again. Then, moments later another police officer burst into the room. He was young, clean-shaven with olive skin, piercing blue eyes, perfect white teeth and a cleft chin. His orange mirrored sunglasses were attached to the right side of his blue shirt, at nipple height, but the padre couldn't tell how. Was there a loop? Velcro? He barely had time to ponder this irrelevant detail before the officer started to speak.

'*Sei libero di andare.* You are free to go.' He held out his open hand which contained the padre's wallet.

'What?'

'*Non dire a nessuno cosa è successo. Capisci?* Tell no one. Do you understand?'

'Um. Yes. It is secret?'

'Sì. Classificato. You go now.' He flashed a warm handsome grin, like a restaurant owner bidding goodnight to one of his dearest customers. After removing the handcuffs, he started making sweeping arm gestures which meant, 'off you go now, *pronto*' as if he urgently needed the room for something else.

Father Jones had returned to his digs on the outskirts of the city, exhausted and confused. Early next morning, urgent rapping woke him from a deep sleep. It was two police officers – ones he hadn't met before. They formally arrested him for pressing inappropriately against two young women on the metro carriage and placing his hands on their bottoms and chest. A closed court sentenced him to house arrest for fifteen months at a Vatican training college.

After completing his sentence he had returned to the UK last autumn in disgrace, at least that's how he felt. The British tabloids had been quick to pick up the story, so he assumed that everybody knew. He received pockets of support from his parishioners, but he had opted for early retirement at the age of sixty-two, on a much-reduced pension. That was how he found himself living in a squalid social housing flat in one of the roughest parts of the town for the last eight months. He lived alone, with his Cocker Spaniel, whom he had named Bernie, after St. Bernadette of Lourdes.

Eight weeks ago, Bernie had given birth to six unplanned puppies, so he had cleared out the shed which stood behind his flat – on what was supposed to be a garden, but which could only be described as waste ground – and he had turned it over to Bernie and her brood. He had trailed an extension cable from his kitchen window to run an electric radiator inside the shed, so heating wasn't an issue and he had also built a small, caged area outside. He would have kept them all in his flat, but he didn't have enough room and he didn't think he'd be able to cope with all the mess. It wasn't ideal, but it was the best choice in the circumstances, and they were well-protected with a big padlock on the shed door; the access gate was also lockable, and the tiny patch of scrubland was surrounded by a high semi-circular red brick wall, topped with razor wire. Earlier that week, Storm Gareth had brought strong winds, heavy rain and localised flooding, but the puppies had fared happily enough and had stayed dry and cosy in the shed.

Philip doted on the puppies and Bernie was such a proud mother. Looking after those little animals had been an exhausting responsibility, but they had brought some joy back into his life after suffering nearly two years of undiagnosed clinical depression. Finding the money for vaccinations and all the other costs had been crippling, but at least he hadn't had the expense of a breeding licence. He certainly wasn't planning on doing this again – he'd have to get Bernie neutered – nor did he expect to make any money. He wasn't greedy. He'd had a fair amount of interest and so far, three of them were due to be collected the following week by their new owners.

When Philip was satisfied that he wasn't being followed, he crossed the road and walked away from the promenade in the direction of home. He checked behind him several times, slowed his pace and started to think about late lunch. By now he was ravenous. When he reached his street, he quickened again and stared at the pavement in front of him. He passed two purple-faced men who were sitting on a chocolate brown sofa in front of one of the houses, drinking cans of super-strength lager. The floor was littered with empties. Their torpid heads silently tracked him. Two doors down, net curtains were pulled aside and a nose pressed against the window. He avoided eye contact. This was not the kind of area where you waved to your neighbours.

As he reached his communal front door, an off-road motorcycle whizzed noisily past, making him feel jumpy again. He turned to catch a glimpse of its rider – a twelve-year-old, without a helmet. Once safely inside, he picked up half a dozen fast-food leaflets from the tiled floor and then let himself into his ground-floor flat, jemmying the stiff door and pulling it upwards as he turned the key to compensate for loose hinges. He dumped two small bags of shopping on the kitchen table, quickly made some cheese on toast and a cup of tea and did some washing up. Then it was time to clean out the puppies.

Chapter Three

Meanwhile, back at the hospital, Leah glanced at her phone. A lump of impotent anger rose in her throat. *Nearly four hours already.* She had spent the whole of yesterday waiting for an MRI scan, which had finally taken place at nearly eight in the evening. She had then endured a further inexplicable two-hour wait before being sent home, exhausted. Foolishly, she had allowed herself to believe that today would be different, but she was beginning to realise that it could be several hours before she would become the most urgent case. It was her understanding that this morning's visit should have been a scheduled appointment to receive the results of the scan, but here she was again, back in triage purgatory as if yesterday had never happened.

Suddenly she became aware that the old man sitting opposite was studying her. He was wearing a foam neck brace and was reading the local newspaper – the *North Wales Weekly News*. Every so often, he would lower the paper slightly and squint at her over the top of his spectacles. He made no attempt to disguise his curiosity. Rude. She gazed past him, pretending to be lost in her own thoughts, so she could secretly track his movements with her peripheral vision.

She wasn't mistaken. He *was* staring at her. Maybe she

was bleeding out of her ears. That wouldn't surprise her. She instinctively touched the side of her face and then wiped her moist fingertips on the knee of her jeans. Sweat, not blood. Another bead of perspiration ran down the back of her shirt. Their eyes met briefly but he immediately looked away and had buried his nose in his newspaper by the time her lips had dutifully widened and pressed together into a polite smile. Then she figured it out.

The previous week she had agreed to take part in a photo opportunity for the newspaper with a local counsellor named Charles Price. She didn't agree with his politics, and she certainly didn't trust him, but they had one thing in common, even if their motives were different: they both opposed the threatened closure of the local retained fire station.

He was a career politician who sprayed populist sound bites as naturally as a hydrant spurts water; she was a retained firefighter, the Watch Manager, *The Guvnor*, responsible for a team of eleven other retained firefighters. The journalist had interviewed them both and then they had posed for a photograph, which the local hack had snapped using his iPhone, due to cutbacks at the newspaper.

Counsellor Charlie Price was a self-made multi-millionaire from Cheshire who had amassed a fortune providing 'a wide range of parts and services for the automotive and fire equipment industry'.

At first, he had dominated the interview with carefully rehearsed phrases such as 'industry leading' and 'my expertise'. She lost count of the number of times he said 'I'.

Anyone with half a brain could see through his bluster,

but Leah already knew him. She had sat with him on several Local Authority planning panels and had taken an instant dislike to his brashness and enforced bonhomie. There was no way this man was a champion of localism, except when it directly benefitted him. He was a career politician with his backside already aimed squarely at the hot ticket – parachuting into a safe seat as a constituency MP – hence his eagerness to nail his garish colours to the drill tower of this small coastal community.

Finally, the journalist turned to Leah. 'Now, I'd like to ask you some questions about the day-to-day running of the station, if that's OK?'

'Fire away,' she replied. This was her moment to impress on both visitors, the importance of her team. She did not want to mess this up.

'No pun intended,' interjected Price, grinning inanely.

'This station has two appliances – fire engines – and a crew of twelve firefighters, including me. It takes six of us to operate each appliance and we serve an area of about one hundred square miles. But not many people realise that we're all *retained* firefighters, which means that we all have other jobs. So, I work as a planning assistant for the Local Authority. We also have a landscape gardener, a window cleaner, stay-at-home mum, receptionist, car salesman, an industrial chemist and a gym owner.' Leah had found her stride. She was well used to giving guided tours of the station to groups of school children.

'So, are there any full-time firefighters here?'

'No. This is a retained fire station, which means we're all part-time.'

'Really? But how does that work?'

'Well, each of us carries a pocket alerter when we're

on call, which is activated when we're needed. When our alerters go off, we have to get to the fire station within five minutes.'

'So, you have to stay quite close to the station, then.'

'If we're on call, yes. And that's 24-7 – day or night. Typically, we're operational within nine minutes of receiving the alert.'

'So, what kind of incidents can you attend?'

'All of them. We're fully trained, just like the full-timers. We train once a week, every Tuesday evening – we maintain a high level of physical fitness – so we're fully qualified to deal with the entire range of incidents: fires, floods, road traffic collisions, chemical spills—'

'Not forgetting, cats stuck in trees.' Price grinned again, pleased with his quick wit.

'Yes, and the occasional animal rescue.' Leah grimaced tersely. It hadn't escaped her notice that both men felt mildly unsettled by her.

'I had no idea that an entire station could be re—'

'Retained. Oh yeah. Most of the time this building is empty.'

'Why do you feel it's important to keep this particular station open?'

'Because our community needs us. It's as simple as that. 12,000 front-line firefighters have been lost to cuts during the previous decade, along with a rise in fire-related deaths across the country. Of course, many politicians claim there's no link.'

'What do you think, Mr Price? Do you believe there's a link?'

'Well, I . . . I can tell you that I'm a passionate supporter of all our brave firefighters, which is why I'm here today.'

'But do you believe there's a link between government cuts and an increase in fire-related deaths?'

'Well, of course, any increase in deaths is a tragedy and . . . blights . . . hard-working families, which is why we must all take personal responsibility . . . not to—'

'Catch fire?' Leah knew she should be more diplomatic, but she was starting to feel like she was doing him a big favour in return for very little.

'. . . not to . . . place an extra burden on our fire and rescue service.'

'And how many fires do you attend in a typical year?'

'Well, they're not all fires. We average just under 6 incidents a week, about 300 a year.'

'Some people would argue that's a poor return on taxpayers' money. Wouldn't it be more cost-effective to close the smaller stations and pump extra resources into the bigger ones?'

'Actually, we're highly cost-effective.' She glanced at Price to gauge his reaction, but he was busy composing a text. 'We're only paid for the hours we work, and we are just as professional as our full-time colleagues, plus we're local. The nearest big station is thirty-five miles away.'

After the interview, it was time for the photograph. Leah quickly changed into her full thermal PPE: white helmet with a black central comb and a black stripe, brown tunic and leggings with hi-vis yellow stripes, protective hood, boots and yellow gloves. Price was wearing an expensive dark grey suit with an open-collared lilac shirt.

They stood side-by-side in front of one of the fire engines. She was already taller than him, but her helmet added another four inches, so she towered above him. Price squared up to the camera, legs wide apart in a power stance, hands held stiffly by his side. *That knocked another inch off his height. So much for expensive media training.*

'Leah, that's perfect,' said the journalist, 'but I wonder if we could have you carrying a hose?'

'A hose?' She held a pause and frowned. 'Isn't my outfit *firefightery* enough for you?'

'It isn't that. In this game, it's all about relatability. Mmmm? Trust me. I've been doing this for years. Also, can we lose the helmet?'

'Why?'

'Because our readers want to see your face. It will help them engage with your story.'

Leah grabbed a rolled-up five-inch diameter fire hose and tucked it underneath her arm as easily as if it were a beach towel, even though the compact red coil had a dry weight of 55 pounds. With her free hand, she removed her helmet to reveal a high and tight buzz cut. Then she pouted and mimed shaking out a silky mane of shoulder-length hair.

'Is that more acceptable to your readership?' She was still four inches taller than Price, even though he had closed his legs and was standing straighter. There was no way she was removing her boots, especially since he was probably wearing lifts.

The journalist took a burst of photographs.

'All done. That's great, thank you both for your time.'

'Thank *you*,' said Leah, 'and thank you, Charles, for lending your support.'

'It's my pleasure and please call me Charlie. If there's

anything else I can do, anything at all, just let me know.'

Leah doubted that; up to now, he had only been borderline present. 'Well, there is one thing. Be an angel and pop this back, would you?' She nodded in the direction of the storage locker on the side of the vehicle and held the hose straight out in front of her as easily as if it were a scatter cushion. Then she turned sharply, dropped it into Price's cradling arms and strode away, as he crumpled under its weight.

Chapter Four

After the ex-priest had walked away, Daniel checked the time on his phone.

'I know where dat pussy lives. Fucking nonce. We should go and fuck him up. You wiv me bruv?'

His words were pure bravado, but once he had made this call to arms, he couldn't unsay them. And, since there were three of them, peer pressure and groupthink exponentially increased the likelihood of his ill-considered threat being incrementally ratcheted into deadly action.

Four years earlier, Daniel Lewin had been an angelic-faced little boy, riding a bike with playing cards attached to the wheel forks, pretending it was a motorcycle. Then puberty had coincided with his introduction to alcohol and drugs and now he was a danger to himself and to others, embarking on a journey of petty crime that would inevitably lead to several lengthy prison stretches during his twenties.

Daniel and his mates, were already culturally trapped by the pressure to act tough, repress their emotions and use aggression to dominate every situation to acquire what every immature psyche craves: power, status and above all, '*respec*'. This noxious masculinity had already soaked deep into their marrow and affected every aspect of their lives. Despite their innate North Wales/Merseyside lilt, they strutted about, emulating how they imagined kids walked and talked on the streets of Hackney.

However, at this precise moment, Daniel was at a crossroads. He hadn't been arrested; he hadn't done anything irredeemable or caused anybody the sort of harm that would hang over him for the rest of his life. This afternoon, all that was about to change.

First, they stole a petrol can from a filling station forecourt, then they rode to a lock up where they knew that petrol was being stored. They filled the can. Then they found empty glass bottles in a recycling bin. They tore an old shirt into rags, and within half an hour, they had made two Molotov cocktails. At this stage, there was still no real intent in any individual mind of causing criminal damage. The three lads might just as easily have thrown them against a wall, enjoyed watching them burn, then ridden home for a latchkey microwave dinner. Instead, the momentum they had built up, now made a visit to Philip Jones's house almost inescapable.

Chapter Five

A nurse approached the old man in the neck brace. After checking his name against a list on her clipboard, she escorted him through a set of double doors to receive treatment, *never to be seen again*. Leah chuckled to herself at the melodrama she had just injected into that mundane event. God, she was bored. Then she noticed that he had left the local newspaper roughly folded on his seat, so she leaned forward and snapped it up. She jiggled the pages on her knee to straighten them and then flicked through to find the article.

The 'story' took up half a page. The heading said: 'BAPTISM OF FIRE? NEWLY ELECTED COUNSELLOR COMES TO RESCUE OF LOCAL FIRE STATION.' There was something wrong with the photograph. She kept staring but at first, she couldn't figure out what it was. Then she spotted it. Her face was dirty. There was a palpable brown smudge down her left cheek and another smaller streak across her forehead. That 'dirt' hadn't come from her helmet. Besides, she would have noticed it later. She craned her neck forward and then held the newspaper further away. There could only be one explanation, but why would anyone go to so much trouble? Leah concluded that someone must have photoshopped the picture. But why? To make her look grubby, as if she'd just returned from a shout?

As she continued to stare at the photograph, she realised that the result was subtle but distinctive: it lowered her status and made Counsellor Price – standing in his expensive suit, crisp lilac shirt and clean face – appear for all the world as if *he was her boss*. The anger began to rise in her throat.

Beneath the photo were eight paragraphs of text about Counsellor Price that were so effusive, they may as well have been written by his mother. Then finally, at the bottom, Leah received the briefest of mentions. She was, apparently, preoccupied with losing her job: 'Unfortunately, most of the public don't know that we exist. We're only paid for the hours we work, and we are just as professional as our full-time colleagues.'

That's it? Leah wanted to scream. The journalist had completely misrepresented what she had said to make it sound like a complaint about job security, low pay and a lack of recognition. There was no mention of her professionalism and that of her team, or how the station provided a vital service to the community and saved lives. Leah was furious. She'd been used. The photo had been *photoshopped for fuck's sake*. The entire piece thrust Counsellor Price squarely into the spotlight while she and her grimy mug languished in his shadow.

Leah carefully folded the newspaper and then tossed it back on the old man's empty seat. She exhaled and gritted her teeth. How could she have been so stupid? She knew what the media was like, but she had still let her guard down and let them walk all over her.

Chapter Six

Daniel and his two friends parked behind the house, close to the gate leading from the alleyway into Philip's rear garden. They had a quick peep over the fence; the coast was clear. Daniel kicked open the tall wooden gate and all three entered the rear garden. Daniel took out both bottles from his rucksack, unscrewed the caps and placed rags into their necks.

'Fuck off, nonce!' Daniel threw his first lit Molotov cocktail, over the 3-foot-high mesh fencing to the front of the garden shed. It smashed on contact and ignited the asphalt roof, which was immediately engulfed in orange flames. Heat, oxygen and fuel. The fire triangle was complete.

Daniel threw his second petrol bomb. Unknown to him, this was the enclosed puppy pen/shed. Glass smashed and the hot burning liquid spread everywhere and ignited everything it touched. Suddenly all the dogs were yelping and tearing around the caged enclosure in a desperate panic. There was no escape for them. Bernie was also on fire. She had been doused in petrol when the second bomb exploded. Despite this, she picked up some of her burning puppies in her mouth, but her efforts were futile, as there was no place of safety. The entire area was alight. Bernie's brown eyes were wide with fear. She soon stopped her ineffectual rescue attempts and began to writhe on the ground as she succumbed to her own pain.

Her repeated yelping soon morphed into a single sustained scream, which merged with the high-pitched squeals of her burning brood, echoing off the enclosure walls as she thrashed and rolled. The banshee chorus of dying puppies tore through the air, past the razor wire and away over the rooftops, followed by thick black smoke and the smell of charred fur and flesh.

It was subsequently claimed that people who lived nearly two miles away had reported being able to hear the animals. The noise gradually died away as the frantic activity diminished, until all the dogs lay immobile, either dead or silently burning.

A next-door neighbour, hearing the noise and seeing the smoke billowing up into the clear blue sky, peered over her dividing garden fence to see a scene of carnage. She frantically called 999.

At 15:04 hrs the teleprinter at Stockwood on Sea retained fire station printed out the fire call message and 12 alerters were immediately activated, commanding 12 on-call firefighters to drop whatever they were doing and report to the station within five minutes.

Hearing the commotion from his kitchen, Philip had run outside to see a hellish vision that he couldn't have imagined in his worst nightmares. He ran into Daniel and his two friends, who were trying to escape. Even though he towered over them, it was three desperate amped-up teens against one gentle old man who hadn't thrown a single punch in his life. They quickly knocked him to the ground and then kicked him repeatedly in the face, stomach and back as he curled into a ball to protect himself.

Seconds later, the three lads were gone. The violence they had just shown against a retired priest was as much a lethal reaction to their own fear and confusion as their desire to mete out vigilante justice. Nevertheless, as they fled the scene, they buried their individual fear and guilt with bravado.

'Fucking nonce got what was coming to him. He shouldn't have disrespected us.'

With a broken bleeding nose, cut lip and estimable clarity of thought, Philip got up and limped to his kitchen to fill a bowl of cold water. He went into the fire, grabbed four of the charred little bodies and dunked them into the bowl to cool them down. Unknown to him, the flesh on his arms and hands dripped off him as he tried to save the little puppies. Adrenaline ran through his body; he felt no physical pain. It was utterly hopeless. He collapsed onto the ground sobbing.

Bernie, the mother of the pups crawled towards him, writhing in agony. She was very burnt, her eyes were bulging red, fur and flesh were falling off her small body, but she inched forward until she had reached her master. Philip gently cradled her. Her eyes didn't leave him as she pawed at him weakly. Philip took her paw and held it tenderly. He sensed that in her final moments, she was begging him to protect her pups. They locked eyes until she could no longer hold on to life. Bernie died in his arms.

Chapter Seven

Back at the hospital, Leah had spent the last hour mentally ticking off four patients, as they disappeared behind the double doors, until finally, just when she was about to give up all hope of a hot bath and early night, the nurse with the clipboard approached her.

'Leah Walsh?'

'Yes, that's me.'

'I'm sorry you've had such a long wait, but the neurologist has been delayed in theatre. He's free now and he's been studying your MRI scans. Would you like to follow me?' Leah studied her tone to detect anything beyond the usual platitudes – pity perhaps, but she was overthinking again. There was no reason why this woman should know anything about the results.

Leah stood up and took one last glance at Number Nineteen. He was still fidgeting like a trifle in a wind tunnel. She had won that petty battle, at least. She was being seen first. The nurse skipped ahead and held one of the double doors open for her. *Did she do this for the other patients? Am I getting special treatment?* Leah crossed the threshold and steeled herself to hear the worst.

They walked past several beds with drawn curtains and then the nurse showed her into a side office. 'Here we are. Please take a seat. The neurologist will be with you shortly.'

'Thank you.' Leah sat down and stared at the nurse's back as she disappeared through the doorway. She was just about to settle in for another long wait, when a small Indian gentleman bustled in and closed the door briskly behind him.

'Hello, hello. Sorry to keep you. I'm Dr Srinivasan.' He cleared his throat. 'Erm . . . have you come alone today? Or do you have someone with you?'

Leah shook her head.

'OK, so I have your scans here.' He carefully removed several large acetates from a big manilla envelope, stuck two of them side by side on the wall scanner and flicked a switch. The fluorescent tube flickered into life and she was presented with 16 seemingly identical sections of her blue brain, against a black background. She leaned forward to get a closer look, but she needn't have bothered. A white blob, the size of a walnut, sat intractably in the top right corner of every single image.

'I'm afraid I do have some bad news and I appreciate that this must be very hard. So, um . . . in what appears to be the intersection of the parietal, optical and temporal lobes right here is this unmistakable white mass. This is almost certainly a growth and it is relatively large but at this stage we don't know whether it's cancerous, pre-cancerous or benign. In other words, this does not mean that you have cancer, but there is a distinct possibility. Do you understand what I have said so far?'

'Yes.' *Did she?*

'Good, so what we do know is that it's been causing you a lot of pain. Is that correct?'

'Yes, headache. And I've been feeling sick.'

'Well, the headache is not caused directly by the tumour itself, because the brain has no pain receptors. It's caused by a build-up of pressure on vessels and nerves within the brain. So, the next step: we must perform a biopsy to remove a small piece of the mass, which we will analyse to test for cancer. Even if the growth is benign, we will still require a second procedure to remove as much of it as we can, while minimizing damage to the brain.'

Leah scanned the doctor's face. He had a white stubbly beard, rectangular frameless glasses and large ears. He was wearing a navy blue and silver striped tie and a turquoise shirt.

'My headache started about a week ago. Can you tell if the thing is . . . if the walnut is growing quickly? The tumour.' She blinked away a single tear and tried to focus on the wise face of this tired man with large ears and kind brown eyes.

Katie is only 14. She needs a mother. As the thought hit her, she had to choke back a lump in her throat. Suddenly, she was sobbing. For years she had risked her life, first in the armed forces and then as a firefighter and she had rarely contemplated death, but this was a new threat, over which she had no control.

'I'm sorry,' said Leah, pressing her sleeves into her eyes as if physical pressure alone could keep her emotions bottled up. The doctor looked so exhausted. He didn't need another patient blubbing self-indulgently in his office. He was a busy man and she felt like she was wasting his time.

'There is no need to apologise. It is perfectly understandable. I can't tell how fast it is growing because

I have no baseline to compare it to. You are in pain because the growth has caused a build-up of pressure on the surrounding blood vessels and nerves and it may also be blocking the flow of cerebrospinal fluid—'

An urgent insistent high pitched beeping sound interrupted him.

'—within the brain. What is that noise? Is that you or me?'

The noise was coming from Leah's coat pocket.

'It's me. Shit, shit, shit, sorry. It's me. I've got to go. It's me. It's my alerter. I'm on call. I'm sorry. I've got to go.'

Leah wiped her eyes, sprang to her feet and tore at the door handle.

'Thank you, doctor, for all your help. Thank you so much.'

She started running along the corridor, retracing her steps back to the waiting room. She burst through the double doors, ran through the waiting room and sprinted to her car, slammed the door shut and sped towards the station *She still had time*. It was a four-minute drive. *She could still make it.*

Chapter Eight

At that precise moment, eleven other retained firefighters were either slamming their driver-side car doors and starting their engines, or they were already on the road, with the shared single aim of reaching the fire station.

Five minutes is more than enough time for an elite athlete, to comfortably jog a mile; sticking within speed limits of 30 and 40 miles an hour, it's barely time to drive three miles. Responders are not allowed to break the speed limit, so when the adrenaline is flowing, simply reaching the station in time is a significant challenge that tests their patience and discipline.

When Leah pulled into the fire station, she could see by the array of vehicles scattered around the front and side of the building that she was one of the last to arrive. Five minutes earlier, every one of her colleagues had been going about their civilian lives, like her, tending to their daily business, holding down their normal daily jobs, or looking after their families, walking the dog, going shopping, whatever. Each of them had been interrupted by their alerter and had sprung into action.

Every time Leah's pager summoned her to the station, a little tingle went down her spine when she saw everything coming together: dedicated men and women doing their duty and responding efficiently to the call. The sense of pride in being part of this tight teamwork never wore thin.

The appliance bay doors were open and the first appliance – Sierra Whiskey, SW01 – was already pulling forward. She could see Lee 'Suds' Stones at the wheel, with his unmistakable flock of thick chestnut brown hair and his prominent chin dimple (or 'bum-for-a-chin' as she never tired of calling it, much to his annoyance). She'd already spotted his window cleaning van in the drill yard. Lee was one of four fire appliance drivers at the station. She raised her hand to acknowledge him, then she sprinted to the changing room. Two minutes later, she emerged in full gear.

She had also collected the printed incident report and shouted to the crew, 'Shed on fire, well alight, spreading to garage, both pumps required.' Leah jumped into the cab, alongside Lee. She was in charge of Sierra Whiskey, SW01.

The second appliance, Sierra Whiskey, SW02, was already emerging from the bay, driven by Chelsea Schofield – 32-year-old full-time stay-at-home mum, married with two young kids; she was also one of the best drivers Leah had ever worked with. Sat stolidly next to Chelsea, in command of this vehicle, was Crew Manager John 'Greens' Turnbull, a landscape gardener in his late-thirties, but his buzz-cut and army tattoos told another story. He was hard as granite, still super fit and totally committed to the fire service. He was also prone to sudden outbursts which, although they had never led to a formal warning (since they usually happened in the pub, never while on duty), made Leah suspect that he suffered from untreated PTSD. She had her eye on him. Despite this, she knew that she and everyone else on the crew, could trust him with their lives.

Matt 'Twink' Dolan and Alan 'Steds' Morgan staffed the back doors of her appliance. Matt, as his nickname suggested, was a slim, boyish-looking young man who could pass for ten years younger than his 29 years. He sold cars for a living and was married to Jake, who ran a successful dog grooming business. Like Matt, Alan was also a keep-fit fanatic, although 'Steds' was an abbreviation of 'steroids'. He was the owner of a local gym, but whereas Matt was a self-appointed 'cardio queen', Alan was all about the 'high weight, low reps' end of the training spectrum and he made no secret of his ongoing love affair with artificial hormones, which he also sold to his customers.

Last month, Alan had thrown a big party to celebrate his fortieth birthday, but despite living with his long-term teaching assistant girlfriend, he maintained a well-deserved reputation for playing away from home. But Leah didn't judge, didn't mind him smiling and winking at passing women through the open back window of the appliance, so long as he kept showing up for shouts (in his Ford Sierra RS Cosworth Sapphire track car) and continued to wield a firehose like Hercules wrestling the Hydra.

Jordan Powell and Steve Jones made up the full team of six on her appliance that afternoon. As Lee started to turn onto the main road, Leah flicked on the blue lights and glanced over at the second appliance. She could see Ricky Worthington and Raj Hussain at the back and she assumed that Mike Williams and Sandi Weston were already onboard.

The station doors closed behind them, automatically, and once both appliances had left, all was quiet. Cars, shoes and clothes lay strewn about. Seconds earlier this had been a hub of activity; now the deserted station looked like an alien abduction site.

The blue light drive took just under four minutes. Children waved at them as they flew past; when safety permitted, Lee splayed his fingers to acknowledge them. It was his job to drive the crew to the incident as safely as possible. Some cars sped up to escape the siren; some pulled over and stopped; others froze in the middle of road, the driver racked with indecision. There was no accounting for human nature. Some drivers did the craziest things, such as parking on grassy roundabouts instead of simply pulling over. Lee had seen it all. He also had to be vigilant for pedestrians and cyclists, especially children and the elderly, who might not have been as focused on road safety as others.

'Look at this one, Leah!' A skinny guy wearing Lycra and a hipster beard started sprinting away on his supine bicycle as the 25-tonne appliance bore down on him. 'Is he really trying to race us?' Lee sounded the bullhorn to encourage the absurd velocipede to bail into a hedge. He didn't, but Lee managed to lose the befuddled cyclist by driving through some red traffic lights.

Leah could feel the adrenaline burning in her belly and rising into her chest; she responded by consciously controlling her thumping heart by taking slower, deeper breaths into her diaphragm. There was no way to disguise from her body that she was going into battle, because that was precisely what she and her crew did on every shout, so her physiological responses were only natural and helped her to focus.

There would always be an element of necessary fear; remove it from the equation and complacency and carelessness could quickly take its place, so she took professional reassurance from the fact that her heart rate had increased by 50 bpm. By now, they had left the built-up area of town and were heading onto a notorious council estate, where firefighters were just as unwelcome as the police.

Leah could see black smoke rising into the blue sky, so she knew they were close. At that precise moment, they turned the corner and Leah caught her first glimpse of the mayhem at the end of the street. A couple of young children ran past in triumph; each was waving what looked like a small mirror above their heads. She wasn't mistaken. They were police car wing mirrors, as prized as ivory in the urban jungle.

Three police cars were parked up and several police officers were attempting to clear members of the public from the danger zone, which was a challenge because it seemed as if the entire street had come out to view the spectacle. Some drank cans of alcohol while they enjoyed the entertainment. Leah counted at least eight kids of varying sizes, sat astride their bicycles. Both appliances parked just short of the house where the fire had taken hold. Parked cars stopped them from getting any closer.

Leah sent a radio message to the control room: 'Sierra Whiskey 01, I can confirm a fire is in progress. We're in attendance.' A call came back: 'Police officers already on the scene; met with hostility from the locals.' *No shit.*

Both drivers, Alan and Chelsea, engaged the fire

pumps on their respective appliances. Leah jumped out of the cab and was surprised by the noise – a mixture of shouting, screaming and laughter. A police officer ran up to her: 'The shed's almost burnt out, but the fire is spreading to the house. There are dogs in there; it's fucking mayhem. We have an adult male who has been assaulted and suffered burns to his arms and hands. Ambulance is on its way.'

Leah could see a tall, bloodied male talking to a police officer. He was clutching a tiny clump of charred fur to his chest and sobbing. She ran to the rear of the house. The smell hit her first: the sickly-sweet odour of burning flesh mixed with acrid smoke. Several dead puppies lay inert around the yard. Even though the shed was destroyed, the fire still posed an existential threat to life and to property. Leah ran back to the appliances, where the HPHRs – high pressure hose reels – were now ready for use.

'Matt, Alan, Mike and Sandi get under air.'

The four firefighters wearing their BA tackled the fire. They worked quickly and efficiently and managed to extinguish all visible flames within three minutes. There was no cheering from the crowd. Instead, there were sporadic shouts of, 'Let them burn, the dirty bastard' and other derogatory remarks that were so bovine and lacking in empathy that Leah had to fight hard not to shout back at them. Were they even watching the same scene?

A local vet, who had been alerted by the police had arrived just as the flames were extinguished; she immediately tended the dead and dying animals, administering lethal injections to end their pain. Only one of the puppies had a hope of survival. She had a nasty burn to her lower back, her tail and to her four paw pads and she was unconscious but still breathing. Leah placed a mask over her tiny muzzle and gave her some oxygen.

'I think we may be able to save this one', said the vet. 'Sadly, the rest didn't stand a chance, I'm afraid.' Leah recognised the vet; it was the same woman who had recently treated her daughter Katie's horse.

'OK. Please can you keep me informed about this little one's progress? Nina isn't it?'

'Yes, that's right. Hello Mrs Walsh. I didn't recognise you with the mask. I didn't know you're a . . .' Her voice tailed off guiltily as she realised that this professional firefighter didn't need to hear her mistaken assumption that she was a stay-at-home mum. She carefully rose to her feet, cradling the puppy in a clean blanket. 'I'll . . . stabilize her in the car and then take her back to the surgery. And yes, of course, I'll let you know if she makes it. She may be much sicker than she looks if she's inhaled a lot of smoke. I won't know for sure until I've scanned her lungs.'

Leah walked back to the shed and surveyed the area, committing as much as she could to memory, for her forthcoming report. She overheard the tall gentleman explaining to a police officer that he had been assaulted by three youths whom he had first encountered outside the supermarket. When he mentioned that he was a retired priest, she suddenly realised who he was. She had read about him in the newspaper.

She stared at his bloodied face. Whatever he had done, or had been accused of doing, he didn't deserve this. Assault and arson. Inexplicably, the repercussions of the incident that had destroyed his career were still being played out, here in this town; ignorance compounded ignorance, vigilante justice inflicted deeper wounds on a community that had already been flayed beyond recognition. It was as sad as it was predictable.

That was the moment when Leah remembered, with a jolt, that she had a *brain tumour*. She also noticed that her headache had returned, and as the adrenaline was slowly working its way out of her system, she started to feel nauseous. *Did he say mass or tumour? He definitely used the word tumour.*

She buried those thoughts again as quickly as they had risen. She still had work to do. The crews were making up their equipment, rolling up the hoses and checking in their breathing equipment; the cylinders would be refilled back at base, using an air compressor.

Twenty minutes later, as they drove away, Leah saw the priest climb into the back of an ambulance. Both crews headed back to the station in silence. Everyone had been affected by the incident. Thankfully, there were no human deaths, but that didn't make the senseless suffering of the puppies any easier to bear. Those poor little puppies had died yelping and squealing in agony, with no explanation, no understanding and zero dignity.

After they had returned to the fire station, the appliance doors opened and they saw Tom, the black and white fire station cat strutting across the drill yard. This brought a chuckle from both crews. Tom often made himself at home. He had adopted the crew as his family. They all gave him a little stroke as he purred and wrapped himself around their legs. 'Hey little guy, are you hungry?'

It was about 7:30 pm by the time Leah had completed her report and the debrief to make sure the staff were OK as well as other post-incident duties at the station. She had also overseen the cleaning and servicing of the equipment, ready for the next shout. She waved at Raj and Ricky, the last remaining crew, before turning the corner and unlocking her car. She slumped wearily into the front seat, placed her head and elbows on the steering wheel and started to sob uncontrollably.

Chapter Nine

As Leah turned into her driveway, she was relieved to see Dave's car parked in front of her. She assumed that he had picked up Katie from horse riding as they had agreed that morning, but she was also pleased that he hadn't gone out and left her on her own, on a Sunday evening. The downside was that by now, he would almost certainly have broken into his second bottle of wine. She was too exhausted to get into a fight this evening, so as she turned the key in the front door she thought, *just leave it*. If he wanted to get shitfaced and sleep in the spare room, tonight that was his problem not hers. She had too much to deal with right now.

'Hi everybody, I'm home. Katie?' Leah called up the stairs with false cheeriness. 'Are you OK? Katie?'

There was no reply. Typical teenager. Once she was in her room with her earbuds in, Katie was harder to contact than an exotic aquatic mammal. Leah wandered into the lounge, where Dave was slumped, wine glass in hand, dozing off in front of a procedural police drama.

'Don't fall asleep, you'll spill it.' She was immediately annoyed with herself for opening with this.

'I wasn't asleep. Anyway, white wine doesn't stain.'

'Has Katie had any dinner?'

'Nah. We were thinking about getting a takeaway

when you got back if you don't want to cook. Are you alright? You look . . . really rough.'

'Gee, thanks. Way to woo a woman into cooking a meal.'

'No, seriously. You know what I mean. Are you OK?'

'Yeah, yeah, I'm OK, just tired. Tough shout today. Some kids set fire to a shed on the estate and a bunch of puppies got burned to death. And their mother. They belonged to that priest who was in the newspaper. Remember? The one in Rome who got done for feeling up women on a train? Well, he's living on the estate now. Defrocked or retired. He got beaten up too. Poor man.'

'Fucking nonce probably deserved it.'

'Stop it, Dave. We don't know what really happened. He might be innocent for all we know.'

'No smoke without fire.'

'Oh, shut up. Typical copper. It's always black and white with you.'

'It's called intuition. It's how I catch criminals.'

'Whatever. I'm going to have a quick shower. I didn't have time at the station. What do you fancy for takeaway? I'm in the mood for Chinese.'

'Katie wants a curry. Me too.'

'OK, then I'll have the usual. Can you order it while I'm in the shower? Ah, shit, it's Sunday. There won't be much open. That nice Indian is closed on Sundays. Have a look on Deliveroo.'

As she stood in the shower, trying to wash away the bad memories of the day, she finally allowed herself to explore the issue that she had been burying all afternoon: her position as Watch Manager was now severely jeopardised. She was ill and she had a legal duty to report it to her superiors. There was never a right time to get sick, but this was the worst. Katie was going through a tough time at school, her husband was a high-functioning alcohol dependent, and her station was under threat of closure. Besides, they couldn't survive without her earnings. If she told Dave, then he would become an accessory if she chose to hide it from the fire service. But there was no way she could keep something this big from her own husband even if she wanted to. She didn't know what to do.

Forty-five minutes later, the doorbell rang. Dave answered the door. It was the Deliveroo driver, or rather, the cyclist. It was raining. A soggy manila bag full of Tupperware portions of lukewarm curry sat limply on the doorstep.

'Walsh?'

'That's us,' replied Dave, tersely. 'Cheers.' He carefully picked up the bag, keeping his hand underneath in case it ripped, bumped the front door closed with his hip and scurried into the kitchen. 'Grubs up everyone,' he shouted. 'Leah, can you tell Katie?'

Katie skipped down the stairs, followed by Leah, who was now wearing ivory silk pyjamas and a dressing gown.

'Can I eat in my room?' asked Katie.

'No, we're going to sit and eat together as a family. Can you get the plates, please? They're in the oven.'

'I'm starving,' said Dave as he dug around in the bag. 'Ah, here we are. "Pr K." That must be mine.'

'Take them all out, don't just grab your own. Jesus Dave. It's like a bloody zoo.'

'I wasn't just grabbing my own. Look, I've unpacked it.'

'Only cos yours was at the bottom.'

'Don't argue,' pleaded Katie, moodily. '*Please,* can I eat in my room?'

'I don't mind,' said Dave, 'It's your mother.'

'You are NOT eating in your room. Sit down. I haven't seen you all day.'

'Ughh.' Katie pulled out a chair noisily and flumped onto the seat.

'Why do we have to be so bloody dysfunctional? It's just one meal, for Christ's sake. And Dave, some support would be nice.'

'Ah shit. Does it really matter where we eat?'

'It'll stink the house out. Anyway, that's not the point. It's bad enough I'm the only person who ever cooks a meal around here, so if we're having another takeaway, we're eating it together, as a family.'

They ate in silence for several minutes until Katie pushed her half-finished plate away. 'I don't want any more. I'm going to do my homework. Please may I be excused.'

'Alright, darling,' said Leah, 'well done.'

Dave waited until he could hear Katie's footsteps on the stairs, then he said, quietly, 'I'll save hers for tomorrow. That's at least five quid's worth there. It's such a waste.'

'At least she's eating, Dave. Don't let her hear you say that.'

'She can't hear me.'

'It's important. We mustn't turn food into a big deal. If she feels overcontrolled she could relapse.'

'Which was why she could have eaten in her room. But you had to turn it into a thing.'

'That's different and you know it. Eating in public is an important part of her recovery.'

'Well, I think we've managed to create this big fucking problem around mealtimes, and I still think it has something to do with how you made her clear her plate when she was little. She had to sit at the table for hours sometimes, just because of a bit of broccoli. And now—'

'That's not fair—'

'And now you're still making family mealtimes into a big deal. We're not living in the 1950s for fuck's sake. Stop being such a control freak. Just let her do what she wants. She's a teenager.'

'The psychiatrist said it was important. You know that. Why are you being so obstructive? I know you just want to sit with your stupid wine and block us all out, pretend you're on your own, but you can't. We all live here and we're the adults; we're her parents and it's our responsibility to help her get well again. But if you don't want to, then you know where the door is.'

'Oh, fuck off. Jesus. And here we are again. I'm not going anywhere. This is my house and, believe it or not, I don't happen to want a divorce, OK? . . . I'm sorry, you're right. It's just . . . we seem to spend so much time arguing, it's no wonder Katie is such a fuck up.'

'DON'T you DARE call her that. Jesus, Dave. Is that really what you think? She's fourteen and she needs our support. And of course, I blame myself. There's lots I should have done differently, but we are where we are. Perhaps if you weren't such a fucking alcoholic, we might be able—'

'This has nothing to do with my drinking.'

'Yuh think? Oh no, of course not. Alcoholic copper.'

'DCI.'

'Model father. You're such a fucking cliché. I need some support. I can't do this all by myself. I need you to be sober and present. What if something happened to me? Where would you be then?'

'I'm present. I'm sitting right here. I give this family plenty of support. I work my arse off. I spend all week dealing with low lifes, druggies and the same criminal little scrotes, the same gormless junk-food fed faces, day in day out and when I get home all I want is some peace and quiet but it's like being back at work.'

'You think I enjoy fighting with you? You're not the only one who has a tough job. We both deal with shit, day after day. But I'm worried Dave. You have a problem and it's only going to get worse.'

'I wouldn't have a problem if you'd just leave me alone. It's not like I beat you up, is it? I just enjoy a few drinks to unwind. It's my way of coping. It's my pressure valve.'

'It's pressure alright. What are you going to be like in five years' time? Or ten?'

'I'll be retired by then, with any luck, on a big fat end-salary police pension.'

'It's just a big joke to you, isn't it? Well, I won't be here.'

'Yeah, you will. Don't be so bloody dramatic. You and me, we're keepers.'

'I don't mean that. Ah shit . . . I've got to tell you . . . I'm sorry, but you need to know. . .'

'Need to know? Leah? Need to know what?'

After a brief pause, she lowered her voice. 'I've got a brain tumour.'

'What?'

'I saw a consultant this morning, I had scans, last night. There's a big mass at the top of my brain. The doctor says it could be benign, but it's why I've been having all these headaches, so it's got to be removed.'

'Jesus, Leah. Why didn't you tell me?'

'Well, I'm telling you now aren't I?'

'Fuckety fuck.'

'You could say that. I wanted to get the results first. The consultant said I need surgery, but then my alerter went off, so we didn't finish. You should have seen the look on his face. I bet he's never had a patient sprint out of the room like that after a diagnosis. It would almost be comical if it wasn't so shitty.'

'What are you going to tell work? You've got to tell them.'

'I know. My line manager at the local authority already knows some of the details, but I'm going to have to fully disclose to the fire service as well. Which means I'll be removed from all duties and John fucking Turnbull will get to deputise in my place. He won't be able to stop smiling. He's never got over the fact that I was promoted over him, but what if I never pass another medical? He'll take my job and that matters more to me than planning admin, believe it or not.'

'But you must tell them, Leah. Promise me you will. You'd be breaking the law big time and how are you going to hide brain surgery, anyway? It could take you months to recover.'

'That's just what I'm afraid of. Leave it with me. I'll tell them in my own time. The right time.'

'I don't believe you.'

'Look, just leave it, please. I'm not going to break the law, but I've got to think things through. I'll tell them this week.'

'Leah, there's nothing to think about. You've got to phone them first thing tomorrow. You've probably broken the law already. You oversaw a major incident today in the full knowledge that you were unfit for work. What if you had passed out on duty? You could have put dozens of lives at risk.'

'I didn't think. I just responded. Surely, they can't hold that against me?'

'And we can't hide it from Katie either. The last thing she needs is to be kept in the dark.'

'I know. It's the worst possible timing, but we're going to have to tell her the truth, but play things down.'

'We don't want her anxiety to drive her back into her old ways.'

'Well, at least we agree on that. I'll tell her tomorrow after school. I don't want her lying awake worrying. It's hard enough to get her up on a Monday morning anyway. I'll telephone tomorrow. They might even let me stay in post until my op. God knows when that is. Hopefully within the next month. My thinking isn't affected. Or maybe I should recommend Turnbull to take over. It's going to happen anyway, so I may as well get on his good side.'

'Really? From what you've told me, once he's got his feet under your desk, he could be harder to shift than a dose of the clap. Do you really want to make it easier for him?'

'What choice do I have? He's the most senior and he's well connected enough to make sure he's chosen. I love my job but it's always the politics and the dickheads who make things difficult.'

'Tell me about it. We've got more than our fair share of wankers down the nick.'

'He can't steal my job. There are protocols. And they can't sack me for being ill.'

'Anyway. We need to focus on getting you well. The rest is just bullshit, at the end of the day. Your health is the most important thing. So, you need to phone the hospital tomorrow and make sure they give you a date for your operation. And if it's weeks away, we'll have to go private.'

'We can't afford that.'

'It's a brain tumour, Leah. Please don't start getting stubborn on me. We'll do whatever it takes to get you well, as quickly as possible.'

'I love you.' She hugged him from behind, as he sat in his chair.

'I love you too.'

'Dave. I know you don't want to hear this, but I could get very sick over the next few months and I'm going to lean on you. We're all going to need you, now more than ever. And that means you can't drink two bottles of wine every night.'

'Bottle and a half.'

'Whatever. I mean it Dave. We can't both be ill.'

'I'm not fucking ill. I like a drink and I've always pulled my weight; I've always supported this family.'

'I'm not going to argue. Either you sort yourself out or I'm going to have to face this on my own. I can't be responsible for both of us.'

'I know. I will. I'm sorry. Fuck. Fuck. Fucking

cancer.'

'Well, we don't know that yet.'

'Fuck, yeah, sorry Leah.' He raised his hand, intending to squeeze her arm in a tender gesture of support. Instead, he knocked over his wine glass. The pale-yellow liquid spread slowly across the table until it finally came to rest, in the shape of a giant, curved blade.

Chapter Ten

10:25 Tuesday 19 March 2019

PC Andrew Davies pressed 'record' and spoke with his face towards the recording machine. 'This interview is being recorded. The time is 10:25 am on Tuesday March 19, 2019. I am PC Andrew Davies and I'm based at Stockwood on Sea police station, which is with Denbighshire Police. Also present in the room are PC Laura Gibbons, the suspect Daniel Lewin, his mother Karen Lewin and the suspect's legal advisor, Ms Maria Roberts. What is your full name?'

'Daniel Kai Lewin.'

'OK. You said earlier Daniel that it was OK to call you 'Danny'? Is that OK?'

'It's my name. So yeah.'

'OK, thank you. And *Danny,* can you confirm your date of birth for me?'

'27th February, 2004.'

'Thank you. Before we start, I need to caution you, Danny. You are presently under arrest. You do not have to say anything, but it may harm your defence if you do not mention when questioned something which you later rely on in court. And anything you do say may be given in evidence. What that means is, Danny, any question I ask you this morning, you don't have to answer it if you don't want to, OK?'

Danny nodded.

'You need to say something Danny, I can't record a nod. Nice and clear.'

'. . . yeah, OK.'

'Well then. First, Danny, I would ask you to account for your movements on Sunday 17 March 2019. Where were you at 13:45? That's one forty-five in the afternoon.'

'I was at home.'

'Are you sure? Because we happen to know that's not true. So, I want you to think hard. Where were you at 13:45 on Sunday afternoon?

'I just fucking told you. I was at home.'

'OK. Well Danny, then I must tell *you* that we have CCTV footage showing that you were in ALDI car park, with two of your friends. It also shows you getting into a verbal altercation with a Mr Philip Jones. So, I'll ask you again: where were you on—'

'No comment.'

'OK. And where were you one hour later that same day?'

'No comment.'

'Once again, I must inform you, Danny, that we have further CCTV footage which clearly shows you throwing two petrol bombs at the shed and kennel area in the back yard of Mr Philip Jones's house. PC Gibbons is going to play this footage now.'

Danny stared at the table, glancing up sporadically at the CCTV footage which was playing on an iPad. After it had finished, PC Andrew Davies leaned forward.

'What do you think about that, Danny?'

'Fucking nonce, innit,' replied Danny, after a short pause. 'I hate nonces.'

'We have more than enough evidence here to convict you of arson and assault. But you can make your life easier if you cooperate with us. We're going to need the names of your two friends.'

'I'm not a grass. No fucking comment.'

'OK Danny, have it your way. We *will* be charging you and make no mistake, we will also track down your little pals with or without your assistance.'

'They didn't do nuffin. I started the fire. I admit it. And I nearly sparked out the nonce with one punch. So fucking what? I enjoyed it. And you can't do nuffink to me cos I'm only a kid.'

'Oh, we can do plenty, Danny, so it's in your best interests to plead guilty because the judge will take that into account.'

'Can I go now?'

'No. You'll be released on bail pending a Youth Court judgement in the next fortnight.'

Chapter Eleven

'Shift your arse, Ricky, we're all waiting for you.' John Turnbull bellowed in the direction of the changing rooms.

It was Tuesday evening. That meant fire training. Both crews were chatting in small groups, waiting for Leah to begin the evening's hard graft by calling them to order for a briefing. Usually she would split them into three teams and then allocate a training task to each team, typically involving a burning vehicle, ladders, confined spaces, hot fire training, hose running for water delivery, rescue methods, search and rescue in buildings, breathing apparatus wearing and deployment, Fire Appliance driving and BA control board duties, RTC Incidents, working at height, local area hazard awareness or the dreaded smoke house.

Leah was about to step forward and start her briefing when she heard a cheer go up among the crews, accompanied by clapping and wolf-whistling. She turned to see Ricky, jogging towards her from the changing room carrying something large and flat underneath one arm. At first, she thought it was a tarpaulin, but when he got closer, she realised it was a large piece of cardboard. He stood next to her and set it down on the floor. It was a six-foot-tall colour photograph of Leah and Counsellor

Charlie Price, blown up from the newspaper article, mounted on cardboard and cut into a large silhouette. Someone had used a black sharpie to draw a speech bubble coming from her mouth saying, 'My hero!' and a large penis and a pair of unfeasibly hairy balls hanging out of Price's trousers.

After the laughter had died down, Leah fanned her face, feigning mock gratitude and surprise. 'Well, I don't know what to say guys. I'm very touched but I won't let my newfound fame go to my head. While we're on the subject – and I want to be quick because we've got a lot to fit in this evening – I'm sure you've all got your individual opinions about Counsellor Price, but as it says in the article, he has gone on record to register his commitment to keeping this station open. Now, I know that words come cheap and I, for one, will reserve judgement until I see some action coming from his camp. But right now, we need every ally that we can muster, so let's not burn our bridges just yet. He may yet turn out to be our knight in shining armour.'

'Shining bell end more like,' said Ricky under his breath.

'The Guvnor is right,' said Turnbull. 'As far as I'm concerned, anyone who voices their support for a viable future for this station is my enemy's enemy, if you get what I mean. So, let's trust the guy until he gives us a reason not to.'

'Thanks, John. OK, that's all I wanted to say about that. Now, there's one more thing that it's my unhappy duty to report before we start this evening's training. I haven't even told John about this, because I've been stuck in meetings all day. There's no easy way to say this . . .

I've recently been diagnosed with a small growth in my brain and so I'm hoping to have surgery as soon as possible to remove it and perform a biopsy. That should take place sometime in the next six weeks, but I haven't been given a date yet. I've consulted with my superiors and sadly have no alternative but to step down from my watch command until further notice, but I will be continuing in my role as firefighter and Crew Manager until I go into hospital. As of this evening and during my absence, John Turnbull will take over as Acting Watch Manager. That's it. Are there any questions?'

'Oh God! How long will you be out of action, do you think?' asked Chelsea.

'It's very hard to guess at this stage. If the growth is benign and the surgeons manage to remove nearly all of it, with zero complications, I could probably be back driving a desk within a few weeks, but it could be at least six months, minimum, before I'm declared firefighting fit. If the tumour . . . if the growth is cancerous, then all bets are probably off.'

John Turnbull did an admirable job of containing his excitement. He stood stiffly with his hands behind his back and maintained a neutral facial expression, but Leah knew that he was silently celebrating.

'So, before I hand you into the capable . . . hands of JT, it just remains for me to say that tonight we are all doing the smoke house.'

An audible groan spread around the crew.

'Over to you John. If anyone needs me, I'll be in my . . . JT's office.'

As she walked away, there was complete silence, which was a measure of the high esteem in which everyone in the station held her. Then Lee started to clap. The others quickly joined in, until the drill yard rang with the sound of applause, magnified as it bounced back at them from the surrounding buildings. Leah didn't look back. She didn't want them to see the tears that were streaming down her cheeks. She dabbed her face briskly with her sleeve and disappeared inside.

'Right, you heard what she said. Gaylord Matt, get your BA set on, you're in first with me. Matt didn't question the 'banter' as he was well used to it. He knew that John hated him because he was openly gay.

'Mike and Sandi, you're next in. Chelsea and Lee, you're on the BA board and hose duties outside, Steve, first aider outside.'

The smoke house was a boring rectangular grey brick building, with no windows and a pitch roof; the size of a very large house or a small warehouse. Grey metal doors divided the space into various 'rooms' to mimick and represent houses.

Its bland appearance hid its sinister function. The smoke house was the building where every firefighter had to face his or her worst fears. Inside, the layout and access routes could be altered through the various rooms and corridors and the amount of light and smoke entering the building could be controlled. Overhead beams allowed for rope rescue training. When filled with smoke, it was a terrifying, confining and disorientating hellhole that could push anyone unfortunate enough to be inside to the very limits of their sanity.

Twenty minutes later, everything was ready for the smoke house training. This was a hot fire exercise. Two fires had been set in two metal gurneys inside the building, so by now fire was raging on both floors.

John Turnbull gave the crews their primary objectives. 'This is a hot fire drill. I repeat: a hot fire drill. We will use the ground floor entrance and Mike and Sandi will gain entry by the same door. Matt and I will perform a lefthand wall sweep and head for the stairs; Mike and Sandi will perform a righthand wall sweep on the ground floor. These are your main priorities: there are two sources of fire to locate and two known casualties to recover, but high probability of multi-casualties. Repeat, this is a multiple casualty drill, so keep your eyes peeled. Timer starts now. Let's go, go, go.'

Matt and John slotted the yellow tallies from their breathing apparatus onto Lee's BA board. Using a graphite pencil, Lee wrote their names, location, time of entry and air pressures, and removed the keys from their distress signal units (DSUs). Now that the keys had been removed, the DSUs could not be switched off. Each DSU was equipped with a movement sensor. If it remained stationary for longer than thirty seconds, it would sound an alarm.

'Gauge check,' shouted John.

Matt and John checked their gauges and then entered the smoke house, crawling on their hands and knees. They were followed closely by Mike and Sandi who performed the same safety procedures before entering the building. Visibility was close to zero. By the time Mike and Sandi had crawled into the building, they had already lost visuals on their crewmates, even though they were less than six feet away. Within seconds they were aware of the stifling heat and were breathing heavily. Each firefighter had twenty-five minutes of air, twenty for safety. The BA board kept track of everyone under breathing apparatus and the time they entered the building. Lee maintained radio contact with them all so that everyone was accounted for and monitored in real time.

The two crews spent the next fifteen minutes crawling methodically through the building, moving obstacles, climbing over them, searching in rooms, closets, underneath beds, in every place where a person or child could hide. Their primary search objective was to find the fire and if possible, confine it. Once the fire was confined, they would then search for casualties.

After about fifteen minutes, Mike and Sandi discovered a dummy casualty. Sandi reported to Lee via her radio: 'Adult sized casualty found on the ground floor kitchen area, bringing him out.'

Suddenly, Turnbull's voice, hoarse with anger, broke the calm. 'Dolan, what the fuck are you doing? I've lost Dolan. Repeat I have lost Dolan.'

At that moment, a piercing squealing noise cut through the unremitting black smoke.

'Dolan. Respond. Can you hear me? Dolan?'

There was no reply.

'Abort drill' yelled Turnbull, 'Abort drill. Abort drill. Everyone – locate that DSU. It's on the ground floor, sounds like it's ahead of me.'

The noise of the fans started up as they began to suck the smoke out of the building.

Moments later, Raj spotted an inert form on the ground. When the DSU alarm sounded, he and Ricky had abandoned their righthand sweep and had headed straight for the noise. Raj squatted down to get a better look. He shone his torch into the visor of the recumbent casualty, then he suddenly flinched backwards as if he had seen a ghost.

'It's Matt. It's Matt. We've found him. We've found Matt. He's not moving.'

Raj looked at Matt's air gauge. It registered full. That's when he knew that something had gone horribly wrong.

'Matt's unconscious. He's run out of air. We're bringing him out now. Call an ambulance.'

By the time Raj and Ricky had carried Matt to the nearest exit, Leah and John Turnbull were waiting with an emergency resuscitation kit. Turnbull looked grey with terror. As soon as Matt's lifeless body was safely on the concrete drill yard, Turnbull ripped off Matt's breathing mask and air cylinder and threw them away from him with such force that the pressure gauge smashed. He was breathing heavily.

'John, are you OK?'

Turnbull was already checking for breathing and a pulse. 'Leave it. I'm fine. No breathing, no pulse. Starting resuscitation.' He cupped both his hands just below Matt's breastbone and began to pump up and down. A small crowd of crew members formed in a semicircle around them as each managed to escape from the smoke house. They watched helplessly as Turnbull continued with his chest compressions. After two minutes, Leah checked Matt's pulse.

'Still no pulse, John. Keep going.'

The ambulance arrived within five minutes, but even then, John Turnbull was so agitated that Alan and Ricky had to drag him away from Matt by force, so that the paramedics could do their job.

'He unhooked himself. Why did he unhook himself? What the fuck was he thinking?' He wrestled himself free and then, as he stormed away, he aimed a kick of frustration at Matt's discarded breathing apparatus.

The paramedics continued to work on Matt until he finally regained consciousness.

'What happened?' he asked, trying to sit up.

'Stay down Matt and keep your oxygen mask on' instructed one of the paramedics, firmly. 'Matt, you were pulled unconscious from the smoke house. Can you tell me if you're in any pain?'

'My ribs hurt. And my lungs.'

'OK, Matt, we need to make sure you're stable before we get you into the ambulance and take you to hospital. You're going to need to stay overnight for observation. Matt, do you understand?

'Yeah. Can I have some water? My throat.'

'Of course. Matt, do you remember anything before you lost consciousness? Did you bang your head?'

'I . . . I don't think so. I just couldn't breathe. It was so hot. I felt dizzy and hot. That's all I remember.'

'Just rest up for a bit longer, then when you're feeling better, we'll get you to hospital for a proper check-up.'

Chapter Twelve

11:30 Wednesday 20 March 2019

Matt was kept in the hospital overnight and was sitting, fully clothed, in a wheelchair waiting to be discharged when Leah showed up, carrying a huge bouquet of flowers. Matt's husband, Jake was sitting by his bed, peeling a banana.

'Oh, hi guys. Are you leaving already? I brought you these.' Leah held out the bouquet.

'Aw, thanks Guv,' said Matt. 'You really shouldn't have!'

'How do you feel?'

'Bruised and battered and very tired, but the doctors say I'm good to go.'

'That's great. But do they know why you passed out?'

'One of them said panic attack, but I know that's not true. I didn't hyperventilate. Yeah, I felt panicked when I couldn't breathe, not the other way round. But I filled up the cylinders myself.'

'Maybe your gauge was faulty.'

'But surely the cylinders would have felt much lighter, wouldn't they? You want a banana?'

'No thanks. Well, at least you're OK.'

'Guv. Did Turnbull give me CPR?'

'Yep.'

'Huh. I knew he fancied me! Classic closet case!'

'It was just chest compressions; no tongues.'

'Ew. Now you're making *me* feel queasy.'

'He was really rattled. I've never seen him like that before. Despite the banter, he's got your back.'

'Stop it!'

'I didn't mean, *that*!'

'Just kidding. Besides, everyone knows he's a bottom.'

Jake snorted with laughter and nearly choked on his banana.

'Well, at least your sense of humour's undamaged.'

'Seriously though. I didn't have a panic attack. I know I didn't.'

'Well, we're having an internal enquiry tomorrow afternoon, if you feel up to it. You'll need to make a statement.'

Just then a nurse arrived. 'Matt Dolan? I'm pleased to say you're free to go.'

'Thank you, love,' said Matt. 'Shall we?'

After Leah had carried Matt's flowers to the car park and had waved Matt and Jake on their way, she went back inside the hospital to complete some unfinished business. This meant another two-hour wait, after which she was told that a letter had been sent to her GP and that she would be receiving her own letter within the next ten days to confirm the date of her brain surgery.

Chapter Thirteen

15:30 Thursday 21 March 2019

Leah looked around the station's rec room. Both crews were present, apart from Chelsea, who couldn't come because she had to attend a meeting with her children's headteacher.

'OK, I think we're all here,' said John Turnbull, raising his voice above the general chatter. 'Thanks for coming everyone. Chelsea sends her apologies, and Matt, it's a fucking good job you're used to holding your breath.' He stuck his tongue into his cheek, and shook his clenched fist, miming a blowjob.

Matt shifted uncomfortably in his seat and raised his eyes to the ceiling.

'No, but seriously now,' Turnbull continued, 'we nearly lost you there. No joke. That's why we're here this afternoon to try to figure out what went wrong and to make sure it never happens again. Before we start, I'd like to welcome Graeme Dollins, from HQ, who is here as an independent senior officer to observe today's meeting.

'OK, so wasting no time, to kick off, Alan, have you got the BA log?'

'Yes, Guv—' said Alan. His eyes darted nervously at Leah. She was staring at Turnbull, so he continued. 'Four

BA sets were used at the incident last Sunday, with me, Matt, Mike and Sandi all under air. The BA log shows that all four sets were refilled that evening, initialled MD.'

'I filled up the four we'd used and I did a pressure check on the other four,' said Matt.

'Did you inspect them for damage?' asked Turnbull.

'No. Obviously, I didn't spot any damage, or I would have reported it.'

'But you didn't physically check for damage.'

'No.'

'Right, then that's the first point. We all need to perform a thorough damage check after every shout, understood? Is that understood?'

A murmur of agreement spread reluctantly around the room.

'Thank you for your enthusiasm,' said Turnbull. 'Next—'

'They weren't damaged,' insisted Matt, 'I would have noticed.'

'Well how could you know if you didn't check? So, there's a possibility that the BA equipment was damaged. We can't rule that out. But we'll take Matt's word for it that it was in full working order.'

'I filled each set to capacity, and all the gauges showed full,' said Matt.

'I was coming to that,' said Turnbull. 'Now, if one of them didn't fill up properly, you could have started with only half a cylinder of air, or even less, without knowing it, if your gauge was faulty.'

'Yeah, but I think I would have noticed the weight difference.'

'But again, it's possible. When was the air compressor

serviced?'

'Nine months ago,' said Leah, 'but it's only two years old. John, I'd like to ask Matt a question.'

'Be my guest.'

'So, you were fine when you entered the smoke house, yeah? But can you remember when you started struggling to breathe?'

'I was fine when I went in, yes. So that means I started off with some air.'

'So, that rules out a blockage – you'd have noticed that immediately.'

'You still think it's a faulty gauge? Why didn't I notice the weight difference, then?'

'Oh. Nobody's told you . . . your cylinders were half full. You didn't run out of air and they didn't fail. They were in *perfect working order*.'

'That's impossible,' said Matt. His eyes darted around the room. Most of his colleagues were staring at the floor.

'Hold on,' said Raj. 'When Ricky and I found Matt unconscious, his gauge was on full, even though we'd all been under air for at least fifteen minutes.'

'Where is it now?' asked Matt.

'Smashed,' said Raj. He looked directly at Turnbull.

'That's irrelevant, Raj,' insisted Turnbull, with a note of triumph in his voice, 'because whatever you think it said, the cylinder is still half full.'

'I know what I saw. That gauge was fault—'

'And you didn't suffer a blockage,' continued Turnbull, 'so that only leaves human error—'

'I did NOT have a panic attack. I was fine until—'

'So, if you didn't panic,' said Turnbull, 'why did you untether yourself?'

'I didn't.'

'You don't even remember doing it, do you?'

'I didn't untether. Why would I do that?'

'Well, I didn't do it.'

'I didn't touch that rope. I would have remembered.'

'You were way ahead of me when you passed out.'

'I'm sorry, Matt,' said Leah, 'the facts speak for themselves. At this moment, your BA is still half full and there is no blockage. You entered the smoke house, with your gauge reading full. Even if the gauge was faulty, you said yourself that you would have noticed the weight difference, so we must conclude that you had full cylinders. You were breathing normally, you said so yourself. You didn't fall over or hit your head because the hospital tests ruled that out. So, the only conclusion I can draw is that you had some sort of . . . episode.'

'I did not have a fucking episode. Jesus, Guv, I thought you were on my side.'

'I'm not on anyone's side, Matt.'

'This is bullshit. I ran out of air.'

'Impossible,' said Turnbull, 'because your cylinders are in my office, half full. I'm sorry mate, but those are the facts and we're going to have to apply Occam's Razor to this one. The simplest explanation—'

'Fuck this shit. You're loving this aren't you?'

'I saved your life and, if you remember, two minutes ago I was making the case for equipment damage, which YOU dismissed, not me.'

'How fucking convenient. And Raj told me that you smashed my equipment. So now we'll never know whether the gauge was faulty. I don't know how you've done it, but you've stitched me up good, haven't you, you fucking jarhead prick.'

'Watch it, lad. I suggest you take a walk outside and cool off. Let it go. You're an excellent firefighter, Matt and we're all on the same team.'

'I'm going and here's my fucking statement.' Matt pulled a crumpled sheet of A4 from his back pocket, threw it on the pool table and stormed out of the station.

There was a brief silence while everyone processed what had just happened. Then Leah stood up and was about to speak when Turnbull announced: 'OK, everyone. Thank you for coming. I don't think there's any more to be discussed. Both Leah and myself will be writing a full report, so if there's anything else you'd like to add that we haven't discussed today, please come and see one of us before the weekend. Thank you.'

There was a scraping of chairs as the crew started to leave.

Dollins stared impassively at both Leah and John and then asked: 'Can we move this to your office, John? There's another matter I'd like to discuss. It's highly sensitive. Shall we?'

John looked perplexed, then he spluttered: 'Of course. Follow me.'

As soon as Leah had closed the office door, Dollins began: 'It can't have escaped your attention that the government is putting pressure on us to make further cuts. Thus far, this has meant tightening our belts and, as I'm sure you appreciate, I and my colleagues have made every effort to ensure that where redundancies have taken place, they have for the most part been on a voluntary basis. Unfortunately, recent orders from above have raised the stakes considerably. Now we are obliged not only to look at wage freezes and job cuts, but also to plans for the closure of fire stations. We've drawn up a shortlist, and I'm afraid to inform you that Stockwood on Sea is on that list.'

'So, the rumours were true,' said Leah, quietly.

'This is all highly confidential, so please don't share this information with your crews.'

'Of course not,' said John. 'We wouldn't want to ruin the surprise. May I ask why you've chosen this station? Or is that confidential too?'

'Well, I can't divulge all the details. It's been a very complex consultation process—'

'Well, we weren't consulted, that's for sure.'

'We considered dozens of parameters before reaching our decision. The professionalism and efficiency of this station and the high level of training of its retained firefighters are second to none, but ultimately . . . to be candid . . . it's about value for money. All things considered, there simply aren't enough incidents in this area to justify keeping this station operative.'

'But we attend more than 300 incidents every year and the nearest big station is thirty-five miles away.' Leah could feel herself getting angry.

'We also play a vital community role in fire risk reduction through public relations and education events,' said Leah. 'Do you take any of that important outreach work into account? You can't judge us solely on the number of incidents we attend.'

'I understand your feelings. Believe me, this was a difficult decision. We—'

'What about the land?' asked John.

'I'm sorry?'

'The land. If this station closes, what happens to the land? This is a nice area. The house prices along this road are some of the highest in town.'

'Um . . . the real estate would be . . . sold. But I can assure you that—'

'You can assure my fucking arse. Do you really expect us to believe it had no bearing on your *difficult decision*? Do you think we're fucking stupid?'

'There are numerous factors, but I can assure you that process is rigorous and substantive.'

'When will we know for sure?' asked Leah. 'I mean, when will you make the final decision?'

'Based on past and future cost-benefit metrics, we aim to consolidate this phase of discontinuance by the end of the year.'

'Allow me to translate,' said John to Leah. 'Basically, he's saying we've got nine months to find another job, unless there's a dramatic rise in incidents in this area of attempted suicides, high-speed road accidents and pensioners smoking in bed. Good to get that clear. Are we done?'

'Well, I—'

'Are we done?'

Graeme Dollins rose awkwardly from his seat and walked resolutely towards the exit. Neither Leah nor Turnbull showed him the courtesy of opening the door, so he let himself out. Leah watched him walk purposefully towards a Silver Tesla Model S. *A grey little man with expensive tastes.* Leah's hackles began to rise, along with a kernel of distrust. She didn't mention it to Turnbull, but a seed of suspicion had been firmly planted.

Chapter Fourteen

13:03 Saturday 23 March 2019

It was a beautiful spring afternoon. Single mum, Sandi and gym owner, steroid lover and serial love cheat, Alan were enjoying a secluded shag at the brickfield pond quarry.

'Alan, why the fuck have you brought me here?' Sandi asked, with a rising sense of guilt and discontent, after he had carefully parked the car out of sight of the road.

'Because last week my neighbour saw you in my car, so we can't go back to Splash Point again, or the East Parade, for that matter; it's too risky.'

That was fifteen minutes ago. Now they were semi-naked, two hot bodies locked together on a sweat-stained yoga mat, at the foot of a sheer cliff face, overlooking the deep, cold lake.

'Ahh, ahh, Alan,' moaned Sandi. She gripped onto his carefully curated triceps as she gyrated on top of him. She rode him hard and fast, rubbing her clit against him with every thrust, her mind wild with uncontrolled frenzy. 'Fuck! You're so fucking hard, so fucking deep.'

'You've got great tits,' moaned Alan, pulling on them, trying to suck them as she thrashed on top of him. 'I'm gonna cum on them.'

'No. Fuck. Not yet. Take me from behind.'

Alan paused for a moment, then obediently rolled over and thrust his pelvis forwards, dumping her face down onto the ground. Panting heavily, she pushed herself up onto her hands and knees as Alan grabbed her buttocks apart roughly, pulled aside her red G-string, stuck his thumb in her anus and entered her again with urgency whilst his cock was still rock hard and wet. Now free from her body weight, Alan started to thrust eagerly, with full power; their loins were slapping, the rhythmic glop glop glop of flesh against flesh and the smell of sweaty lust and perfume was overpowering as they reached a noisy mutual climax, which echoed off the limestone wall and ricocheted around the shady concrete abutment.

Buzz, buzz buzz . . . bleep bleep bleep. Both Sandi and Alan's alerters were flashing and bleeping simultaneously just two feet away. 'Shit. Fuck' said Alan, 'we gotta go.'

Meanwhile, in the dark, deserted fire station, the incident printer whirred into action, and typed out another 'shout' for the retained crew. And as sure as night follows day, at 13:07 hrs, twelve alerters started beeping and flashing. Each device commanded its owner to drop whatever they were doing and report to the station. Once again, the twelve fire crew rushed to their cars yet again, slamming their doors shut behind them. The firefighters were drawn inevitably towards the fire station like iron filings around a magnet, to merge into a single fighting unit.

Alan and Sandi sprang into action, hopping around collecting clothes and dressing as they also tried to sprint towards Alan's car.

'I don't believe it' said Alan, breathing heavily. 'Jesus.

Quick. Ah man, what the fuck!' Sandi giggled and squealed as she deftly rescued her bra from behind a rock and whipped it over her tits in a single move.

'Leave the mat, I can fetch it later. It's rank anyway. Let's go.'

Alan and Sandi were the last to arrive at the station. Alan screeched to a halt and reached the kit room just as Sandi arrived on foot, having bailed out of his car twenty seconds earlier. Their discretion was futile; everyone in the station knew that they were having an affair.

The bay doors were open and both appliances were ready to leave. John Turnbull stared at the printed incident report and bellowed instructions to both crews: 'Location is the railway bridge, town centre. Body on the track. We are providing medical assistance to ambulance crews. Police also attending.'

It was the same setup as before: Lee at the wheel of Sierra Whiskey, SW01, with Crew Manager Leah sitting alongside. Matt was beckoning for Alan to join him at the back doors of her appliance. Jordan and Steve made up the full team of six. John Turnbull was Crew Manager of the second appliance, Sierra Whiskey, SW02, driven by Chelsea. Raj and Ricky were on the back doors and as soon Sandi climbed onboard next to Mike, both vehicles began their blue light journey.

The station doors closed behind them, automatically. The building had been populated for less than four minutes; once both appliances had left, all was quiet again. Once again, cars, shoes and clothes lay scattered around. Seconds earlier this had been a hub of activity; now the deserted station looked like a derelict factory.

The two engines roared through the busy town centre

traffic: Saturday shoppers, weekend revellers and fans in town to support the local football team, with kick-off at 3:00pm. Police had stopped all road traffic in the centre, so they arrived at the railway track within a few minutes. As they drove over the Vale Road bridge at speed and entered Morrisons car park, Leah caught a glimpse of a group of paramedics on the track below, tending to a casualty. Both engines parked up as close to the incident as possible. Several police officers were clearing members of the public from the area.

Leah sent a radio message to the control room to state that they were in attendance: 'There's a casualty on the rail track. Paramedics and police officers already on the scene.' Then she jumped out of the cab and approached the nearest police officer, who was guarding a wooden gate – access to a rough path down to the track. 'Has a stop been placed on the line?'

'Yes,' replied the police officer. 'All trains in both directions have been stopped.'

'What's happened?'

'A male jumped from the bridge onto the tracks and has sustained serious injuries to his head and legs. He's in a bad way but at least he wasn't hit by a train.'

Both fire crews were out of their engines, awaiting further instructions from Leah and Turnbull, so the two Crew Managers walked down onto the tracks, where they could see lots of blood and several paramedics working on his injuries. Paramedics had immobilised his head and had already managed to stem the flow of blood. He also had an open fracture of his lower right leg, with the bone sticking out of the skin. The paramedics were applying a tourniquet to stop the bleeding. In total, three ambulance crews were working hard to save the young man's life. He was dipping in and out of consciousness and screaming in agony.

Leah approached a senior paramedic. 'I've got two crews here. How can we help?'

'We'll need assistance moving him once we've managed to make him stable. The air ambulance has already been called and is about 20 minutes away. The landing zone is the Matalan car park.' He raised his chin and gestured over his shoulder. 'It's about 500 metres away.'

'OK' interjected Turnbull. 'In the meantime, my crew will help the police to yellow tape the LZ and clear members of the public and we'll sweep the car park for debris and obstructions prior to landing. Leah, can you brief four of your crew to assist in transporting the casualty?'

Leah climbed up the grassy bank and jogged back to her engine. 'Matt, Alan, Jordan and Steve. Listen up. The paramedics are stabilising the casualty now. The air ambulance is landing in the supermarket car park over there. You four will be the stretcher-bearers once the helicopter had landed so you've got about ten minutes to get yourselves down there and ready. Turnbull's crew is clearing the LZ. Any questions? OK, off you go.'

As the four crewmembers made their way down to the casualty, Leah walked towards a couple of police officers who were taking an eyewitness statement from a young woman who was gesticulating, shrugging and shaking her head. Even if Leah hadn't known what had happened, it was clear that the young woman was telling them that a man had climbed onto the 6-foot-high bridge wall and, he had stepped off before she could reach him and fallen forty feet before hitting the metal track. Leah caught the end of her sentence as she came within earshot: '. . . terrible thumping sound. He was so quick. There was nothing I could do . . .'

'That's alright, love,' said the stockier of the two police officers, 'You didn't do nothing wrong. In fact, you could have put yourself in danger if you'd tried to grab him. This one couldn't be talked down. He'd already made up his mind. You did the right thing calling the emergency services so quick.'

'Is he going to be alright?'

'Well, the paramedics are working on him now, Miss. I'm afraid I can't tell you any more at this present junction. But we'll need to take some more details from you – name, address, phone number – because you're a primary witness.'

While the young woman was giving the police officer her particulars, Leah could hear the distant sound of an approaching helicopter. She looked up and scanned the sky. Seconds later a red Airbus H145 passed overhead as it made its noisy descent into the car park; it was already low enough that she could make out the distinctive flash of green on its flank and tail. From her vantage point, she was able to watch it land. She could see Turnbull gesticulating towards the safest spot before backing away towards the sizeable crowd of onlookers, which had formed into a semi-circle some distance away. Even so, many of them turned their faces away to protect their eyes from the grit that was churned up by the downwash from the descending rotor blades.

Once the air ambulance had landed, as the rotors

slowed to a halt, the medic and navigator exited the aircraft and started jogging towards the train tracks to join Leah's four crew members. The pilot stayed with the helicopter.

It was another ten minutes before the casualty had been stabilized and strapped into his stretcher ready to be evacuated. Matt, Alan, Jordan and Steve assisted with the physical lift and carry to the waiting helicopter, whereon they carefully manoeuvred him inside. A few more minutes passed, then the helicopter doors closed, the rotor blades started to pick up speed until the aircraft finally lifted a few feet off the ground. It remained there for a few seconds, before rising further upwards, then diagonally backwards to a safe height, ready to embark on its journey to hospital. Leah's Royal Navy training had taught her that this diagonal lift-off was a standard safety procedure that allowed the pilot to lower the aircraft safely back on the landing zone in the event of an emergency.

Once it had reached its safe height, the aircraft turned and flew off into the clear blue sky; the engine noise receded quickly and within less than a minute, the helicopter was a speck in the distance.

Leah spoke into her personal radio: 'Lee, put the stop in, over.'

'Roger that, over,' replied Lee. 'Sierra Whiskey 01 to Fire Control. Casualty airlifted to hospital. We'll be here for another twenty minutes clearing up. No further resources required.'

As Leah walked back to the engine, she overheard a police officer talking on his personal radio to what she assumed was the British Transport Police: 'Yeah, we've just inspected the track and it's clear. You can reopen the line for trains both ways. I repeat: you can reopen the line for trains both ways, over.'

And life carries on as normal, thought Leah. Meanwhile, a young man with a broken body and mind is beginning a journey of recovery that will take months and even years, that's if he even survived. All for want of a joined-up healthcare system, that would now have to spend thousands of pounds to physically piece his body back together, dwarfing the savings supposedly made by the systematic neglect of mental health funding. The air ambulance alone would have cost over £3,000 for its lifesaving mission, funded almost entirely by donations from the public.

Leah climbed into the cab next to Lee and they were soon threading their way through the post-match traffic on their way back to the station. She stared blankly at the road ahead and continued to reflect on the future of the young man they had just saved. She couldn't reconcile her belief in the decency and generosity of humankind – with its conflicting instinct to elect shower upon shower of sociopaths to defund everything in sight and to grind the country into the ground. If the cuts continued, there wouldn't be a fire station within twenty-five miles to attend similar incidents and the cost of repairing broken lives would rise exponentially, wiping out any so-called savings.

She'd lost count of how many attempted suicides she had attended this year alone – seven, eight, ten maybe – two women; the rest were men under the age of thirty of whom three had died. These men were likely known to the overstretched mental health services and, prior to their suicide attempts, had most probably been judged to be 'not sick enough' to access the kind of specialist support that they urgently required. Her mind drifted towards her own daughter's eating disorder, which was never far from her mind – a key part of her burden of parental worry. Then inevitably her own diagnosis sprang back into her consciousness.

Chapter Fifteen

10:05 Monday 25 March 2019

'Welcome to Stockwood on Sea fire station. My name is John Turnbull and I am the acting Watch Manager, which means I'm in charge of everything that happens around here. Now, you lads are here today because your offending behaviour has brought you to the attention of the police. Not only that, but there was also a fire component, which is why they passed you onto us.'

Turnbull paused for effect while he surveyed the room, imperiously. He scanned the semi-circle of five seated youths and looked each one in the eye. Only one – Daniel Lewin – stared back defiantly, head cocked to one side. His two accomplices in the kennel fire incident – Kyle and Liam – nodded obediently. The other two lads were only thirteen years old, so they just looked terrified.

Turnbull loved this shit – not helping disaffected youths to find a better life and to take the honest path. Fuck that. He didn't care whether they lived or died. What he loved was scaring the crap out of these little scrotes, just for the fun of it. If it just so happened that a short sharp shock was what they needed, that was an added bonus because it made him look good, but that wasn't the reason he was standing in front of them this morning. He loved the feeling of power and he also got paid good money for running these six-day courses.

'Now, I'm not here to judge whatever it is you've done. I don't give a shit about that. My job is to teach you how to become a Fire Cadet, to introduce you to the fire service and how we operate and ideally to get into your thick skulls how fucking dangerous fire is. As a Fire Cadet you will be treated as a young trainee firefighter. You will learn the basic skills required of a firefighter while taking part in activities in and around this fire station. You will be provided with your own uniform and fire set which you will take good care of. You will be treated with respect and you are expected to show respect in return.

'This isn't school so I'm not going to treat you like kids, but I expect you to act like young adults. I also expect you to demonstrate discipline and commitment. If you piss about or don't cooperate, then not only will you be in deep shit with me – which, believe me, you do not fucking want – your attitude will be reported back to the police and that will be seriously bad for you.

'We are going to meet twice a week – Mondays and Thursdays – for the next three weeks and you will also be required to attend a weekly drill night at your Fire Cadet Unit, i.e. here, on Wednesday evenings. At the end of the course, it's your choice whether you want to be a permanent member of our Cadet Force. But you must come to every session because you are here on a 'must attend' basis. That means that if you skive off, even once, I will report your absence to the police and once again, you will be in deep shit. Is that understood?'

'Hopefully, by the end of this course you'll have a newfound respect for fire and you'll certainly have tested yourself physically and mentally. Being a firefighter is hard work and it takes a lot of balls, but I promise you, if you're willing to give it a go and push yourself, you will get back far more than you put in. You may even decide that you want to become a firefighter. Great. Some of our best firefighters started off where you are now. So, in conclusion – this is a golden opportunity for you. Don't fuck it up. OK, are there any questions?'

On cue, all five lads stared earnestly at their feet just as Sandi appeared in the doorway.

'OK then. This is Sandi. She's one of our firefighters. She's going to take you to get kitted out, so if you follow her, get your stuff and then come back here. Daniel, wait behind, please. I want a word with you.'

Daniel sat with his arms folded while the four lads obediently followed Sandi out of the room. After a brief silence, Turnbull turned a wooden chair around and sat, with his arms resting on the back of the chair. Then he lowered his voice and spoke in an almost conspiratorial tone.

'I like you, Daniel. You're smart, you're tough, your two friends look up to you and they'd probably do anything you say. You're a born leader. You've got a bright future, but only if you start making the right choices. I was like you when I was your age – bored, pissed off, directionless, always getting in trouble with the police. I used to get into fights and I'd usually fucking win them too. I also used to deal drugs – just like you. It was great for a while. I could afford to buy expensive trainers and clothes. And that mountain bike of yours didn't come cheap, eh? But then I got pissed about by a couple of my customers and it didn't matter how much I threatened them, they couldn't pay me, so I ended up in debt to a fucking criminal gang. Sound familiar?'

As Turnbull had been speaking, Daniel's body language had softened. He was now sitting with his hands on his lap and was looking at the older man's rugged face. His defiance had quickly changed to attentiveness. Daniel nodded.

'The only way I escaped was to join the army. Best fucking thing I ever did. You don't have to carry on like this, Daniel. I see a lot of me in you and I want to help you. Short term, all I ask is that you give this cadet course your best shot, OK? Really fucking throw yourself into it. I promise you'll enjoy it. Longer term, I've earmarked a little job for you – a well-paid job that doesn't involve selling drugs. I can't discuss it with you yet – you'll need to earn my trust first. But trust me, you won't regret it. OK, good lad. Now run along and get your kit and I'll see you back here in fifteen minutes.'

Twenty minutes later, all the lads had returned carrying a uniform and boots stiffly in front of them, as if they were prison clothes. But despite this, they were starting to look more comfortable in their surroundings. Sandi had helped to put them at their ease. Turnbull cleared his throat and they fell silent.

'Now, there's one more thing before we take a break. I'm hoping that all of you have already been contacted by the Fire Liaison Officer, yep? Is that right?'

Everyone nodded.

'There's a bit of business we've got to attend to. In a moment, I'm going to introduce you to a young lady called Joanna. She's the Psychiatric Liaison Nurse and she's going to give a little talk to explain the dangers of setting fire to people's property and the consequences of such behaviour. I expect you to listen and cooperate and I sincerely hope what you learn from her will have a positive effect on your future actions. Once we've got that out of the way, that's when the real fun begins.'

Turnbull winked at Daniel, who responded with a half grin. He felt secretly pleased with himself. He'd broken the ice. His bullshit 'bright future' speech always had the desired effect on delinquents like Daniel. It was his superpower. It wouldn't be long before he'd have the fire-starting little scrote eating out of the palm of his hand.

Chapter Sixteen

Daniel, Kyle and Liam walked briskly away from the fire station in the direction of the town centre. They were wheeling their mountain bikes.

'Fuck bruv, I thought that was never going to end. Give me one, I'm gagging.'

Liam helped himself to a cigarette from the packet that Kyle was clutching.

'Gimme a light?'

Kyle handed Liam his disposable lighter and held out the cigarette packet to Daniel, who deftly snatched two, poked one behind his ear and lit the other from Liam.

'Fuck. I've got four left now. Gimme my lighter.'

Liam tossed the lighter in a wide arc, forcing Kyle to skip forward a couple of paces to catch it, leaving his bike to clatter to the ground.

'Thanks a lot, you fucking gimp.'

'I didn't fink it was too bad', said Daniel. 'In fact, I kind of enjoyed it. That nurse fire safety bullshit was rank, but after he'd given us a bollocking, John seemed alright. When he took us round the fire engine? Showed us how to use the hoses, you get me? That wasn't even boring.'

'That Sandi is peng as fuck,' said Liam.

'Yeah . . . for a MILF. She's older than your mum,' said Daniel.

'So? I would do her any day. All day, innit?' Liam made a grinding motion with his pelvis.

'Me too,' offered Kyle.

Daniel snorted. 'You'd last about five minutes.'

'Nah, he'd jizz in his pants.'

'Fuck off. I'd last longer than you. I'd smash her up with my monster cock. She'd need surgery after I'd finished.'

'After you'd finished, the only thing she'd need would be getting railed by me. I'd destroy her womb then I'd take her up the arse.'

Daniel's phone rang. He didn't need to look at the screen to know who was calling. 'It's Coke Dick. Shit. I'm fucking late.'

'Hello? . . . I'm here, I'm coming. I'm on my way now. Yes. OK . . . yeah. I'm sorry, I . . . yeah. Yes, yeah . . . I understand. I'll be there—'

Daniel leaped onto his mountain bike and accelerated away from his two friends. 'I'm dead. He's in McDonald's waiting for me. He's fucking pissed off and he's leaving if I'm not there in five minutes. Shit. Fuck. I'll never make it.' He checked the time on his phone and then started pedalling as if his life depended on it.

Chapter Seventeen

Kwang Lin Choy, also known as 'Coke Dick', was a short pot-bellied man with brown eyes and overplucked eyebrows. His resemblance to a laughing buddha belied a psychopathic streak and a fierce temper that had earned him notoriety, fear and respect that extended well beyond his chosen profession. He was a hitman – an essential part of any drug gang. He and his goons meted out violence and threats of violence, either to collect money that was owing or to defend turf from rival gangs.

He was known as 'Coke Dick' on account of a persistent rumour that he had once been forced at gunpoint to snort cocaine from the erect penis of a rival drug gang member. Legend had it that he bided his time for several months before exacting his revenge. He and two other men kidnapped the gang member, removed his penis with a machete and then used meat hooks to hang him by his torso from the ceiling of a lock-up garage. Two weeks later, police recovered the bloated decomposed body. A post-mortem identified several chewed fragments of partially digested penis inside the victim's stomach. Another rumour doing the rounds was that Coke Dick and one of his heavies threw a man to his death off the three-storey car park of the White Rose Shopping

Centre, another drug-related death in the area.

Daniel had, on a few occasions, tried to verify the rumour on Google using search terms such as 'meat hook death' and 'murder swallowed penis' but he'd never been able to corroborate the story. His searches always returned the same results – German cannibal Armin Meiwes who chopped up and ate a man after advertising on the internet for a willing volunteer; and 'Death On A Meat Hook' (feat. M.M.M.F.D.) [Explicit] by the Butcher Brothaz. Regardless, he wasn't taking any chances. Coke Dick terrified Daniel, which was why he was pedalling towards McDonald's like an EPO junkie.

Coke Dick was sitting in a wooden booth facing the door with his back to the wall. He was reaching the end of a triple cheeseburger which had been preceded by a Large Big Mac Meal with Diet Coke. His face was beginning to droop in anticipation of the sad moment in approximately fifteen seconds' time, when the meal would reach its inevitable conclusion. That was also when he intended to stand up and storm out.

To his left sat an eighteen-stone, pink-faced man in his early forties. He had a thick neck, a buzz cut and a black goatee beard flecked with grey and was wearing a tight black T-shirt. He looked ex-army. Tough as fuck. The skin on his massive pink forearms was almost completely covered with monochrome tattoos. On his right sat a rangy youth in his early twenties who was fizzing with nervous energy. He was wearing a plaster cast from ankle to crotch and shiny white joggers with one leg cut short. A pair of aluminium crutches stood propped up beside him.

The three men couldn't have dressed more like East

Coast drug dealers if they had tried. It was a strong classic look that was woefully out of place in a small fast-food outlet in North Wales.

Just as Coke Dick's stubby fingers were delivering the final morsel into his gaping maw, he heard crashing metal outside. Moments later Daniel Lewin burst through the door. He had dumped his bike on the floor outside. One of the wheels was still spinning. Daniel scanned the room urgently, spotted Coke Dick and with a huge feeling of relief, started walking slowly towards him.

'Where the fuck have you been?' Coke Dick's voice was disconcertingly monotone.

'I'm sorry, I had to—'

'Shut up. I don't want to hear your excuses. Where's my money?'

'I don't have it yet. I'm still trying to get it.'

'I know you are, Daniel. But when will you get it, do you think? This week? Next week?'

Daniel said nothing. Frozen with fear, he couldn't think of anything he could say that would get this guy off his back, but he knew better than to lie.

'Don't look so scared. I'm not going to hurt you. Sit down.'

'I'd rather stand if that's—'

'Sit . . . the fuck . . . down.' The pink-faced man mountain stood up menacingly. Daniel immediately plonked his backside on the nearest chair.

'Now. I understand that one of your clients is having problems paying, is that correct?'

Daniel nodded.

'Well . . . that's a problem, isn't it?'

Daniel nodded again.

'But at this present moment, this is your problem, Daniel, do you understand?'

'Er . . . I think so.' Daniel was confused.

Coke Dick smiled paternally. 'Let me clarify. Right now, your client's problem is your problem and yours alone. Lucky for you it hasn't yet become my problem. That means you still have time to sort it out. But if it becomes my problem then it stops being a problem for you.'

'It stops? You won't be angry . . .'

'Oh, I'll be angry. Fucking kick-you-in-the-stomach-until-you-cough-blood angry. Stamp-on-your-fucking-head-until-you-stop-breathing angry. As I said, it stops being a problem for you . . . because instead, it becomes a *fucking disaster*. Are we clear?'

'But . . . I can't force him to pay.'

'You grossly underestimate your abilities, Daniel. Word on the street is that you're handy with a Molotov cocktail. Use your imagination. Play to your strengths.'

Chapter Eighteen

19:35 Wednesday 27 March 2019

Jake Edwards sat on his parents' cheap leather sofa watching *Fake Britain*. The episode was about fake protein shakes and a vacuum servicing that ripped off thousands of customers. Jake loved consumer rights programmes, but this was his clear favourite. As a bonus, he was alone in the house, so for the moment at least, he could watch what he liked without his dad switching over to the news or his mum nagging him to do his 'A' level homework.

There was a knock at the door. He ignored it at first, but when he heard a second, more urgent knock, he sighed heavily and stropped into the hall. His sister might have forgotten her keys.

It was Daniel.

'What do you want?' It was a stupid question, but he had to say something.

'You know what I want. Where's my £300?'

'Look kid, I've told you, I don't have it.'

'Do you fucking know who you're dealing with?' asked Daniel, brazenly.

'Er . . . I think so,' replied Jake sarcastically.

'Not me. There are important people higher up, nasty

fuckers who don't want this to become their problem, because if it does, then it will be a *fucking disaster* for you. You get me, Jake?'

'Look, my parents will be home any minute. You'll get your money, just not today. I don't have it, OK? In the meantime, why don't you piss off.'

He closed the door in Daniel's face and went back to watching the television. He cursed as he realised that he'd missed the end of the vacuum servicing segment. The chimp-faced ex-con presenter was now discussing exploding head torches.

Moments later he heard the flap of the front door letter plate, followed by a loud fizzing noise. He wandered into the hall and watched with horror as a six-foot flame extended from the floor almost to the ceiling. It had already spread to the draft-excluding curtain and a rack of coats. The smoke detector activated, adding its high-pitched bleeping to the chaos. Jake staggered backward in shock as his brain became clouded with panic.

His first instinct was to call the emergency services, but how would he explain the cause of the fire – an argument over drugs? He had to put the fire out himself. He ran to the kitchen, half-filled a bowl of water and ran back to the hall, sloshing water all over the kitchen floor on the way. During those thirty seconds, the fire had spread to the ceiling and the wooden front door was also ablaze. Standing ten feet away, he hurled the depleted contents of the bowl in the direction of the flames. It was futile. Most of the water hit the floor before it even reached the front door. That's when Jake came to his senses and dialled 999.

John Turnbull was already at the fire station when his

alerter started beeping. He and four of his five wayward cadets were halfway through the first Fire Cadet Unit weekly drill night. Daniel was conspicuous by his absence.

'OK lads. I'm sorry but I've got to wrap it up early this evening. But this is perfect, cos here's your chance to see how we operate. See this alerter? It's beeping. That means we've been called out on a shout. The next eight minutes are going to blow your mind. Stand over there and don't move a muscle, just watch.'

The four young cadets stood rooted to the spot and watched in awe as retained firefighters appeared as if from nowhere. Each of them had been interrupted by their alerter and had sprung into action. They screeched to a halt and ran from their cars dressed as ordinary people to reappear from the locker room moments later in full firefighting uniform. A frisson tickled Liam's back and he felt a lump rising in his throat. There was something deeply moving about what he was witnessing that he was unable to articulate. It was like they were superheroes. They all knew precisely what they were doing. They all clicked together.

By the time the last firefighter had arrived, Liam had counted eleven cars. Then shortly afterward, John Turnbull's voice rang out across the drill yard: 'House fire at 56 Patagonia Drive, persons reported inside, PDA: both fire appliances required.'

Liam recognised one of the firefighters – Sandi – boarding a fire engine. Just before the two fire engines left the station, John Turnbull ran over to the four teens.

'Impressive huh? OK lads, you're dismissed. You can let yourselves out! See you tomorrow morning at 10:00am sharp.'

Both fire engines left the station together. The station doors closed behind them, automatically, and then all was quiet. The four lads cycled home, buzzing with the excitement of what they had just seen.

The blue light drive took just under four minutes, with blues and two-tone sirens on along with the bull horn. Children and pensioners waved at them as they flew past; when safety permitted, Lee and Chelsea splayed their fingers to acknowledge them. The two engines roared through the busy town centre traffic, contravening 'keep left' signs and tearing past pedestrians, cyclists and other vehicles to reach the fire.

As they approached Patagonia Drive, Turnbull noticed a young lad on the pavement. He was wearing a grey hoody and sitting on an expensive mountain bike, watching the two engines pass by. Turnbull didn't need to see his face to know that it was Daniel but at that moment, the lad obligingly looked up at his cab and their eyes briefly met.

Gotcha! Now you're mine. He smiled with delight but Daniel had already pulled up his hood and started to cycle away. Chelsea was too busy driving to notice, which was just what he wanted. This was their secret and he could use it to his advantage.

As the fire engines arrived at the property, a few neighbours were lingering outside, eager to see what was going on, but there was no obvious fire. Turnbull booked in attendance with the fire control room: 'Sierra Whiskey 02, I can confirm a fire has occurred. In attendance.'

Leah and John interviewed the occupants of the house and pieced together the story. An incendiary firework had been dropped through the letterbox, while a 17-year-old schoolboy was home alone. He had alerted the emergency services before dousing the flames using a washing-up bowl. Luckily, his father had arrived home shortly afterwards and ran a garden hose from the back garden, through the kitchen and hall to extinguish the blaze before it spread to the rest of the house. It was a clear case of arson. Leah requested police attendance and declared that the incident was now a crime scene. She also requested an ambulance as a precaution because the schoolboy had inhaled a considerable amount of smoke.

Since there was no fire to extinguish, Turnbull instructed his crew members to 'leaflet' the street, which was normal procedure after a domestic house fire. Raj and Mike also knocked on doors and explained: 'This leaflet highlights the importance of early smoke detection, which saves lives, and offers a free home safety check so that the fire service can supply and fit smoke alarms in your homes for free.' They were usually met with polite equivocation or indifference, despite what had just occurred a few doors away.

'Raj, are we doing something wrong?' asked Mike in exasperation after repeating their script on a dozen doorsteps.

'You don't get anything for nothing these days. There's always a catch. They're afraid of being ripped off.'

'Or maybe they're just racist.'

As Leah and Turnbull were assessing the fire damage around the front door, two uniformed police officers arrived in a marked police car. They interviewed Jake and his parents and opened a criminal investigation.

Jake kept quiet about Daniel's visit, but he broke into a cold sweat when he overheard one of the police officers asking a neighbour if there were any private CCTV cameras in the street. Lucky for him, the answer was 'no'.

Chapter Nineteen

14:55 Thursday 28 March 2019

'OK, lads, I'm going to stop there. Congratulations. You just completed your first week of fire cadet training. You four can go. See you next Monday. Daniel, wait behind, please. We need to talk.'

They sat in silence until the four other lads had filed out of the room, then Turnbull stood up and walked towards the door. 'Follow me.'

When they reached the far end of the drill yard, Turnbull stopped and leaned his back against the metal boundary fence with his hands in his pockets and stared at Daniel. Daniel stood with his head slightly bowed, nervously biting his thumbnail, waiting for him to speak.

'I was quite impressed by your handywork last night.'

Daniel frowned. 'I don't know what—'

'Don't fucking bullshit me, you little prick. I saw you on your bike and you saw me. Patagonia Drive. Firework through the letterbox. How did you get your hands on fireworks at this time of year? Also, you look about twelve, so I'm assuming you nicked them, which is no mean feat.'

'What do you want?' asked Daniel, sulkily.

'Don't worry, I'm not going to grass you up. In fact,

the police phoned me this morning and I gave you an alibi – told them you were attending cadet training with me.'

'Why?'

'Isn't it obvious? You were in a spot of trouble and, as I said before, I like you.'

'Are you a nonce?' Daniel suddenly looked nervous again.

Turnbull laughed. 'Don't be ridiculous. Just shut up and pay attention. Remember I said I earmarked a little job for you – a well-paid job – that doesn't involve selling drugs? But you had to earn my trust first? Well now you don't because I own you.'

'I didn't ask you to lie for me.'

'If I hadn't, you'd be in the nick right now, lad. I did you a big favour but I want something in return.'

'What if I say no?'

'Then I'll tell the police that it was you playing Guy Fawkes last night. But when you've heard what I've got to say, I don't think you'll need much persuading. This is right up your alley.'

'What is it?'

'First of all. How much does that kid owe you?'

'What kid?'

'The one whose house you fucking torched, of course. How much? . . . Come on—'

'Three hundred.'

'Is that all? Here, take this.' Turnbull passed Daniel a small brown envelope.

Daniel started to look inside.

'Don't fucking open it. Put it in your pocket. There's £400 in there. You can count it when you get home. Use it to pay your debt and consider this an advance against your future employment. Now, I'll let you into a little secret. This fire station is earmarked for closure, because apparently, we're not busy enough. So that's where you come in. You're going to make sure that by Christmas, they can't use that bullshit excuse because we'll have been so busy fighting fires that they won't be able to close us down. From now on, I want you to use your fire-starting skills for good not evil. Cross over from the dark side.'

'And you're gonna pay me?'

'I already did. Four hundred – twenty quid a pop – that's twenty fires right there. Three or four a week.'

'What sort of fires?'

'Whatever you can get away with without being arrested or caught on CCTV, because if you do, it's all over. No more easy money for you. Dumpster fires are the best because they create lots of flames and smoke without causing too much collateral damage, but we still get called out. If you see an old sofa lying around, torch it. Just don't fucking get caught. And no more house fires – I don't want anyone getting killed or injured. And it goes without saying that if you do get nicked, you're on your own.'

'So, you want me to start twenty fires?'

'No, I want you to start a hundred fires. I'll pay you £20 for each one. That means there's another £1,600 coming your way this year if you're smart and you don't get caught.'

'How can I start a hundred fires without getting caught?'

'I dunno. That's your problem. Use your imagination. Dream big. Anyway, it's your fucking hobby, so stop whining. But there is one other thing: I want you to stop dealing drugs.'

'I can't do that. I make good money and . . . there's no way they'll let me just quit.'

'You make a bit of cash, sure, but what I'm offering you is much better – a guaranteed payday of two grand, and you won't have to chase any snivelling losers who can't pay. Which means you won't get your kneecaps smashed in by Coke Dick.'

'How do you—'

'Everyone knows Coke Dick. He's been running kids like you for years. Paying them shit, treating them like shit. I'll have a little word with him. Tell him to leave you alone. There's no future for you selling weed, so I'm doing you a favour, Danny Boy.'

'DON'T call me that.'

'Alright. Calm down. Jesus. So, do we have an agreement?'

'. . . S'pose.'

'Excellent. And no drugs. I'm serious. If I find out you're dealing again, we're done. And for Christ's sake, cheer up. This is a great opportunity.'

Daniel nodded. He was trying to look miserable, but he was secretly delighted. Easy money for something he would do for free and no more threats of violence.

'Can I still *smoke* weed?'

'What you do in your spare time is your business. If you want to waste it getting high, that's your choice. But strictly no dealing.'

'OK, OK, I got it, no dealing.'

'And a piece of advice: it's really dumb to hang around the scene of your crime. Set a fire and get the fuck out of there. No sitting around with a boner watching the flames.

Understood?'

Daniel nodded again.

'Right, off you go. Light up the town; don't do anything stupid. I'll see you back here next Monday. Must attend, remember?'

'I won't forget.' Daniel collected his bike and wheeled it away from the fire station. As soon as he was out of sight, he pulled out his phone and smiled. *You think you fucking own me?* Daniel had recorded every word.

Chapter Twenty

10:15 Monday 1 April 2019

Just as Leah was leaving her house, the postman arrived.

'Anything for us?' she asked as she closed the front door.

The postman handed her a small bundle of letters, held together by a red rubber band.

'Ooh, thank you. I'll take them with me.' Why she felt the need to explain her actions, she didn't know. He'd seen her coming out of her house, so he must have figured out that she lived there and wasn't trying to steal someone else's post, but still Leah felt a little guilty about interrupting its rightful journey – through the letterbox.

'Whatever.' The postman shrugged and walked away.

'Feeling a little stupid, Leah flicked through the letters: bills and junk, apart from one official-looking window envelope. She sat in her car and opened it. It was from the hospital, giving her a date for her brain surgery – Monday 13 May. Exactly six weeks away. Was that an urgent appointment? If so, six weeks was a long time to wait, even though her headaches appeared to have eased off. Maybe she *should* go private.

She started the engine and typed the postcode of the

veterinary surgery into her satnav. It was nineteen minutes away. She was way too early, but better to be early than late. She had an appointment at 11:00am to check on the progress of the little puppy who had survived the arson attack two weeks earlier. To kill some time, she grabbed a latte from a drive-through Starbucks and arrived at the vets with ten minutes to spare.

'Hi. I'm Leah Walsh.' She smiled at the receptionist. 'I'm here to see the little puppy who was rescued from the fire? I'm a bit early. Can I drink this in here?'

'Yes, of course. Please take a seat. Nina's seeing another patient, but she'll be with you soon.'

'How's she doing?' The receptionist looked confused. 'The puppy I mean.'

'Oh . . . very well. She's put on some weight, which is a good sign, but she's had a terrible shock. But animals are very resilient. Especially dogs. And she's so cute. We've named her Bells.'

'That's pretty . . .' Leah couldn't think of any more small talk so she busied herself inspecting a display of cat and dog toys, then she started reading a leaflet about ticks and worms: 'Many kittens have roundworm because it's commonly passed on to them in their mother's milk.'

That's a bummer she thought. Then she read another fact that took her by surprise: 'Fleas can carry tapeworm eggs.' *Yuck.*

'Hello, Mrs Walsh.' It was Nina. 'It's nice to see you under happier circumstances.'

'Yes. I can honestly say that it affected all of us. Those incidents stay with you. It's terrible of course when people get injured but seeing animals suffering is very disturbing. Well, I don't need to tell you that.'

'Would you like to come through? Bells is just down the corridor.'

'I'd love to. I'm feeling a bit nervous.'

'Here we are. Meet Bells.' Nina pointed to a metal cage. In the far corner, a tiny brown and white puppy was curled up asleep on a small lambswool blanket.

'Oh. Look at her,' Leah whispered. 'Is it OK to wake her up?'

'Just this once won't do any harm.' Nina reached into the cage and gently picked up the blanket, cradling the puppy inside. Then she passed the little bundle to Leah.

'She's so gorgeous. Hello, little one. Ah. She's opening her eyes. Hello. Aw, she's closed them again. Hmm. Well, I've made a huge impression on *her*.'

Bells opened her eyes again and yawned. Then in a sudden frenzy of excitement, she started wagging her tail and jumped up to lick Leah's face and neck.

'Oh, she's so wriggly. I don't want to drop her. She won't stop licking me. She's so friendly, aren't you? Yes, you are!'

'She's really doing remarkably well. Thankfully her lungs haven't been permanently damaged and as you can see, the fur is already starting to grow back where we shaved her. She's had all her jabs now, so she won't be here much longer. We're putting feelers out to find her a new home.'

'What about the owner?'

'He doesn't want her. To be honest, I think he feels guilty, responsible, even though what happened was obviously not his fault. He told me he was thinking of leaving the area.'

'Another fresh start. Poor guy. I mean, I know the

rumours but . . . he didn't deserve . . .'

'Absolutely.'

'He'd do well to move anyway. He's living in one of the . . .' Leah chose her words carefully: 'roughest streets in the town.'

'Well, anyway, do let us know if you know anyone who wants a puppy.'

At that moment, little Bells start suckling the tip of Leah's nose. Then she nuzzled into her warm neck and started to drift off to sleep again. Leah could smell that gorgeous 'puppy smell'. Bells' fur coat was so silky and soft, and as she stroked her she could feel all the puppy fat Bells had yet to grow into. Leah's heart melted. Without thinking, she blurted: 'I'll take her.' It made no sense to be adopting a puppy six weeks before major surgery, but she and Dave had talked seriously about getting a dog on several occasions and Katie loved dogs, so she would be over the moon.

'Really?'

'I think so. I'll have to run it past my husband first. Can't just spring a puppy on him. I mean, we've already talked about getting a dog . . . lots.' Leah didn't want the vet to think that she was making a rash decision.

'Of course. Well, that's excellent. Can you let us know as soon as possible?'

'Yeah, I'll . . . um . . . either way I'll phone you tomorrow. Is it alright if I cuddle her a bit longer?'

'Be my guest. Take all the time you want. I'll be down the corridor if you need anything.'

Leah sat down, closed her eyes and enjoyed the feeling of the silky-smooth fur against her neck, trying to remain calm. Her blinding headache had returned.

Chapter Twenty-One

Leah was woken by the sound of the front door slamming – not in anger – it wasn't loud enough for that. It was most likely the result of a casual back kick from a teenager too lazy to close the door with her hand. She could hear Dave's voice. In the confusion of waking, Leah's first thought was that she had forgotten to collect Katie from school, but she quickly realised that it was Dave's turn. Which was just as well because she had been in a deep sleep.

After a head-splitting journey home, Leah had taken the maximum safe dose of paracetamol, flopped onto the bed in her clothes and had slept for four hours. Dave came up the stairs and into the bedroom.

'Everything OK? You've been asleep?'

'Oh God, yeah.' She yawned. 'I felt terrible. Feel a bit better now. I got a letter from the hospital. My operation is exactly six weeks today – Monday 13 May. Lucky thirteen.'

'Oh right,' said Dave.

'What do you think it means? Is that their idea of emergency surgery? Or am I low risk?'

'Nah. They're just busy, with long waiting times. That's an urgent booking, for sure.'

'Gee, thanks.'

'Well, you asked my opinion. I'm not going to lie. You know how I feel about going private.'

'And we still can't afford it. Even less now my job's under threat. Also, for a few weeks I'm only going to get Statutory Sick Pay. It's less than £100 a week. It's £94 something. It's miserable. If I was having a baby instead of a tumour, I'd be getting almost twice as much. It's mad isn't it? I can't afford to be ill. We certainly can't afford to go private.'

'We could take out a loan. You'll earn even less if you're dead.'

'Alright, Joe Wicks. Thanks for the pep talk. Where's Katie? Is she still downstairs? I don't want her to hear this.'

'Yeah, she's making a sandwich.'

'Oh, good.'

'She didn't need any encouragement from me.'

'Assuming the tumour is benign, I should be able to go back to desk work within a few weeks, but I won't be able to get my command back from John until well into the autumn. Oh, that reminds me – I forgot to tell you: John suspects the closure has more to do with the value of the land than how busy we are. He even confronted a superior officer about it. I know John can be a drama queen, but this time he just might have a point. The fire station is in a prime position. Those big Edwardian houses further down the road are worth a fortune. Imagine how much a developer could make by building commercial property on a footprint the size of the fire station.'

'I hate to give Turnbull the credit, but he could be right.'

'I'll keep my ear to the ground at work. I wonder if

there's anything in the digital archives worth digging up. I could easily check to see what applications have been granted and refused in the vicinity of the fire station in the last few years. If we – the local authority – refuse planning permission or impose conditions, we must give written reasons, so a keyword search of 'Coast Road' cross referenced with 'Fire Station' might throw up some interesting reading. Well . . . it's a start. There will either be nothing at all or else, too many results to read in any detail. Anyway, that's what I shall do tomorrow. It'll be fun. A bit of sleuthing. Oh, and I must give them the date of my surgery.'

'Did you go to the vets?'

'Oh my God, yes! Oh, she's so gorgeous, Dave. She's so tiny and she was asleep in my arms and then she woke up and started licking me. I've fallen in love with her. She's called Bells; in fact . . . I've told them that we want to adopt her . . . but that I had to talk to you first.'

'Woah.' Dave puffed out his cheeks and exhaled.

'Well? Oh, come on, she's beautiful and she needs a home and Katie would love her. Please?'

'I'm not saying no . . . but is this the right time?'

'There's never a right time. It's like having kids – if we had waited until everything was perfect, we would never have had Katie.'

'That's true but dogs aren't cheap. The food alone will be over £1,000 a year, then there's vets' bills and pet insurance—'

'I thought you didn't care about money.'

'That's different. That's your health.'

'Oh, come on, don't be so boring. It'll be fun. She'll take our mind off things. Plus, she really does need a home. I've got a good feeling about this. It feels right.'

'Easy for you to say.'

'What do you mean.'

'Well, don't take this the wrong way, but you're going to need a lot of support after your operation and having a dog on top of all that . . . it complicates everything.'

'You mean, it's extra work for you.'

'Well, yeah, alright, yeah . . . it is.'

'Katie will help out.'

'She's a teenager. She'll say one thing and do another.'

'Let's ask her. *Katie!*'

'What?' Katie was standing in the doorway looking mildly annoyed.

'Blimey, that was quick.

'I was in the kitchen. What?'

'How would you like to have a puppy?'

'Are we getting a puppy? That would be l-u-s-h. For real?'

'Ask your father. I've just been to see this gorgeous little thing who was rescued from a fire two weeks ago. She's a Cocker Spaniel and her name is Bells.'

Katie screamed with excitement and started jumping up and down on the spot. 'Dad? Dad? Dad? Can we? Dad . . . p-l-e-a-s-e . . .'

Dave smiled broadly. 'Oh, what the hell—'

Another scream, this time from Katie and Leah.

'Yes! I knew you couldn't resist your darling daughter!'

'M-u-m—'

'Thank you.' Leah kissed Dave on the cheek. 'It's going to be great. I'll phone them now and tell them the good news.'

Chapter Twenty-Two

The lift was still broken. Paul Gray started tramping up the piss-stained stairs to his seventh-floor flat. His arms and legs ached, and his neck was stiff. He was fifty-eight next month and would be collecting his free bus pass in two years' time. He was too old for this.

Paul was known as the Hydrant Man, Water Man or even The Bat. He worked all hours, not just at night, so the latter was a misnomer, but it sounded cool. Besides, he enjoyed working nightshifts, when he could go about his business unnoticed without being bothered by idle members of the public spectating. It was his job to inspect and maintain all the council-owned fire hydrants on his patch. There was nothing much to see, so he couldn't fathom why he frequently drew small crowds. He often joked that he should put a hat on the floor for people to throw money into. Or he could sell popcorn and ice creams.

He could understand cocky kids on bikes – kids will be kids. But the grown-ups who had nothing better to do than to gawp – they were annoying-as-fuck. Standing scratching their arses and asking stupid questions: 'Oi mate, is that a fire hydrant? What ya doin'?' and most frequent of all, 'How did you lose your hand?' He didn't get any of that at night. Working in silence in the cool air without any interruptions. Today had been a day shift, so he'd had his fair share of nosey bastards. All he wanted to do now was to heat up a microwave dinner and watch telly.

Breathing heavily, he turned his key in the lock. He could already hear the television blaring inside. He walked into the hall and kicked the door shut behind him. 'Is that you?' he called. No reply.

Paul shuffled into the lounge. On the sofa sat a rangy youth in his early twenties. He was wearing shiny white joggers, with one leg cut short to accommodate a plaster cast that swathed his entire leg from ankle to crotch. He was fizzing with nervous energy.

'Jesus, what the fuck happened to you?'

'It's nothing, Dad, don't worry about it.'

'It doesn't look like nothing. When did it happen?'

'About two weeks ago.' He stared at the telly.

'And?'

'I told you, I'm fine.'

'No, Dean. You can't show up here with a broken leg and pretend nothing happened. Is it drugs again?'

'No.'

'It's fucking drugs. Look at me. Who did this to you?'

'I fell over. Look, can you just leave it?'

'Fell over my arse. Only racehorses and old ladies break their legs falling over.'

'I don't want to talk about it.'

'Well, that's tough, because I do. I thought we'd put all that shit behind us. You worked so hard to get straight. Are you using again?'

'It's not as simple as that. And no, I'm not using.'

'So, why won't you tell me who fucked you up?'

'It's complicated.'

'No, having a junkie son is complicated. If you're lying to me, I'll fucking break your other leg, you hear me?' He took a step toward his son.

'Dad, please, no. I swear on Mum's grave. I don't do Class A no more . . . just some weed . . .'

'. . . OK, I believe you. But how can I help if you don't tell me what happened?'

'I don't need your help.'

'Er . . . I beg to fucking differ. Look at you. Please Dean, let me help you.'

'You can't help me. I think I need to disappear. Until things . . .'

'You're a Gray, son. Grays don't disappear. We face our problems. Whatever they are. Otherwise, no matter where you run, your problems will always run faster. You understand?'

'You can't fix this, Dad.

'Try me. You got clean. So, you can do this. Just tell me what you need.'

'CAN'T YOU . . . *fuck* . . . can't you *understand*? You can't fix this.' Dean's eyes welled up. He quickly wiped away a tear with his sleeve.

'Tell me what you need. Tell me. Just tell me. Tell me.'

'Dad—'

'Tell me Dean. Fucking tell me. Dean, fucking tell me—'

'TWENTY-FIVE THOUSAND POUNDS. ALRIGHT??' Dean leapt off the sofa, ran into the kitchen and slammed the door.

The words had tumbled out of Dean's mouth so quickly, that Paul had to pause for a moment to let them settle in his mind.

When Paul finally opened the kitchen door, Dean was sitting at the dining table in the dark with his head in his hands. He didn't look up. Paul stepped over the threshold, but he didn't turn on the light, because he didn't want to do anything to agitate his son any further. After a few moments of silence, he spoke quietly.

'Leave it with me, son. I'll raise the money. It won't be pretty, but if the goons who did this will give you three more days, I can fix you up and make this go away. Don't ask me how. That's my business. OK?'

Dean nodded.

'So, was it Coke Dick? Did he do this?'

'No. It wasn't Coke Dick.'

'So, who then?'

'He doesn't know anything. I mean, he knows I broke my leg, but he doesn't know why. He'd literally kill me if he found out. I've been so fucking stupid. I went behind his back. I tried to move some drugs, County Lines, but for another dealer, not him. I don't know his name, but I know he's big. Bigger than Coke Dick and like . . . much, much more dangerous – if that's even possible. It was supposed to be one easy job, low risk. My cut was £2,000. Easy money. But the fucking feds seized the drugs. Right in front of my nose. I nearly got caught. But they didn't get all of it. If they had, I'd already be dead. They got twenty-five grand's worth. So now I've got to pay it back.'

'One easy job? There's no easy way to make money. Not for people like us. Not without huge risks. And now look where you are.'

'I'm sure somebody grassed us in. There's no way the

feds could have found out any other way. It was solid gold, tight deal. Hardly anyone even knew anything about it, you get me? And I didn't tell nobody. So, it's not my fault the drugs got seized. But I'm the one that's got to pay, cos I was supposed to pick them up and keep them safe like. I think they suspect I nicked them or something. Which is crazy. I'd have to be really stupid to do that. Anyway, they know the feds swooped, so I don't know why they think I nicked anything.'

'That's how it works, son. Those are the rules. It's always those at the bottom who take all the risks and get the smallest cut. Look, if . . . after I sort this, you've got to cut ties with everyone, including Coke Dick. Learn a trade, get an apprenticeship, work in fucking McDonald's, I don't care. It's not worth it. Meantime don't tell another soul. If word gets around that you went behind Coke Dick's back, you're fucked. What were you even thinking?'

'What are you going to do?'

'I told you. It's none of your business. This is *my* problem now.'

Paul walked purposefully into his bedroom. He closed the door and listened to make sure that Dean was still in the kitchen. Then he lay on his front and reached underneath his wardrobe and moved his hand around at full stretch until it made contact with a small package. He slid it out carefully and laid it on the bed. It was a black drawstring gym bag. Paul prized apart the string and tipped the contents onto the bed.

There was a SIG Sauer P226 full-sized service pistol and a matt black Glock G19 semi-automatic 9mm pistol, with a trigger sheath and two magazines – one 19-round magazine and the other filled with 33 bullets, a total of 52 units of live ammunition. First, he checked in the chamber. Empty. Then he took a pair of socks from a drawer, wrapped the Glock in one and the 33-round magazine in the other and stuffed them both into his trouser pockets. Then he went down the hallway, pushed his arm into the sleeve of his coat and reached for the front door.

'I'm going out. You can stay the night if you like but don't wait up.'

Paul closed the door softly behind him and walked to the end of the road, until he was out of sight of his house. Then he took out his mobile phone and dialled a number from memory.

'Hello? It's Paul . . . Yeah, it has been a long time . . . Yep . . . I'm glad to hear it. Yeah, I'm good. But I need to call in a favour. Sorry to spring this on you, but it's kind of urgent . . . I've got a piece I need to move . . . Glock G19, Gen 2, two mags, 50 live rounds. Yeah. Yeah. No, it's the real thing, not converted. Can you get 28 and take a 3K cut? Three days. Yeah. I know, if it wasn't serious, I wouldn't ask. OK, yeah. Got it. Thanks. OK. I'll meet you there in twenty minutes. Cheers.'

Chapter Twenty-Three

Mike had two reasons to celebrate. Today was his 34th birthday and he had hit his sales target for the first quarter – C1 – which meant that in July he would be one of three employees enjoying a spa weekend in Cheshire. He'd have preferred a pay rise but at least he wasn't in danger of losing his job any time soon.

He was an industrial chemist – but really, he was a glorified sales rep, touting 'technology-based performance materials' – pigments, powders and oxides – it was highly technical and too boring to explain so he identified primarily as a firefighter. It was a more interesting subject than specialty chemicals. Besides, it was usually misconstrued as code for 'drug dealer'. Either that or the conversation would meander towards a discussion of chemtrails or big pharma. So, being a firefighter had saved him on many occasions. On the bookshelf behind the television in the lounge, sat two framed photographs: one of him dressed in a fur-lined robe on the day he graduated with a First in Chemistry from Manchester University; the second was him, five years older, in full firefighter set. He was most proud of the latter.

He was also Chinese. His parents still ran a thriving takeaway restaurant in the town. He had worked there many times when he was growing up but didn't want to make it his life and neither did his 'tiger' parents, who had pushed him hard at school. As a result, he had developed a fierce work ethic and always applied himself one hundred percent to whatever he did. He loved firefighting because it was the perfect blend of the mental and the physical. It demanded bucket loads of common sense and a high level of physical fitness. It took him out of his head and it also demanded a very practical application of knowledge. Mike gave classroom talks to the crew on fires and its deadly smoke products and was one of four fire appliance drivers at the station.

Tonight's celebration took the form of vegging on the sofa enjoying a delivery meal from his parents' gaffe (he wasn't allowed to patronise any other establishments, but it was always free, so he didn't object) whilst binge-watching some Scandi Noir on Netflix. He had split up with his girlfriend a month earlier, so he was enjoying the freedom of a night in. She would have insisted they go to a restaurant, which would have cost at least £80 and meant the wearing of clothes. This was much better. Prawn balls with sweet and sour sauce, chicken in a black bean sauce, half a crispy duck with pancakes, egg fried rice and two small vegetable spring rolls. All free and there would be enough leftovers for breakfast tomorrow.

There was a sharp knock at the door. It was his takeaway. From a white plastic bag, Mike carefully removed five containers – four plastic and one corrugated aluminium – plus one Styrofoam cup of bright red sauce and placed them neatly on the kitchen table. Then he collected his plate which had been warming in the oven. He was about to start spooning food when he heard the unmistakable beep of his alerter, which was sitting next to the television.

'Fuck! No!' Mike hopped around the kitchen as he slipped on a pair of trainers without undoing the laces, then he closed the kitchen door, so the cat couldn't eat his food. He was almost at the front door when he realised that he'd shut the cat *inside* the kitchen. He grabbed her from underneath the table, then popped her on the sofa, or rather, the cat made a giant leap to escape from his arms.

With the cat sorted, Mike grabbed his car keys, ran out of the house and jumped into his car. At that precise moment, eleven other retained firefighters were either slamming their driver-side car doors and starting their engines, or they were already on the road, with the shared single aim of reaching the fire station by 15:05. One minute had already elapsed since their alerters had started flashing and beeping.

When Mike pulled into the fire station, he could see by the array of vehicles scattered around the front and side of the building that he was one of the last to arrive. Five minutes earlier, every one of his colleagues had been going about their civilian lives, like him, tending to their daily business, holding down their jobs, or looking after their families, walking the dog, going shopping, whatever. Each of them had been interrupted by their alerter and had sprung into action.

He rushed from his car to the changing room, passing Ricky on the way. Ricky snorted with laughter. It was only then that Mike realised that he was wearing his SpongeBob SquarePants pyjamas.

Four minutes later Mike, along with the rest of the crew, had changed into his fire kit and boarded a fire engine. Reading from the printed report, John Turnbull shouted out the incident to the crew: 'Waste dumpster on fire behind the Westminster Hotel, Stockwood, one appliance required.'

Since John Turnbull oversaw this incident, he commanded appliance SW02, which began its blue light journey, this time with Mike driving and four other crew members – Chelsea, Sandi, Raj and Ricky – on board. The other appliance and its crew remained on standby at the station.

After a short fast drive, Mike parked the fire engine in front of the hotel. Several staff members came out to meet them and to direct them to the dumpster fire at the rear of the five-storey red brick building. This wasn't necessary because the thick black smoke rising from the blue dumpster was clearly visible, even from the road.

Mike watched as Raj and Ricky readied the HPHR – high pressure hose reel – for use as Turnbull radioed the control room to book 'in attendance'. As driver, this time it was Mike's job to engage the fire pump.

'Raj and Ricky, get under air.' At Turnbull's instruction, Raj and Ricky donned their breathing apparatus and slotted their ID tags onto Mike's BA board.

'Gauge check,' shouted Raj. They both checked their gauges and then the two men ran towards the dumpster, as the yellow and black hose unfurled behind them.

At that moment, Turnbull heard the fire control room radioing a request for SW01 to attend another dumpster bin fire only half a mile from the Westminster Hotel.

They applied whoosh water to the dumpster, half of which had melted, so that there was a small lake of flaming molten plastic on the tarmac that was threatening to spread the fire to the surrounding debris – two broken fence panels, a pile of scrap wood, half a wooden pallet, two filthy orange traffic cones and several parked cars. The entire area was littered with flammable wooden waste, most of which was contained behind a red-brown welded wire mesh fence. If they didn't extinguish the flames quickly, there was a strong chance that the hotel building would become engulfed in flames. So, there was no such thing as 'just a dumpster fire'. The sheer quantity of builders' waste meant that without intervention, the situation would have quickly developed into a major incident.

Working quickly and efficiently, Raj and Ricky managed to extinguish all visible flames within five minutes. Taking no chances, they also hosed down the flammable debris.

Turnbull barked into his personal radio: 'Mike, put the stop in, over.'

'Roger that, over,' replied Mike. 'Sierra Whiskey 02 to Fire Control. Dumpster fire extinguished. We'll be here for another fifteen minutes clearing up. No further resources required.'

Sierra Whiskey 02 never made it back to the station. Before the night was out a further three dumpster fires were lit, and several wheelie bins torched across town and at 1:30am, an abandoned sofa was set alight beneath a fire escape. Eight fires were lit in total in different parts of the town, keeping both crews busy for nearly six hours.

Mike got home the following morning at 3:15am. He was greeted by a hungry cat and a table full of cold takeaway. He zapped his dinner in the microwave and while he ate, he reflected on a busy shift. He had a hunch that these wouldn't be the last bin fires they would have to tackle this month. It never crossed his mind that one of his trusted colleagues was responsible.

Across the town, John Turnbull was relaxing at home with a large whisky, delighting in his young protégé's handiwork. In a single evening, Daniel had earned £160 of his £400 advance. If he could continue his arson spree without getting caught, the lad was going to turn around the fortunes of Stockwood on Sea Fire Station. As expected, the police were treating the incidents as arson, but they would have their work cut out trying to gather a case against an individual, not least because fire destroys most forensic evidence and firefighting destroys the rest. John would make sure that each arson crime scene he attended would be severely compromised by the conscientious application of gallons of water at high pressure.

Chapter Twenty-Four

10:30 Wednesday 3 April 2019

After spending Monday evening and well into Tuesday morning fighting dumpster fires, Leah had postponed her sleuthing until today. But now that she was in her office at the planning department, with a cup of black coffee steaming beside her, she was already starting to feel foolish.

Nevertheless, she logged into her computer and started to search the online register of planning decisions. She could have done this at home, since it was all in the public domain, but she figured that if she did find anything that she wanted to explore further, then she could switch to the mainframe for details to which only she and her colleagues had privileged access, but even that was merely for reasons of confidentiality and issues surrounding data protection. She was already starting to doubt that she would find anything since nearly all the information was hiding in plain sight. Everything from the last 12 years was freely available online; anything earlier than that was unlikely to have any relevance to the attempted closure of the fire station in the present day.

A keyword search of 'Coast Road' cross-referenced with 'Fire Station' returned nothing of interest. She came across an application for a caravan park, which had been declined six years earlier, but it didn't look suspicious, and the same applicant had successfully acquired an alternative plot of land the following year further along the coast. Next, she ran a few searches using the postcode of the fire station and nearby properties, which also drew a blank. After an hour of aimless searching, interrupted by several telephone calls, Leah's neck was stiff, her eyes were sore, and she realised that her efforts were hopeless.

What am I even looking for? Leah asked herself. She could only search using postcodes and planning application reference numbers. She couldn't type in 'Graeme Dollins', the little grey man with the expensive Tesla, and get a result. It was worse than looking for the proverbial needle because she didn't know what she was looking for, or even if she was searching in the correct haystack.

She was going to have to come at this from another angle. What if she assumed that her suspicions were true? What if someone – let's say a property developer – wanted to close the fire station and acquire the land cheaply using unscrupulous methods like bribery? This hardly narrowed the field. She could name at least six individuals who had a reputation for using cash bungs under the table to get things done. And one or two who had been brazen enough to flash their cash above the table too.

Two years ago, she had been in a planning meeting for the restoration of a large seafront hotel. Negotiations had reached an impasse; tempers were fraying and both sides were unwilling to compromise. After a short coffee break, Leah returned to find a large brown envelope on the table in front of her chair. Thinking quickly, she waited until everyone was present and then drew their attention to the envelope.

'Does anyone know whose this is?' She looked around the room as she began to open it. She pulled out a wad of cash in twenty-pound notes, easily about £5,000. The barrister for the property developer whipped around and glared at her client, who shrugged and blushed deeply. The large brown envelope and its contents were hastily returned to its rightful owner, who in a subsequent public prosecution, pleaded guilty to attempted bribery. He had clearly watched too many movies because up to that point he had truly believed this was how all local planning decisions were decided.

Whoever the crooked property developer was, he or she would need someone who could bend the ear of the Fire Authority to encourage the closure and sale of the fire station, rather than simply bribe an individual like Dollins. And who would be able to do that? A local councillor who was not only involved with local planning decisions but also had a seat on the Fire Authority Committee.

The full Fire Authority comprising all 17 councillors met a minimum of three times a year. The Chief Fire Officer and directors sat at the table with the Fire Authority members and acted as advisors. Also present was a legal adviser and the Fire Authority treasurer (Dollins). As well as the full Fire Authority meetings, there were also several committees made up of smaller groups of Fire Authority members, which looked at certain aspects of the fire service. These committees made recommendations on the delivery of the Service and made decisions about issues relating to their specific field.

Her heart pumping with excitement, Leah googled the Fire Authority membership and scanned all the names of those who attended the various committees. One name immediately caught her eye because it came up time and time again. This individual was involved in all but one of the committees as well as playing a prominent role in the full Fire Authority meetings. His name was Charlie Price.

Leah wanted to shout with joy. She'd always suspected that there was something dodgy about that oily self-serving little try-hard. This didn't prove any wrongdoing, but his deep level of involvement was more than a little suspicious. She knew Price had zero interest in public service, so sitting on all these committees – as well as the Local Authority planning committee, where she had first met him – screamed vested interest with a capital V. There was no criminality here, but she had at least most probably exposed him in a lie, in his public support to save the station. But her discovery meant the odds had shifted: he was probably more invested in closing the station than fighting for it to stay open.

At that moment, Leah's thoughts were interrupted by her mobile phone ringing. It was the receptionist from the vets.

'Hello, Mrs Walsh? It's Tilly from Broadway Vets. I've got some good news. Bells is all ready for collection this week, whenever you are.'

'Oh, thank you, yes, that's great. I'll pick her up on Friday afternoon if that's OK? About five o'clock?'

'That's fine. Just to let you know, we close at five-thirty so try not to be late. Thank you. We'll see you then.'

Leah looked at the time. *Damn it.* This would have to

wait until she got home, but at least she had Price's measure. Now she just had to figure out what he was up to and how he stood to benefit personally from the closure of the fire station.

Chapter Twenty-Five

08:15 Thursday 4 April 2019

Paul Gray had reached the 'collecting the floating stragglers' stage of a large bowl of Crunchy Nut Clusters when he heard his son, stirring in the lounge. A few moments later, Dean shuffled into the kitchen. He looked rough, not only because he'd been sleeping on his dad's sofa for the last three nights, but also because he was scared. He knew that his dad had promised to settle his debt, but they hadn't spoken of it since Monday evening. No one knew he was here, so he felt safer staying off the grid for a few days, but he couldn't doss here forever. Just as he was about to raise the subject, his dad pre-empted him.

'Hi. Take a seat. You look like shit. Didn't you sleep?'

'Yeah, it's alright, I've just got stuff on my mind.'

'Well yeah, about that stuff. I've got your money, in cash of course. All of it, the full 25K.'

Dean nodded. He wanted to say thank you, but it didn't seem appropriate. He mainly felt embarrassed.

'So, I need you to set up a drop.'

'It's OK, I can take it . . .'

'No, I'm going to deliver it myself. It's not that I don't trust you. Actually, I *don't* trust you, but—'

'Look, Dad, I swear—'

'Whatever, I'm delivering it myself. No discussion. If any shit kicks off, then it comes through me. I used to have a . . . reputation around these streets . . . and I'm hoping some of it still sticks. So, please get on your blower and make the call.'

'Now?'

'Yeah. I don't want this money hanging around. I've let the dust settle for a few days, but now I want rid of it as soon as. Tell them I can deliver this morning.'

'They won't like it if you turn up instead of me.'

'Well, that's their problem. If they want their money, then they deal with me. Go on. Make the call.'

Dean sighed, glumly. He walked into the hall to retrieve a burner phone from the pocket of his jacket which was hanging by the front door. After making a quick call, he returned to the kitchen.

'Nine-fifteen, now, this morning. They said the waste ground just before you get to the old steelworks. There's a massive stack of old tyres. They said something about a single tyre in front of the cage. They want you to put the money underneath it and walk away.'

'Jesus. Why can't they just deal face to face?'

'You haven't got much time. Nine-fifteen.'

'Yeah, yeah. OK, whatever. But that's you straight, right? Done. Finished with all this shit. I cannot bail you out again. So, you'd better tell me if there's anything else I should know.'

'No that's it. I swear.'

'Right, well, I'd better make a move then.'

Seven flights of stairs and twenty-five minutes later, Paul Gray had changed the flat tyre on his Fire Service hydrant van and was finally ready to leave. *Bloody kids.* This was the third puncture in as many weeks, but he had to use his van for the drop off. Although it made him a target for casual vandalism, Paul knew the police would never suspect the driver of a trusted partner agency vehicle. But now he was late. He was definitely too old for *this*.

He crawled tediously around the city centre, stopping at every set of traffic lights, before finally reaching the coast road to make the long straight journey to the steelworks in the next town along. Paul kept checking his watch, nervously. *Get a fucking move on.* He frequently tapped the rucksack on the passenger seat to reassure himself that the money was still there. After an interminably long and stressful journey, Paul spotted two grey steel stacks thrusting into the sky and parked the van.

It was 09:12. He had three minutes to reach the tyre dump, which was nearly four hundred yards away. He walked as quickly as he could. He knew he was being watched so he didn't want to look weak by breaking into a run. He reached the tyre cage with seconds to spare. A rubber slag heap of tyres loomed over him like a single brooding entity. Sure enough, a single tyre was propped up against the mesh fence.

Paul nonchalantly scanned a wide arc, to make sure he wasn't being watched by a member of the public, then quickly pulled a grey plastic A3 envelope out of his rucksack and stashed it underneath the tyre. He felt ridiculously conspicuous and hated leaving so much money, however briefly. *They'd better be here.*

As he turned to leave, he heard a noise behind him and spun round. A stocky young man with ginger hair was walking slowly towards him.

'Hello Paul. How have you been?'

'Fuck, you gave me a shock' was what Paul wanted to say, but instead he opted for: 'Should I know you?'

'You don't know me, but you know my boss.'

'OK, whatever. The money's all there. Twenty-five grand. That's my son's debt paid in full. You can count it if you like, otherwise, I'm leaving.'

'I said, you know my boss.'

'I heard what you said. And like I said – whatever. Are we done?'

'BASILEUS.'

The word hung in the fresh morning air like a toxic gas.

'What did you say?'

'You heard me.'

'Alright. But that doesn't change anything. I've paid my son's debt. In full. That was the deal.'

'Is that what your son told you?'

'Look, what's happening here? Do we have a deal or not?'

'Your son still owes us.'

I fucking knew it. 'How much?'

'Well, you tell me. What is his life worth? We inflicted a penalty on his leg because he couldn't pay. And you've settled his debt, so we can draw a line under that. But if Coke Dick found out that he tried to deal with us, he's a dead man.'

'Why is that any business of yours?'

'Your, forgive me – clueless son – is way out of his

depth. At first, we thought he was an undercover cop, but then we found out that he worked for Coke Dick. We don't want another turf war. A broken leg here, a lost hand there.' He nodded at Paul's stump which Paul instinctively moved from the other man's gaze. 'That's acceptable. That's collateral damage . . . but when people start dying . . . well let's just say a turf war is bad for business and it disturbs the status quo. Do you understand?'

'Look, I don't have any more money and my son has nothing. I can't pay you to keep quiet.'

'If it was up to me, I would say yes, but as you know, my boss doesn't do anything by halves.'

'You just said that dead bodies are bad for business. If Coke Dick . . . finds out . . . surely, it's in your best interest that he doesn't.'

'Well, that's a logical theory but . . . are you prepared to take that gamble?'

'I can't . . . I just can't pay anymore. Look, what can . . . what do you need me to do?'

'You can pay us another way. Do a drop. One big drop to clear the slate.'

'Jesus.'

'I'll take that as your tacit agreement. It's nice to have you back in the firm, even if it's just for a short while. Run along now. We'll be in touch.'

The man turned around and strode away without looking back. Paul stood, feeling winded and angry. *What just happened? Shit. What the fuck?*

Chapter Twenty-Six

16:45 Friday 5 April 2019

The waist-high stone wall outside the church curved in a wide crescent around the freshly laid red brick parquet. The old concrete benches had been supplanted by wooden picnic tables. Nearby, a hexagon of grass and shrubbery was neatly fenced off. The facelift had been a municipal success, but Bartek Kaminska preferred the way it had been before when he could drink his vodka without being disturbed. Now, the police turned up every day to move him and other homeless drinkers away from the area. What were they supposed to do? They had to be somewhere.

Bartek chuckled to himself as he scanned the faces of his five drinking 'przyjaciele'. They weren't 'friends'. Bullies within the group knew Bart was a soft touch. There was a pecking order and Bart was right at the bottom of it. They would steal his alcohol; if he refused to hand it over, they would beat him up. Once a week at midnight they marched him to the cashpoint to steal his benefit money, leaving him with a few pounds to live on.

If the bullies were at the bottom of the soup kitchen steps, and only 14 people were let in, and Bart was at the top of the steps, which he often was, he would be shoved and pushed to the bottom, past others waiting in line. As a result, he had spent many wet cold lonely nights sleeping rough in Stockwood on Sea. He often had a black eye and a cut lip but would never tell police officers what had happened. He didn't want any trouble; he just wanted to be left alone and to stay under everyone's radar.

Life hadn't always been this difficult. Ten years earlier, Bartek – or Bart as he was known – had moved to the UK to look for better-paid jobs and to send money back home to his family in Poland. He had spent a few years in London labouring on construction sites, but he had been fired countless times because of his drinking. He had often been drunk on the job but never violent. He was always polite and courteous to everyone including police officers. He usually kept himself to himself but still sought the company of like-minded street drinkers.

He had moved into the area on the promise of work in the nearby steelworks. He had held down a job there for 2 years, paid his rent on a flat and only drank vodka on his days off. Life had been tolerable for Bart back then until a single lapse when he turned up to work drunk and was fired on the spot. That meant that he couldn't pay the rent on his flat and so he was eventually evicted and had spent several months sleeping rough on the streets of Stockwood on Sea.

Finally, a few weeks ago, his luck had changed. The Local Authority had judged him to be highly vulnerable, so he had been given a room in an HMO (house of multiple occupancy). His building, like many others, had been converted from an old bed and breakfast establishment from the bygone age of mass UK home holidaying. Bart started to receive state benefits and was given some new clothes but vodka still ruled his every waking moment. He would drink it every day, no matter what time it was: vodka for breakfast, lunch, dinner, supper and in between. Like so many in the many town-centre HMOs, Bart lived at the margins of society, unable to work due to his poor health brought on by alcoholism, unwanted by society in general and viewed as a stain on the town by do-gooders and town council members who were vociferous in the vanguard. Police would often receive complaints from shop owners and the public about their drunken behaviour and then move them on to a place where they were less likely to be seen.

Most would go to the bandstand area in the park, where they would meet up with other drinkers and a few teenagers who went there to see the entertainment, as very often fights and arguments would break out in the group. Bart's only involvement with the police was receiving a caution for exposing himself to a parent and his daughter a few years ago. He'd only been peeing against a wall. Members of the public would often cross the street to avoid this group of down-and-outs. Parents gripped their children's hands a little tighter and always avoided eye contact.

Daniel and his little posse often went there to see the show. Bart also continued to mix with the same group of street drinkers and his flat had quickly become a drinking haven for them but on this Friday afternoon, the drinks remained *al fresco* until the storm clouds began to darken the sky.

'Hey, Barty boy.' A red-faced ginger-haired Scottish guy called Jock, prodded Bart aggressively in the arm as he announced his plan in a guttural rasping voice: 'Hey pal, let's go. It's gonna rain. Let's get to your gaffe before it soaks the fucking lot of us. Eh? Bart. Do you fucking hear meh?'

'Yes. I can hear you. You want to go now?'

'That's wa a fuckin' said. Come on, move.'

Bart obediently shifted his weight forward and his legs slid stiffly off the wall. He swayed on his feet as he addressed the group: 'You all come to my flat. All you are welcome. It is going to rain soon.'

As he was speaking, the first drops began to fall; the other four drinkers started to stir themselves. Within thirty seconds the drops had turned into a torrent; they were getting soaked. Pulling dirty clothes tight around them, the liminal group of misfits limped, swaggered and cursed their way to Bart's flat.

The bedsit was a set of six flats above a shop. All the tenants had issues of some kind – drug abuse, alcohol abuse or mental health – many had all three. As soon as Bart had located his keys and opened his front door, there was no room for niceties. Bart might have said, 'make yourself at home' but they didn't need an invitation. They barged past him and sluiced into his flat like a muddy squall. It made little difference to its appearance since similar chaotic groups composed of transient individuals had already trashed Bart's home on earlier visits. The floor, table and most other surfaces were strewn with the debris from those drink and drug sessions. Jock immediately hailed his arrival by pissing copiously in a corner, before ransacking the empty fridge and kitchen cupboards in search of food. The toilet was the cleanest place in the flat because it was rarely used; there was human waste in the corners of every room.

By 7:00pm all the alcohol had been drunk and everyone was beyond smashed. The three left Bart's flat and headed for the pecking order steps at the local night shelter to take up a free bed and breakfast for the night. Bart sat on his couch, smoking a cigarette and drunkenly lapsing in and out of consciousness.

At 8:00pm, other tenants in the building could smell smoke and began to leave via the communal hallway, to gather outside on the street. As is common in HMOs, someone had removed the batteries from the smoke detectors in the communal hallways, so there was no facility for early smoke detection to save lives with early evacuation. A passer-by called 999 and asked for the fire service: 'There's a first-floor flat on fire. We think a man is still inside.'

Chapter Twenty-Seven

Leah rang her own doorbell. She had it all rehearsed in her mind: Dave, or even better (though highly unlikely), Katie would open the door to find her standing with a huge smile on her face, carrying their new canine family member. As usual, reality played out slightly differently. First, there were no signs of life inside, even though she knew that both were home. She rang again, three times, holding the third ring for a few seconds. She still couldn't hear footsteps or Katie bounding downstairs.

'Sod this,' said Leah out loud. Bells was already squirming in her arms, wanting to explore the smells at ground level. She scrambled in her bag for her keys and let herself in. She had to pick Bells up again because she didn't have her lead and she didn't want to drag her by her collar.

'Hello? Anyone home?'

'In here.' Dave was in the lounge, watching television, wine glass in hand.

'Why didn't you answer the door? Look what I've got. Surprise!'

'Holy shit! It's a dog!'

'It's Bells. Isn't she gorgeous?'

'Is it . . . have you . . . are we having her now?'

'Well, yeah. We agreed, didn't we?'

'Yeah but . . . it's OK, I just . . .'

'What?'

'Well, I didn't think it would be so soon, like this week.'

'I said she'd had all her jabs and was good to go, didn't I? Anyway, thanks for answering the door. Are you pissed off?'

'No, of course not. It's just . . . you could have warned me.'

'It was meant to be a surprise. What's wrong? You *are* pissed off.'

'Don't tell me I'm pissed off. Fuck. Now I am. Stop telling me what I'm feeling.'

'And here we go again. This was supposed to be a nice thing. Meet Bells. She's our new best friend. Jesus. Where's Katie. Is she in?'

'She's in her room, I think.'

'Katie!' Leah yelled up the stairs. 'KATIE!'

'What?'

'Come downstairs. I've got a surprise for you.'

'It's OK, I had a sandwich. I'm not hungry.'

'Come here. It's not food. Come down, now, please.'

Katie exhaled noisily with exasperation and stood at the top of the stairs. Then she saw Bells and burst into tears.

'She's beautiful, hello Bells.' Katie rubbed her ears and nuzzled her face into hers. 'Is she staying, now?'

'Yes, I've got all her stuff in the car, plus dog food. Be careful though, don't crowd her too much, she's been through a lot, remember.'

'She's fine. She loves it, look. You're so cute.'

'She's very friendly, but don't put your face too close

to her for now, until she knows you better. Can you keep her in the lounge? I'm going to fetch the rest of her stuff from the car, plus I did some shopping.'

Once Leah had emptied the car and unpacked the shopping, she looked at the kitchen clock. It was 8:05pm. Time to make some dinner.

Suddenly, her alerter began to beep as the printer at Stockwood on Sea fire station printed out another incident for the retained crew.

Three miles away, Ricky was about to cut into a medium-rare pan-seared sirloin at the intimate Bistro restaurant where he and his wife were celebrating their wedding anniversary. His alerter activated.

'Another bloody night ruined, I'm sick of you being called out all the time. What about me?'

'Sorry, Lin, we'll have to talk about it later. You'll have to get a taxi home, I need the car.'

All other alerters activated around the town. Twelve retained crew members abandoned their places of work or homes, said their goodbyes, and entered their cars for the short but fast drive to their fire station. Twelve driver's doors opened and closed and they were off to a deployment, mobilized.

Watch Manager John shouted out the incident to the crew: 'Flat on fire at 56 North Street, Stockwood on Sea, persons reported, both appliances to attend.' *Persons reported.* The words no firefighter ever wants to hear.

The high-adrenaline blue light drive took three minutes, with blues and two-tone sirens on along with the bull horn. The two engines roared along the coast road, hitting speeds up to 60 mph before turning off and heading through the busy town centre traffic, where the flashing lights of the appliances painted patterns on every building and were reflected from every shop window.

Lee was driving appliance Sierra Whiskey 01. As he approached the scene, he could see that the police had already taped off the road ahead. Two police officers in high-viz jackets were standing on either side of the road. Lee had less than a second to decide: he could either brake hard and wait for the two officers to remove the police tape cordon, losing thirty precious seconds, or smash through the tape without even slowing down. He chose the latter. The police officers were stupefied. They looked up to witness a grinning Lee drive straight through the tape, which stretched and snapped as they raced to those who needed help. After the wailing red fire truck had passed, a sliver of yellow and black tape fluttered back to earth to land artlessly across the face of one of the officers. It displayed the instruction: 'LICE LINE DO NOT CRO'.

Then a second fire truck screamed past, as driver Chelsea waved an apologetic 'thank you'.

Two hundred yards further on, a small group of heavily outnumbered police officers was managing the pedestrian onlookers. Despite the rising fear and hysteria among the crowd, most people quickly complied with police orders to move behind the cordon. Despite this, the scene felt chaotic. Some people were screaming and pointing up at the first-floor window, where it appeared that a figure of a person fully on fire had their hands pressed flat against the window in a surrender pose. A distraught woman was fighting to get past the police to enter the building. The police officer pulled her away and pushed her back towards the crowd.

'But it's Barts flat,' she screamed, 'you got to get in there, for fuck's sake do something, you're just standing around doing piss all.'

The woman ran up to Turnbull in tears: 'I think Bart is still in his flat. He was there with his friends earlier.' She pointed up to the shattered window. It was a redundant gesture; the bright orange flames and thick black smoke told the whole story: Bart was in all probability already dead.

Turnbull sent a radio message to the control room: 'Sierra Whiskey 02, I can confirm a fire is in progress and well alight. Persons reported. Smoke and fire is issuing out of several first-floor windows. In attendance.' The call came back: 'Police officers already on the scene. Ambulance on its way.'

Raj, Ricky, Jordan and Steve quickly got themselves and each other ready with 'no skin on show' and donned their BA sets ready to enter the gates of hell. Their brief was to save survivable lives and to extinguish the fire. They handed their ID tallies to the BA control board operator. 'Gauge check,' shouted Jordan. They all checked their gauges and ran towards the fire, with the yellow and black hose behind them.

The pumps from both appliances were engaged and the revs increased.

'Water on' shouted Lee from SW01. 'Water on' echoed Chelsea from SW02. Mike linked up a fire hydrant to SW02 to feed it with water.

The two pairs of BA wearers walked through the ground-level entrance door, which was already open. Despite poor visibility, they quickly climbed the stairs to the first floor, dragging their charged high-pressure hose reels. Then they trudged towards Bart's flat, shining their torches and shouting brief instructions to each other above the muffled sound of their own heavy breathing. Even before they reached the flames, this was a highly toxic environment, as alien and as deadly to life as the surface of Mars.

They reached the door to Bart's flat. Beyond it lay a shard of dislocated time and space, a seething conflagration of ghostly otherworldliness. Primal fear and the instinct for self-preservation told the four crew that they had no business being there, exposing themselves to this lethal malicious energy. Then, adrenaline and years of training, locked away all their mundane human responses.

'Once we open this door, there's no going back,' said Ricky. 'Are you ready?'

They all gave a nod. Ricky took a half step back and then landed a single brutal kick on the door, which flew open to reveal thick black smoke from waist to ceiling as a fire ball erupted from the flat and roared up the staircase. They had already accepted the grim certainty that they would be recovering a dead body rather than rescuing a casualty.

Suddenly, a burning figure, swaddled in flame, eyes wide with fear, lunged toward them screaming in agony. Its hair and clothing were ablaze, burning flesh fell from its face, its hands and forearms were exposed to the bone. It careened into them, shunted by a dense cloud of acrid smoke as another huge orange fire ball burst out of the room and tore up the stairs, forcing the four crew onto the floor.

As the burning man collapsed on the stairs, the second

crew – Jordan and Steve – drenched him with water with their high-pressure hose as he lay screaming in the smoke-filled hallway. Steve and Jordan took hold of the burning casualty. Steve had his legs and Jordan supported him under his armpits. They carried him down the stairs, still smouldering and screaming in agony, into the open air and onto the pavement, where he was treated by paramedics until he went quiet. His final tortured words were 'help me, help me.'

Steve and Jordan re-joined Raj and Ricky at the entrance to the first floor flat. The foursome entered the flat on their knees, shouting Bart's name, their voices muffled by their rubber face masks. Deadly radiated heat pulsed from the room, which was fully ablaze. They could feel the intensity. The only thing standing between them and certain death was the thermal protection of their multi-layered fire kit, which allowed them to operate in such hostile conditions.

The crew performed left- and right-hand searches of the flat, shuffling and sweeping their way through the darkness and smoke and eventually reached the living area, where everything was burning bright orange, including an inert mass on the sofa. It was Bart.

Both teams squirted water everywhere with their HPHRs and opened a front window for smoke ventilation. The extreme heat had already shattered several windows, sucking in more oxygen to feed the inferno. Large plumes of black smoke cascaded through the open window, accompanied by rivulets of brown water as they set about bringing the fire under control.

Leah and John remained outside, directing operations and listening to their crews over their radio comms system. Finally, the two crews exited the building with smoke and steam emanating from their hot clothing. It had been a tough firefight.

Lee put the stop in to the control room: 'Sierra Whiskey 01. Fire under control. No further resources required.'

Now that the fire had been extinguished, Leah and John entered the flat as the smoke had now cleared and had been replaced by a strange ghostly feeling. Leah and John looked at Bart's burnt remains. He had fallen asleep whilst smoking his last cigarette. The flesh and fat from his charred body had melted from his bones and melded with the remains of the old couch. A single snag of black curly hair sat atop a skinless skull. One eye socket was fused; the other was clean hollow bone. Teeth were poised like a row of old skittles. Ears, nose and lips were gone. Smoke was coming out of his mouth. Leah bit her cheek hard to suppress her gag reflex. Turnbull clenched his jaw and puckered his lips. The reek of cooked flesh hung in the air.

The crew remained on site for a further six hours. After officers from CID and CSI had preserved, documented, and photographed the scene. Crew members assisted HM Coroner staff. They placed Bart's remains into a rubber body bag before carrying him down the stairs into a private unmarked ambulance for transportation to the morgue at Stockwood General Hospital.

Stockwood on Sea retained fire crew returned to their station at 4am. Despite being tired and affected by the harrowing incident, they had to service the equipment and the appliances to make them ready for the next shout. The crew eventually headed home to their families at 6am.

Police officers remained on scene all night to protect its integrity pending the joint Police and Fire Service investigation the following day. The other residents were placed in the Westminster Hotel in East Parade.

In the coming days the crew discussed and dissected the incident, and after a week or so it was established that Bart had died from smoke inhalation, rather than burning in agony. One significant component was that Bart's couch was made many years before the introduction of non-flammable upholstery. The other casualty was identified as a man called Ivan who had travelled from a neighbouring village to join the drinking session at Bart's flat.

HM Coroner recorded a verdict of Accidental Death, with a cigarette as the probable cause of the fire. The Polish Embassy in London contacted Bart's family in Poland to inform them of his death. The Local Authority gave Bart a pauper's funeral. None of his family in Poland was present, because of the cost of travel and accommodation. However, a small group of street drinkers attended. At Stockwood on Sea cemetery, his grave was marked with a small wooden cross, with lettering in English and Polish, along with an empty bottle of vodka.

Chapter Twenty-Eight

10:00 Saturday 6 April 2019

Daniel was going up in the world. Two days ago, Coke Dick had paid him £1,000 cash. All he had to do in return was to keep a small package safe (under his bed) until he asked for it back. Easy money. His mum never came into his bedroom and his nine-year-old sister knew better than to trespass on his territory. He didn't care what was inside. Drugs most likely, or maybe even a gun. He was curious to know, but the package was wrapped in thick black duct tape and Coke Dick had told him that on no account was he to open it.

Whatever. The first thing Daniel had done was to ditch his bike for an off-road motorcycle, for which he had paid two hundred pounds, but it wasn't taxed or insured and he didn't even have a licence. He'd spent the day riding it around his estate. He didn't even care about getting stopped by the police. They couldn't catch him, and the residents would never snitch on him. Daniel also kept stashed under his bed the stolen five-litre plastic petrol can, so he had plenty of fuel.

This morning was like many others. He rode from his house to meet up with a drug dealer so that he could make some deliveries. Turnbull had told him to quit the drug scene, but there was no way he was going to cut off one of his income streams. Daniel saw himself as a businessman, a cool-headed entrepreneur from the streets, and he intended to make easy money wherever he could.

Setting bin fires for that idiot Turnbull must have been the easiest gig he had ever blagged. But today he had bigger plans. He was going to take out a *pig's* car. He smiled. Daniel loved a bit of retro. It was fucking mint.

As he rode past a row of shops on Chester Street, he spotted two police officers entering a shop. Their patrol car was parked nearby. This was his chance. He knew they'd be in there for a while speaking to the shop owner, at the back of the shop. They were responding to a complaint from the Asian shop owner, who had been verbally abused and threatened the previous night after refusing to serve alcohol to a group of drunken youths. The reason he knew this was because he was one of them.

'Fucking pigs,' Daniel said to himself. He pulled his bike around and sped home to fill a bottle with petrol. Then, with his scarf covering his face, he drove back to the patrol car. He didn't even have to smash a window because dumb plod had left one open. He lit the fuse, threw the bottle onto the dashboard. The bottle shattered with a whooshing sound as the petrol ignited, the car lit up, and without even looking back, Daniel sped away, all in fewer than ten seconds.

As soon as he had rounded the corner, he slowed down. He didn't want to attract attention. He made a few turns just in case a do-gooder member of the public was following him, then he drove to McDonald's. They were still serving breakfast, so they wouldn't give him a burger. But he was feeling pleased with himself, so he didn't kick up a fuss. He didn't even swear. He'd just come back later.

John Turnbull was happily singing along to the radio, whilst cutting a client's lawn in South Drive, when his alerter activated.

Moments earlier, back at the shop, a neighbour had called 999 and asked for the fire service. At 10.35 hrs, the printer at Stockwood on Sea fire station disgorged another incident for the retained crew. Twelve alerters activated at twelve different locations around the town, and twelve ordinary people responded.

John was the first to arrive at the station. As soon as he read the computer readout he couldn't stop himself from cursing out loud: 'The stupid little shit.' He knew immediately that Daniel was responsible. Petrol bomb in a police car? The police might be too stupid to collar Daniel immediately, but Turnbull knew it was him. *The stupid little twat was going to get himself caught.*

When his colleagues had arrived and changed into their kit, John shouted out the incident to the crew. Both appliances to attend.

Blues and twos activated, both drivers negotiated the morning traffic as they made their way to the 'Asian shop' on Chester Street, on the same housing estate where the puppies and their mum had died. When they arrived at the scene, two other police cars were already in attendance and several officers were busy keeping members of the public well away from the blaze and the thick black smoke bellowing over their heads. They were powerless to stop the fire from destroying the patrol car and had to watch, consumed by embarrassment and impotent anger.

Once again, residents were out enjoying the spectacle

– grown-ups, teenagers and young children – united in their excitement at seeing the police being so publicly humiliated. A cheer went up when the first tyre exploded, and the small crowd surged forward to get a closer look.

'Get back. Move back,' yelled the police officers, roughly shoving people away to safety, turning their anger and frustration into bullish physical action. They knew it wouldn't be long before the fuel tank exploded: a BLEVE – (boiling liquid expanding vapour explosion) – was moments away.

Leah radioed the control room to book 'in attendance' and to confirm the fire. Then, as she jumped down from the cab, the fuel tank exploded, sending a fireball shooting up into the morning sky. Two firefighters from each crew went under air and began to squirt water onto the burning vehicle using the HPHRs. Smoke quickly turned to steam and after a few minutes of activity, the fire was out.

John called a stop into the control room. He wanted this shout to end as quickly as possible so that he could track down Daniel and knock some sense into him. It was all he could think about. He barked orders at his crew to hurry up, because he was so impatient to get away. He scanned the area. He wouldn't have been at all surprised to see Daniel somewhere in the crowd, grinning inanely at his dumb criminality.

Eventually, all the equipment was stowed away on board the appliances and they returned to the station. Turnbull tore off his kit, showered and dressed in a flash and drove away without saying goodbye to any of his colleagues.

When Leah realised Turnbull had gone, she was frustrated. She wanted to tell him what she'd managed to uncover about Charlie Price, but now it would have to wait until Monday evening, when she was being honoured for 20 years of service. She didn't feel in the mood for celebration. It felt like a kick in the teeth to be presented with a long service medal and then be made redundant a few months later. Anyway, John would be there, so she'd have to pull him aside and talk to him in confidence. She hadn't even bothered to tell her husband yet because she wanted to gather more evidence.

Turnbull's strange mood didn't go unnoticed with the rest of the crew.

'What's got into him?' asked Alan, flexing his arm muscles and brazenly admiring the ripped V shape of his deltoids, where they met his biceps, triceps and brachialis.

'Buggered if I know,' replied Sandi, with a cheeky wink. 'Maybe he has other plans.'

'Yeah. Maybe he's rushed home for a big fat wank.'

Sandi snorted with laugher. 'Stop it! You're wicked you are. Talking of which . . .' She looked around, lowered her voice and grabbed his cock. 'What are you doing later?'

'Well, what are you doing now?' he replied.

They both hung back until the rest of the crew had left the station and they were alone. They made their way to the fire engine and scrambled to the back seat where they eagerly tore at each other's clothes.

'You know me too well, I can fuck you any time.'

He responded by pulling at her gym leggings and turning her around so she was facing away from him with her cheeks pushed against the BA sets. He quickly shagged her from behind.

Chapter Twenty-Nine

John Turnbull had already wasted the best part of an hour driving around the town searching for Daniel, but he wasn't in any of his usual hangouts. He had checked in McDonald's and several other places where he knew Daniel liked to loiter; he had driven up and down the promenade, in the hope of spotting Daniel pissing away the afternoon on the seafront or in one of the amusement arcades. He had also driven past his house several times, which he knew was futile because even if Daniel was at home, he couldn't just knock on his front door. Besides, he needed to get Daniel on his own so that he could teach that little shithead a fucking lesson.

Just as he was about to give up, he made one final slow pass of McDonald's and *there he was.* Sitting in the window, head buried in his phone, shovelling fries into his gaping maw with his free hand. Turnbull clenched his jaw and parked on double yellow lines just around the corner. He knew that Daniel would have to walk past him on his way home.

Sure enough, ten minutes later, Daniel appeared, but instead of walking past Turnbull's car, he approached a beaten-up off-road motorcycle about two car lengths away and mounted it. Only then did he realise that he wasn't on foot.

Without thinking, Turnbull leapt out of his car, put his arm paternally around Daniel's shoulder and guided him towards his car. 'Hi Daniel, it's good to see you. Jump in, I want to have a little word.'

Sensing something was wrong, Daniel jabbed his elbow sideways and bucked his shoulder hard to break free. 'Get off me. Don't touch—'

'It's OK Dan. Everything's fine. No need to cause a scene. Sh, sh, ssh. In fact, I think you deserve a little bonus.'

Daniel looked confused. 'What do you mean?' He softened a little.

Turnbull smiled. 'Hop in and I'll explain. Go on. I won't bite!'

'What about my bike?'

'No worries. I'll drop you back here after we've finished. Look, just get in. People are starting to stare.'

Against his better judgment, Daniel climbed into the front passenger seat and closed the door gingerly. Turnbull started the engine, pulled out quickly and within seconds was doing thirty miles an hour. He feared Daniel might do a runner if he remained stationary.

'So, what did you want to talk about? And what's this bonus?' Daniel looked at Turnbull's face. It was tenser and angrier than before. In fact, it was trembling with rage. Daniel suddenly felt terrified.

'Let me out. Let me go. Please—'

'SHUT THE FUCK UP!' Turnbull was gripping the steering wheel so tightly, his knuckles were white. Daniel imagined he was going to rip it away from the dashboard.

They drove in silence for about five minutes until they reached the outskirts of the town, down Marsh Road and past Marine Holiday Centre into a derelict building on waste ground. Turnbull parked the car behind the building so that nobody could see them. They were completely alone. He turned off the engine. Silence.

'Get out.' Turnbull had no need to be polite anymore. 'Get the fuck out of my car.'

Daniel sat pinned to his seat with fear. Turnbull barged his way out of the car and walked around to the passenger side. For a second time, Daniel quickly set his mobile phone to record, as he was dragged out. Using the back of his hand, Turnbull slapped Daniel hard across the face. Daniel fell sideways onto the floor. He could taste blood on his lip.

'Please no. Don't kill me.' Daniel started to cry.

'Stand up. Fucking stand up. I'm not going to kill you. I need to talk to you.'

Turnbull grabbed him again and yanked him to a standing position using one hand. They were hopelessly mismatched. Turnbull was a trained fighter and could easily kill a teenager like Daniel with a single punch.

Suddenly Turnbull remembered that he was dealing with a child. He lowered his voice and tried to restore some calm.

'OK, look. We have a good arrangement, right?'

Daniel nodded and dried his eyes. He stood as tall as he could muster, trying to blank from his mind that he had just been grovelling for his life on the dirty ground.

'But . . . what you did today was completely out of order.'

Daniel frowned quizzically, in a misguided attempt to look innocent.

'I know you torched a police car today. Outside the

Paki shop.'

'I thought you wanted me—'

'Not a police car. Bins. Bin fires, old sofas. No chance of injuring anyone or getting caught, so no house fires and certainly no fucking police cars.'

'You never said. I thought you'd be impressed.'

'Well, I'm not. And I'm not your jailbird dad, OK? Impressed? We have a business arrangement. What did I say above all else? Don't get . . .?'

'Don't get caught yeah, I know. But nobody saw me and I didn't stay like before. I was gone.'

'It doesn't matter. It's too risky. If you really want to impress me, stick to bin fires and lots of them. That's what I'm paying you for. It's easy money for you and it's low risk. Why screw that up? If you get caught, it's all over. Is that clear?'

Daniel nodded.

'Right then. Get in. I'll take you back.'

In silence, Turnbull drove him back to his motorbike. The atmosphere in the car was still tense. Daniel hated him more than he had ever hated anyone. He was a psycho. Daniel had genuinely feared for his life. He didn't have to put up with this shit. He could use the recording on his phone to get Turnbull arrested any time he wanted, and if he guessed correctly, he could use the package under his bed for extra security.

Daniel jumped on his motorbike and raced home as quickly as the engine would allow him. He was still amped up with adrenaline. When he got home, he took the big scissors from a kitchen drawer and sat on his bed, carefully cutting through the layers of duct tape. A few minutes later he had liberated its contents which he immediately recognised from hours of playing *Call of Duty* on Kyle's PS4. It was a Glock 19.

There was a piece of metal covering the trigger which slid off quite easily, but beyond that, Daniel didn't know what to do. Nothing a few YouTube videos couldn't fix. After two hours of binge-watching instructional videos and playing around, he was an expert at removing the magazines, loading and unloading the rounds, pulling the slide back (with index finger extended along the frame) or pulling down the slide catch to load. *If only they taught this stuff at school,* he thought. *I'd be top of the class.* Now the only thing he didn't have real-time knowledge about was aiming and firing, but how hard could that be?

If Turnbull ever tried to hurt him again, he'd get a big surprise. Daniel stood up and pointed the gun at his reflection in the mirror. 'Get down on the fucking ground. I said, get on the fucking ground. NOW.' He imagined Turnbull on his knees, looking scared, with a wet patch where he'd pissed himself. 'I'll blow your stupid face off.'

The gun fitted easily into Daniel's tracksuit pocket without bulging. He practised pulling it out quickly a few times, then he sat on the bed, let the weapon rest in his palm on his lap and just stared at it, admiring its brutalist stylings and matt black finish.

Fucking gangsta.

Chapter Thirty

19:00 Monday 8 April 2019

'So, will you please put your hands together and show your appreciation for the guest of honour this evening, Leah Walsh.' Graeme Dollins beckoned for Leah to come up onto the stage to receive her medal for 20 years in the Fire Service.

The Chief Fire Officer is too busy to present my award, so he sent along Graeme Fucking Dollins. Forcing a smile, Leah kissed her husband on the side of his cheek, then squeezed his hand, stood up and made her way to the stage through a cluster of tables, around which were seated every member of her team, some with family, others without. But everyone was there, without exception: Lee was already smashed. He was punching the air and clapping so enthusiastically, it looked like sarcasm, but she knew it was heartfelt, albeit driven by his perilous blood alcohol levels. Matt was also worse for wear, red faced with a wide smile and dressed in a very expensive Paul Smith floral shirt; Sandi and Alan were almost sitting in each other's laps and were making no attempt to be discreet; Jordan and Steve scrubbed up well; Raj and Ricky, thick as thieves, both had huge green foam hands with 'Go Leah' written on them and were thrusting them into the air. Chelsea and Mike let off a couple of party poppers, which decorated a glowering Turnbull with multicoloured streamers. She welled up with pride as she approached the lectern.

She loved these people; they were like a second family. She trusted every single one of them to have her back in a crisis. They were some of the bravest and most incredible people she had met in her life, and yet they just looked like an ordinary bunch of townies on a night out in the function room of the Marine Lake Seaside Hotel. She suddenly felt so proud to have been given the privilege of leading this extraordinary group of unsung heroes and she had to concentrate hard to stop the lump in her throat from making her sob out loud.

Graeme Dollins shook her hand awkwardly using both his hands. Maybe he was trying to copy politicians and was trying too hard to project seniority and leadership but whatever he was attempting, he reminded Leah of a creepy uncle. After his ridiculous handshake, inexplicably he removed the medal from its presentation box, and attempted to place the red and yellow ribbon around her neck. Dollins managed to misjudge the depth of her head bow as well as her height, so that he nearly pressed his thumbs into her eyes. With hand-to-eye coordination that poor, *no wonder he was doing a desk job*, Leah mused. How does a grey little man like him afford a Tesla Model S? *He must be on the fiddle.*

After Leah bowed her head lower than she would have liked, Dollins managed to discharge his duty without further mishap. Then he offered her up to the lectern. Leah turned towards the lagoon of expectant faces and smiled. It was rare to have a night out with her colleagues away from work and be able to leave the alerter at home. Full time crews from 30 miles away were providing cover at Stockwood on Sea from 6pm to 9am to allow this one night out for the retained crew. It had been a tough few weeks but this evening was something of which she could be truly proud.

She hadn't prepared a speech, so she took a deep breath and was about to make a joke, when her temples began to throb, and she lost half the vision in her left eye. *Not again, not here.* Feeling a wave of nausea, and rocked with pain, Leah kept her thank you speech short. She was amazed that no one in the audience had noticed that she was close to passing out. She rattled through some platitudes and walked back to her seat to another boisterous round of applause, trying not to lose consciousness.

'Well done,' said Dave. Then he realised something was wrong. 'Are you OK?'

'Headache' Leah replied. I'll be alright in a sec, just give me moment. As Dollins droned on with a list of announcements, Leah regained her composure and started to feel more normal. She refused to let a brain tumour destroy her evening. More importantly, she needed to talk to Turnbull. Being so close to Dollins and his incompetence, she now trusted him even less than before and she was itching to unburden herself.

With the formalities of the night finished, the disco began and everybody moved onto the dance floor. Sandi was drunk and dancing and rubbing herself against Lee; he responded happily by groping her arse. Alan watched from the bar as jealousy began to take hold.

It was an hour before Leah saw her opportunity. She wasn't subtle. When Dave was deep in conversation with Alan about high resistance weight training, she slipped away, grabbed Turnbull by the shoulder and practically marched him outside. 'Come on,' she said, 'we need to talk.'

Once they were outside and Leah was confident that no one was eavesdropping or having a smoke nearby, she confided in him everything she had discovered about Charlie Price and his ardent committee work. Turnbull listened patiently without interruption. As she concluded, she said, 'I know this isn't proof of criminal activity, but it only makes me want to dig deeper. I know Price is a crook and is somehow linked to the closure of the fire station. And that joke Dollins must be on the take as well. I'm sure we'll be able to find enough so that I can take it to the police. I need to find out who is pulling his strings.'

'That's easy,' replied Turnbull. 'You must have heard of a property developer called David Alexander?'

'Of course.' Leah sneered. 'Alexander the Great.'

'Yep. But what you may not know is that he's a big drug dealer, and he uses his property empire to launder his drug money. He makes good money from both, but his property company serves the drug revenue stream, not the other way round. In the drug world he's known as "Basileus".'

'How do you know all this?'

'Only because an old mate of mine from the army used to work for him. He's six years older than me – forearms covered in prison tats so his nickname was Blackout. We both quit the army at the same time. I went into the fire service and landscape gardening, and he became a heavy for hire, doing Alexander's dirty work – dishing out punishments, kneecapping, collecting debts. But some things went wrong. First, one of the crew lost a hand, as punishment for fucking up on a big drug deal. And I mean really fucking up. The police seized some drugs, the usual thing, but they came this close to implicating David Alexander with rock solid evidence.'

'So, what happened?'

'It went missing from the police evidence room. Inside job. Alexander probably bribed a police officer with a stack of cash. Easy enough. Man like that will always have a few bent coppers on his payroll. Alexander was still livid that he'd come so close to getting arrested, so he lashed out at an easy target: he ordered Blackout to chop off the guy's hand and he did it. Blackout was nothing if not loyal. Years of army training teaches you that. Anyway, *that guy* was Paul Gray.'

'I know that name. Why do I know that name?' Leah frowned.

'It's Paul, Paul the Water Man.'

'Oh God. *Him*! That's how he lost his hand?'

'He's straight now but yeah, he used to be one of Alexander's men. Paul quit after that obviously. But he was lucky he didn't lose his life. But I doubt that he's forgiven Blackout or Alexander for that matter. Anyway, shortly after he quit, there was another fuck-up, only this time someone got killed – a teenager, drug mule.'

'Yes, I remember that. It was huge at the time. Gary something . . .'

'Gary Tomlinson.'

'Didn't the police find him hanging by his skin from the ceiling of a lockup? His dick was missing, but it showed up during the post-mortem, in his stomach.'

'The same. Everyone knew that it was Coke Dick's revenge for how he earned his nickname, but police never managed to pin it on him.'

'Hang on. Who's Coke Dick?'

'Rival drug dealer. A few months earlier, one of Alexander's men had forced him to snort coke off his erect penis. Hence the nickname. Anyway, that's not important. What is weird, though is that shortly after that murder, Blackout also parted company with Alexander and eventually, after a few months of gardening leave – i.e., being a bouncer around the town – he ended up working for none other than Coke Dick, which is fucked up because everyone knew what he had done. They should have been arch enemies. As far as I know, they're still together, but I haven't run into him in years, so I've never been able to ask him about it.'

'OK. But how does all this link with Charlie Price?'

'Charlie Price likes to remind people that he's a self-made man who started with nothing, but when he set up in business fifteen years ago, he couldn't get a dog to piss on him. Alexander was his sole financial backer, literally his angel. He showered him with six-figure start-up capital and injected further cash along the way to support Price's fledgling business. Without Alexander, Price's multi-million-pound parts and services empire wouldn't exist. In return, Alexander has laundered millions of pounds of his drug money through Price's company since then. It's a win-win. The only trouble is, now Price wants to go into politics, so he's probably keen to cut his criminal ties, plus his pride must take a knock every time he looks in a mirror, knowing that he owes everything to Alexander. He won't want to be Alexander's whipping boy all his life, but there's no escaping the fact that they're joined at the hip, no matter how much Price wants to break free. They know where each other's bodies are buried and they could sink each other with that knowledge, but it's self-preservation, isn't it?'

'So, do you think that Alexander is involved in getting the fire station closed?'

'I wouldn't be surprised. But you've still got nothing, Leah. Unless you can find a pile of Alexander's planning applications that have been waved through by Price, all you have is a hunch.'

'I know.'

'You need to be very careful. David Alexander is ruthless. He's a clinical psychopath. I've met plenty of people like him in the army, so trust me, if you start making his life difficult for him, your life will be in danger. I'm serious. These pricks don't mess around.'

'So, what do we do? We can't let him close the station.'

'Can you prove that he's involved?'

'No, but something dodgy is going on because Charlie Price sits on at least four planning application committees, maybe more as well as the Fire Committee. He's ideally placed to pull strings, bribe people and influence decisions.'

'But where's your proof? From what you told me, you can't even link Price with Alexander, let alone demonstrate any wrongdoing.'

'I know. I know. But I'm not giving up. I know it's

needles and haystacks, but there must be shell companies, stacks of proof if I can just find it.'

'And then what?'

'Then I'll go to the police.'

'Better find someone you can trust, then.'

'I trust my husband.'

'Oh yeah. Of course. Well, good luck with that. But we're not finished yet. They can't close us down now our shout rate's increased.'

'A bunch of bin fires? That's not gonna make the blindest bit of difference.'

'Course it will.'

'Well, I'm not going to rely on that. I'd start a few bin fires myself if I thought it would help.'

Turnbull smiled weakly and held Leah's gaze for a second too long. It was a guilty tell if Leah had been looking out for it. At that moment, their conversation was interrupted by the sound of screeching furniture and breaking glass. Leah and Turnbull exchanged a glance, then hurried back inside the building in time to see Lee and Alan fighting. Leah couldn't believe what she was seeing. Alan threw a wild haymaker which missed and knocked him off balance. Lee immediately attempted to get Alan into a headlock so that he could knee him in the face. Then Ricky, Turnbull and Raj intervened to break them up. It was all over very quickly.

Leah glanced over at Sandi, who was sobbing. That's when Leah realised that they were fighting over Sandi. It was common knowledge that Alan and Sandi were shagging; they hadn't been able to keep their hands off each other all night. Leah hadn't known that Lee and Sandi had also been at it. *Grown men fighting over a woman. Jesus.* Leah shook her head in despair.

'Come on, we're going.' Leah tugged at Dave's arm. 'I don't want Katie going to bed too late.'

'But you're the guest of honour. You can't leave yet. And it's half term.' Dave's speech was slurred. She looked at the bottles on their table. He must have necked at least a bottle and a half of wine.

'Come on, piss head. Let's go. We'll save ten pounds on the babysitter. I'll drive.'

Chapter Thirty-One

11:30 Tuesday 9 April 2019

Four teenage boys and two girls were making the most of their half-term holiday by playing with a football, showing off their skills on the bridge that spanned the tidal river in west Stockwood on Sea. One of the lads flicked the ball from ankle level onto his knee, then punted it ten feet into the air. It was supposed to sail into the sky and then fall vertically back to him, so that he could bounce it a few times off his head, which was an unlikely feat, even on a calm day. This morning, however, the wind was up. A sudden gust caught the ball, sending it thirty yards off target. It fell forty feet to the muddy flats below, accompanied by the groans and taunts of the other children.

'Ryan, you knob head. That's my ball.'

'It's OK, the tide's out. Chill.'

'Yeah, but there's quicksand out there. It's not safe.'

'Dare you to fetch the ball. You're not chicken are you?

'Fuck off. It's easy. I've just gotta be quick.'

Ryan ran along the bridge and when he had nearly reached the edge, he jumped eight feet onto the bank and slid down to the level of the sand. Ignoring a warning sign that forbade walking on the sand as well as three small boats that were half buried in the mud, stranded by the low tide, Ryan started running along the mud flats towards the centre of the bridge, without a second thought for the danger.

Almost immediately, he ran into trouble. He had barely jogged twenty steps before his right leg suddenly sank into the mud just above the knee. He lurched forward and instinctively slammed his other leg into the sand to stop his knee from over flexing. In seconds his left leg was also caught in the mud and he teetered in a half-split, waggling his arms to maintain his balance.

'I'm stuck.' Ryan laughed, still unaware of the mortal danger in which he had placed himself. The other children echoed his laughter and started taunting him. They didn't know that the tide was turning and heading back into the harbour and that if Ryan didn't escape, he would soon be under twenty feet of water. Ryan was already stuck up to his waist in the mud and was starting to sink even further. That's when his bravado turned into cold fear.

'Fucking bastard, I'm sinking. Get me some help NOW!'

One of his mates realised just how much danger Ryan was in; he grabbed his phone and dialled 999.

Steve Jones, one of the retained crew members, was midway through his weekly haircut at the Queen Street barbers, chatting about the latest Manchester United game, when his alerter vibrated in his pocket. Jumping from his seat and throwing off his apron, he grabbed his car keys which were on the small shelf in front of him. 'Sorry mate, I've got to go, my alerter's gone off. Can we finish this later?'

At 11:41hrs the printer at Stockwood Fire Station printed out the incident. Twelve alerters activated at twelve different locations around the town, and twelve ordinary people responded. The twelve retained crew members responded to their alerters and left their places of work or home, said their goodbyes and entered their own cars for the short but fast drive to their fire station.

Twelve cars arrived almost at the same time at Stockwood on Sea retained fire station. The drivers ran into the fire station as normal members of the public and emerged two minutes later transformed into firefighting superheroes. At least, that's what a casual observer would have seen. In reality, at least four individuals should have been at home recovering from the excesses of the previous night. Lee and Alan hadn't spoken since they had been pulled apart, but they both knew they had a job to do, so they got on with it.

John Turnbull shouted out the incident to the crew: 'Person trapped in mud under Dragons Bridge at the Harbour. Both appliances to attend.'

The blue light drive took just under four minutes, with blues and two-tone sirens on along with the bull horn. The two engines roared along the promenade, en route to the west end of Stockwood on Sea and tearing past pedestrians, cyclists and other vehicles to reach the harbour bridge. On the way, Leah radioed Fire Control to find out the time of high tide. The answer came back: 'One pm.' Leah spoke to her crew: 'We have less than one hour to get him out of the mud or he will drown.'

The wings of the bridge could be raised to allow larger vessels into and out of the harbour. As her vehicle – SW01 – approached the incident, Leah could see a gaggle of police officers already on the scene. They were busy keeping people off the bridge. Several bystanders were filming with their mobile phones.

Leah also noticed that the bridge was down. That meant that fishing vessels outside the harbour would be waiting to catch the flood tide to land their catch. Most of the vessels would be medium-sized trawlers and fishing vessels, as the site had a large fish cold storage facility where vehicles took the catch to restaurants and to the cities and fish markets. Both appliances parked as close as possible to the bridge and booked in attendance with Fire Control. Then Leah and Turnbull walked onto the bridge, leaving their crews on their respective appliances.

'Ryan!' John shouted through his cupped hands. 'Can you hear me?'

'Yeah,' replied Ryan. 'I can't move. I'm sinking. Please help me, get me out of here. I'm so cold. I'm going to die.' Ryan's dark eyes, wide with fear, contrasted starkly with his pallid face. He was shivering.

Leah radioed Fire Control again: 'We've made contact with the subject. Possible hypothermia. Request ambulance. Over.'

'Alan, I need you over here!' Alan was the station's knots and ropes trainer; he was already on it. With Matt's help, he quickly assembled a rope rescue kit on the bridge. His large hands worked deftly, looping and pulling the rope with lightning speed to create a belay rig with two harnesses.

'We'll lower Jordan and Sandi over the side of the

bridge down to Ryan. They will secure him with another rope and the rest of us will pull him out.' Leah turned to see a burly man limping briskly toward her. He had a white beard and a tawny face as weathered as a lobster trap; she guessed that he was the harbour master.

'There's a large fishing trawler waiting to come in,' he bellowed, as if he was speaking in force nine gale. 'I've told him to stay put for the moment.'

'Nice and easy, Alan.' Leah patted Alan hard on the shoulder. 'Safety first. We've only got one shot at this, so let's go steady and get it right.' Alan smiled and nodded. His left eye was bruised, a reminder of the previous evening's disagreement with Lee. An ordinary person would have been at home nursing a hangover, not rescuing a child from a tidal estuary.

As soon as Jordan and Sandi were strapped into their harnesses, the other ten crew members picked up the carry rope and braced themselves to support their combined weight. Then they climbed over the guard rails as if it was the most natural thing in the world, despite the forty-foot drop. They peered down at Ryan and then started belaying to him.

Ryan had gone quiet, eyes closed, locked into his body's involuntary paroxysms of shivering. But once they had descended, he started to panic, grasping at them weakly and jabbering: 'please get me out of here.'

'It's OK Ryan, we're going to free you. But you need to stay calm. OK?' Jordan and Sandi were soon caked in oily sand. Jordan placed the rescue rope around Ryan's upper body, underneath his arms and tightened it to the carabiner. Then she shouted up to the crew, 'haul aloft' with her thumbs up.

Pulling as one, the ten began to lift Ryan free from the mud. The rope pulled taut and at first Ryan remained firmly stuck. But the experienced crew kept applying steady pressure. By now, Ryan had sunk in the mud up to his armpits. His eyes still wide, shone richly with a mixture of hope and terror. Then, like a cork from a bottle, he sprang free from the enveloping sludge to begin his undignified climb to safety.

Ryan was a pathetic sight. Despite his body being flooded with endorphins, being rescued and the relief, he felt stupid and turned his face away from the cheering, clapping crowd. He needn't have bothered. He looked like an abandoned puppy yanked out of a drain, dangerously cold and unrecognisable from the cocky teenager who had marched onto the mud flats so confidently thirty minutes earlier.

Ryan was carried to the waiting ambulance, where he was diagnosed with mild hypothermia and taken to the local hospital as a precaution. Leah later learned that his parents visited him there and that he was discharged into their care the same evening, fully recovered. Ryan could smell oily mud in his nostrils for the next three weeks.

After Alan and Matt had collected the rescue gear, the bridge raised both its giant arms to form a 'V' shape as if in salute to their bravery. In its raised state, it also resembled the mouth of a giant crocodile, devouring the mast that rose from its central pier. Needing no invitation, the tide swept in, covering the spot where minutes earlier Ryan had been buried, and then the fishing trawler safely landed its precious catch. Both appliances and their crews headed back to the station for a clean-up, coffee and cake and to service the equipment ready for the next shout.

Chapter Thirty-Two

08:16 Thursday 11 April 2019

Leah rubbed her eyes and peered at her computer screen. She had arrived at the planning office early so that she could do some snooping on David Alexander without being interrupted by the telephone. Ever since her conversation with Turnbull on Monday evening, she had been desperate to run his name through the database. Leah's neck was already stiff and her eyes were sore. She didn't feel right. Maybe she was coming down with the flu.

Her first search, the previous week had uncovered no overtly dodgy dealings, but she had made the important discovery that not only did Charlie Price sit on all but one of the Fire Authority committees and played a prominent role in the full Fire Authority meetings, he was also a member of the Local Authority planning committee. She hadn't found any criminality, yet, but she was convinced that there was a conflict of interest; Charlie's involvement at the heart of both the Fire Authority and Local Authority Planning was unlikely to be a coincidence, especially since Charlie was not a committee kind of man and she imagined he didn't lift a finger unless there was something in it for him. It also indicated that his support for the fire station was empty words; he was probably actively working towards its closure. All she had to do was to find a link between Price and Alexander.

Leah logged into her computer and started to search the online register of planning decisions. As expected, a keyword search of 'David Alexander' cross-referenced with 'Fire Station' returned nothing, since Price was the man on the inside there, not Alexander, but she couldn't resist a gratuitous punt. She smiled at her laziness. She was going to have to try harder than that!

She googled Alexander's property development company. As she would have expected, for a drug dealer laundering money, he appeared to be connected to several satellite companies, but his main business was registered with Companies House as 'Macedon Enterprises Ltd'. The company number was 01645639. *This is borderline pathological.* Leah shook her head. *He's holding a boner for an ancient Greek hero. Talk about delusions of grandeur.*

She searched the planning database using the company name and number. She got a few hits, but nothing that rang alarm bells and not a sniff of a connection between *Alexander the Great* and Charlie Price. Once again, Leah started to feel disheartened. After another twenty minutes of directionless searching, she was forced to accept that once again, she had drawn a blank. By now, her colleagues were arriving for work and the telephone on her desk rang for the first time.

Fuck off! Leah was in no mood to start work. She grabbed the phone tetchily. 'Hello?'

It was the receptionist. 'John Turnbull on the line for you. He says it's urgent.'

Leah's heart began to pump faster. *Why is Turnbull phoning me here?*

'Thank you. Hi, John?'

'Leah. Sorry to phone you at work, but I couldn't get through on your mobile. You'll never guess what . . .'

'Yeah?' Turnbull's dramatic pause went on a bit too long. 'Well?'

'Well, I'm at the station doing some admin and I've just opened a letter from the father of Ryan – that lad we rescued from the sand – turns out he's a wealthy businessman and he's written us a cheque for £1,000. His name is David Alexander.'

'What?'

'Yeah, I couldn't believe it either. Small world, huh?' Have you got a signal there, cos I'll take a photo and text it to you.'

'I've got one bar. That should be enough. Send it over.'

'OK, doing it now. Talk to you later.'

Leah stared at her phone until it pinged. She opened the photo and started reading:

Dear All,

I am writing to express my gratitude and admiration for your incredible team. I cannot thank you enough for rescuing my son, Ryan from the estuary. I am happy to say that he has made a full recovery, but he is very shaken by the whole experience. He owes you his life.

My wife and I owe you our sincere gratitude for the professionalism, bravery and skill which you all demonstrated.

I enclose a cheque for £1,000. Maybe you could use it to buy the station an Espresso machine or a small pool table. Also, if there is anything I can do to prevent the threatened closure of the station, I give you my assurance that I will leave no stone unturned.

With kind regards,
David Alexander

Leah couldn't believe what she had read. Family man! Here was a deeply human and slightly clumsy letter of thanks, direct, vulnerable and completely at odds with the mental picture she had formed. She had imagined him as an old-school Bond villain, complete with facial disfigurement, underground lair and a shark tank.

She was completely disarmed. Then, as she studied the letter more critically, her distrust returned. He knew that the station was under threat of closure. It was public knowledge but was his interest significant? Was he taunting them or was this an innocent gesture of thanks, albeit from a drug dealer who made his huge fortune out of the misery of others and who thought of himself as Alexander the Great. *Remember that.* Leah refused to be taken in by his generosity. People like him always threw their money around. *So, what's really going on here?*

The letter was written on company paper. Leah's gaze wandered to the embossed letterhead: 'MACEDON ENTERPRISES LTD' written in navy blue in an approachable sans serif font that was strangely at odds with what she thought she knew about the man and his vaulting ambition. The company number, 01645639 was underneath. That at least was beyond question.

She scanned the letter again. Something niggled her. It was the final sentence, pledging his undying support for the station, with a promise to 'leave no stone unturned'. It was empty hyperbole. It was gushing, over the top . . . why did it bother her so much?

Suddenly, Leah made the connection. Even as she thought she had reached another brick wall, her subconscious had been hard at work. Stone unturned. *Unturned.* A tingle of epiphany ran up her spine and fizzed at the back of her skull. *Unturned. Of course. Why hadn't she thought of that before? She had been searching in the wrong place.*

Leah clacked away on her keyboard. She typed in the company number 01645639, only this time she searched planning reports where the initial officer recommendation to refuse had later been *overturned by Committee*. Such decisions usually had to be ratified by a meeting of the Full Council, but most often went by 'on the nod'. She needed to identify a pattern where Macedon Enterprises Ltd and its satellite companies were the planning applicants who benefitted from overturned decisions.

The first page of results alone almost made Leah whoop with excitement. Macedon Enterprises Ltd featured in no less than four separate developments in which the initial planning permission had been refused, only to be overturned later by Committee. Leah clicked on one of the results. It was for a sea-front hotel conversion into a block of apartments called Barsine Heights, which had been completed three years earlier.

Leah copied the name and then searched online news for planning reports and suddenly there it was – 'August 19, 2015 Controversial plans for 15 apartments

recommended for approval'. She clicked on the link:
This week a hybrid planning committee gave the green light for a controversial application for Barsine Heights – 15 apartments in Stockwood on Sea. Mr D. Alexander had unsuccessfully sought to demolish a Victorian hotel set in a prominent position on the seafront to the south of Beechwood Road but this latest decision overturns the earlier refusal. Committee chair, counsellor Charlie Price said, 'This is the correct decision. This development will not only bring much-needed jobs into the area, but it will also provide a welcome face-lift to an important segment of the promenade.'

Leah sat back in her chair and stared at her screen. She couldn't believe it. Here was the proof she needed, in the public domain, that Charlie Price was David Alexander's inside man on the planning committee. She went back to the first page and clicked on another result featuring Macedon Enterprises Ltd. This time it was for a smaller development, a residential home run by Parysatis Care, which had been completed two years earlier. Leah copied this name and then searched online news for planning reports and up popped another reversal of a previously declined planning application – 'February 24, 2016 Parysatis Care successfully secures planning permission for a 64-bed care home in the Green Belt just outside Stockwood on Sea. She clicked on the link:

This week a satellite planning committee granted planning permission to Mr D. Alexander for a 64-bed care home designed to provide accommodation for specialist dementia care, managed by Parysatis Care.

Whilst officers had recommended that planning permission be refused, the Special Planning Committee accepted that the need for specialist care accommodation outweighed the harm the development would cause to the openness of the Green Belt. Committee spokesperson, counsellor Charlie Price said, 'This is the right decision. We acknowledge the importance of the Green Belt designation but in this instance, we felt strongly that the urgent need for this sort of accommodation outweighed the harm caused by building in the Green Belt.'

Here it was, hiding in plain sight, another undeniable link between counsellor Charlie Price and a notorious drug dealer. Leah looked around the office, which was filling up with staff as they wandered in to begin their working day. None of them could guess the enormity of the information that was on her screen. They brought down Al Capone by chasing down his tax affairs; this felt the same. Here was clear evidence of corruption within the Planning Department, with Charlie Price reversing decisions to favour his benefactor and money-laundering drug baron, David Alexander.

Surely there was enough here for Leah to share with her husband. She picked up the phone and was about to ring Dave when she remembered what Turnbull had said about how ruthless Alexander was. This would end Price's parliamentary career before it had even begun but it would also give the police justifiable grounds to call in the auditors on David Alexander's business interests to uncover a paper trail of bribes, corruption and money laundering. She put the phone down and stared at her screen.

I can replicate this at home. I can show Dave tonight, but first I'd better print this . . . no, then there would be a record in the printer cache. She quickly cleared her screen and clicked on her browser history. Nobody must see what she had uncovered. She was about to delete the previous hour of search results, when suddenly the amyl-nitrate head-crushing feeling returned like never before. It was so intense that she cried out with pain. She felt as if someone was crushing her head in a vice but also that she was experiencing everything through the wrong end of a narrow tunnel. She was dissociating. She was losing consciousness . . .

Chapter Thirty-Three

Leah opened her eyes. Suspended ceiling tinged with green light. Florescent strip lights. She was lying down. In bed. Her eyes closed again.

Chapter Thirty-Four

Leah couldn't open her eyes and she couldn't move. She could hear the ping of a monitor that she sensed was tracking her blood pressure and heartbeat. Two men were talking. One was telling the other that he had to take a decision. She couldn't make sense of the words because she was drifting in and out of consciousness. *Authority to operate. Emergency brain surgery. Next of kin. Fitness for an anaesthetic. Kidneys working. ECG healthy heart. No time for an echocardiogram or lung function tests. Possible brain damage . . . make a good recovery from surgery, but MRI shows . . .*

Chapter Thirty-Five

06:15 Friday 12 April 2019

Leah opened her eyes. Suspended ceiling tinged with green light. Florescent strip lights. Breathing rapidly. She was lying down. In bed. Someone was gently calling her name.

'Leah, can you hear me? You've had an operation. Emergency surgery. You were in surgery for nine hours. The surgeon removed a tumour. You're going to be fine. We're looking after you. Try to stay calm. Dave is here. Your daughter is here.'

Am I alive? Suddenly she remembered. She tore at her oxygen mask and tried to speak. *I need to talk to Dave. Call the police. Dave. Where is he? I need to talk to him in private. My life is in danger. Alexander the Great tried to kill me. Charlie Price. Am I talking or am I thinking? I know what they've been doing. I have the proof now.*

'Shh now. Try to get some rest. We're going to sedate you to help you to sleep. You're completely safe. Nobody can harm you here.'

Chapter Thirty-Six

15:10 Saturday 13 April 2019

It was a typical mid-April day: dry, sunny and cold. The homeless street drinkers were in their usual place – sitting on the wooden picnic tables outside the church. A few feet away, where the red brick parquet met the stone wall crescent, there was a large wet patch, peppered with drink cans and empty vodka bottles – the area served as both a recycling dump and a urinal. The police were late today. They had usually moved the drinkers on by now.

It was eight days since Bartek Kaminska had died and Jock was feeling wistful. 'He was a fuckin' mate he was.' There was a murmur of agreement from the assembled company. 'I'll fuckin' miss him.' His brief eulogy complete, Jock staggered to his feet, tugged at his trousers and started to piss against the wall. Then he spotted four uniformed police officers walking purposefully towards them.

'Ah fuck. Here they are.'

'Good afternoon, gentlemen and lady,' said the smallest of the four officers, 'How are we today?'

'Fuckoff.' Jock was in no mood to be patronised.

'You know the score. Time to move on. Come along. Shift yourselves, please.'

'Ya fuckin' scuffer cunts. Why canna you leave us alone? We're doing no fucker any harm.'

'All right, that's enough. Come on, move it. I won't tell you again.'

Jock and his five companions shuffled away from the police and then when they were out of earshot, he said, 'Let's try The Duke.'

The Duke was a disused pub just outside the town centre. It was a popular site for the homeless to use as a drinking place and also for overnight sleeping, especially during the autumn and winter. It had been closed for just over two years; its windows were boarded up and covered in posters and graffiti tags. The police wouldn't bother them there.

After a twenty-minute amble, with a stop-off at a corner shop to buy alcohol, Jock and his gaggle of five other rough sleepers reached The Duke. Jock bashed his fist three times on the board next to the side entrance, which was out of sight to passing motorists and pedestrians. There was no answer. He shouldered open the heavy wooden door and in they all went.

Daniel Lewin and his friend Kyle were sitting slouched in the corner in the near darkness, drinking vodka and smoking dope.

'Hey kid. Fuck off wi ya. We're here now.' Jock staggered over to the two lads and gestured clumsily toward the door.

Daniel didn't want to start a fight. 'OK, that's calm. But can we finish our scag first?'

'Wa'ever. Just fuckin stay out of my way.' Jock turned away, ripped the tab from a can of Special Brew and pushed it needily to his mouth.

Daniel thought Jock looked pathetically comical, plugging the can into his face as if it was an oxygen mask. *Fucking pisshead.*

Jock took a deep slug, coughed and spat on the floor. 'Hrrrr. Tha's better.'

Half an hour later, by the time Daniel and Kyle had finished smoking, Jock had forgotten they were there, so they slunk out of the side door without further confrontation. Once the two lads were outside, blinking hard in the afternoon sunlight, Daniel started grinning in a way that Kyle knew meant he was thinking something bad.

'It's time to liven things up.' Daniel cocked his head and Kyle obediently followed him to the other side of the building. There was another way in, but it meant crawling a few feet, using their elbows to propel themselves forward. They soon found themselves in the main bar, out of sight and sound of the others who were drinking in the staff area behind the bar. Daniel collected some old newspapers and bits of broken wooden furniture and laid a fire on one of the red curved banquette seats. Then he used a disposable plastic lighter to set it alight. He was surprised at how quickly the fire took hold. Within two minutes the kindling had turned into a blaze.

'Come on, let's go' said Kyle nervously. 'It's not safe.'

The fire was already spreading along the modular seating and was inches away from catching the thick velvet curtains. Black smoke started to billow across the ceiling. Daniel loved experiencing the havoc he could unleash with the merest flick of his thumb and index finger.

'Dan', hissed Kyle, 'Let's go.'

'All right' whispered Dan, 'I've just got to do this.' Daniel quickly knelt behind the bar, pulled back a piece of old carpet and deftly unlatched two bolts in the lino. He carefully lifted out the wooden door and leaned it against the bar, leaving a three-foot square hole in the bar floor.

Daniel wanted to watch the fire spreading some more, but it was time to escape. They wriggled back the way they had come and moments later they were running away in the direction of the bandstand, laughing with nervous excitement.

'Dan, you're a *ledge*.' Kyle stared at his friend with genuine admiration. 'That trapdoor should fuck up the first police officer who arrives. I wish I could be there to watch.'

As they ran, they looked back to see thick black smoke rising into the sky in the distance.

The fire consumed the public lounge, where the seats burned quickly due to years of combustible material left behind and beneath them. Flames spread up the wall to the curtains and across the ceiling into other rooms, burning everything in its path. The drinkers in the back room were forced, coughing and spluttering out of the building.

Lee was busy setting up the BBQ in his back garden for his ten-year- old son's birthday party. Children had already started to arrive with their parents and Lee's wife was happily serving drinks and mingling with her guests. The sun was shining and she was looking forward to a lovely afternoon. Suddenly she became aware of Lee's alerter. He was fumbling in his pocket to quickly turn it off.

'You must be joking Lee, not *today*.' He threw her an

apologetic glance to acknowledge her exasperation and said 'OK, OK.' He grabbed his car keys and slammed the front door behind him.

At 16:15 hrs the teleprinter at the retained fire station printed out the fire call message and 11 alerters were activated, commanding 11 on-call firefighters to drop whatever they were doing and report to the station within five minutes.

By 16:21 an array of abandoned vehicles lay scattered around the front and side of the station building. Eleven people who had been going about their civilian lives, tending to their daily business, were now either waiting on an appliance or in the locker room changing into their uniforms. Each of them had been interrupted by their alerter and had automatically sprung into action.

John Turnbull shouted out the incident to the crew: 'Fire at The Duke pub, on Wellington Road, Stockwood on Sea, both appliances to attend, persons reported.' The station doors closed behind them, automatically, and once both appliances had left, all was quiet, the station deserted.

The blue light drive took six minutes. With blue lights on, bull horn two tones on and with headlights flashing, the two drivers, Mike and Chelsea, made their way carefully through the traffic at speed.

As soon as they arrived at The Duke, Turnbull booked both appliances 'In Attendance' on Wellington Road with Fire Control: 'I can confirm that smoke and flames are issuing from the building. Request ambulance, possible casualties inside, over.'

Outside the police were already busy diverting traffic and controlling the bystanders, who were increasing by the minute, as shoppers and drinkers from a nearby pub indulged their curiosity. Turnbull approached a local police sergeant who was with the group of street drinkers who had been inside The Duke.

'Is there anybody left inside?' He wanted to shake some coherence from Jock, but a mixture of booze and smoke inhalation meant that whatever he attempted to say didn't make much sense. That went for the rest of the drinkers.

'There's an ambulance on its way. They'll check you out. Make sure you're OK.' He may as well have talked to a fire hydrant. 'Do you know if there is anybody left inside? Are any of your friends missing?'

'Missing?' Jock sat on the ground, coughing and spitting, then managed a moment of lucidity: 'I din tek a fuck'n head count, pal. Why don't you ask those two bairns?'

'What? Are there children inside?'

'Nah. I told 'em to fuck off. Fucking potheads.'

Turnbull clenched his jaw. How many times did that feral little scrote have to be told? Bins. Bin fires, old sofas, not police cars and buildings. As soon as this shout was over, *Daniel Lewin was going to wish he'd never been born.*

Turnbull called three of his colleagues under air: 'Matt, get under air with me. Second Team, Alan and Raj also get under air. We need to check for casualties. The four men handed in their BA tallies to the BA controller, Mike Williams.

'Matt and I will carry out a right-hand search, Second Team will carry out a left-hand search. Gauge check.'

Both hose reels were charged and the engine noise

increased on both fire appliances as the pumps were switched on. The water was ready to pump out at a high pressure once the branches were opened. Both teams entered the building together carrying high-pressure hoses and separated, two left and two right, shuffling and sweeping into the darkness and smoke.

Visibility was zero, with thick black smoke at waist level as they headed into the unknown, looking for the fire and anyone trapped inside. All they had to guide them were small torches on their upper body and their sense of touch. They could feel waves of heat and smell the acrid smoke, whilst the crackling of the flames provided a disturbing background to Turnbull's barked instructions.

Meanwhile, the remainder of the crew outside located the nearest fire hydrant and attached a 6-inch hose from it to feed the fire appliance pump. Inside the burning building, the repeated call of 'Fire Service – anyone here?' competed with the roar of the flames as both teams searched each room methodically. Turnbull tugged gently on his line to check that Matt was still attached and focused on search and rescue.

Suddenly he spotted the light from the fire in the room ahead of him. Visibility had improved because he was closer to the source of the flames. He and Matt began to squirt water onto the fire, so that the thick black smoke was soon replaced by steam and white smoke as the fire was knocked down. That's when he reached the area behind the bar and stepped into the open cellar door. His heart leaped into his throat and his spine tingled with shock as he realised he was falling. His line snapped. He put out his hands to break his fall but his face mask hit the floor first as he bumped through the trapdoor and plunged another nine feet to the cellar below.

At least, he would have fallen nine feet if the cellar hadn't been flooded. As Turnbull hit the icy water, he thrashed out with his arms to try to grasp anything solid that would stop him from sinking. He was convinced that he had fractured his jaw. He had partially broken his fall squarely with his face mask, which had at least slowed him down and given him a fraction longer to brace himself so that he didn't sink, but he was now drifting in and out of consciousness. He had also badly grazed his back on the trapdoor opening and jarred his right knee, which was sending pulses of prickly pain into his groin.

In the darkness Matt lay flat on the bar floor with his feet braced against a base unit. 'John – grab my hand.'

Turnbull reached upwards and made contact with Matt's gloved hand. Matt was using every ounce of his strength to keep his injured crew mate afloat as the BA and fire kit equipment was heavy and now full of water. He managed to activate his distress signal unit. As the high-pitched bleeping alarm began to sound, he sent a radio message to the BA control board operator, Mike: 'Mayday, firefighter down in the cellar area of ground floor.'

The flames raged around them and the ceiling above was beginning to lose its structural integrity. The entire upper floor seemed to be on the brink of collapse.

Turnbull shouted to Matt through his BA face mask. 'Leave me. Save yourself.'

'YOU GO I GO' shouted Matt, pulling hard to keep Turnbull's face above the water.

After Mike received the distress call, he immediately radioed the Second BA Team inside the building to head for the bar area on the ground floor, to locate and assist Matt. They abandoned their left-hand search and fought their way to the front of the bar area, where they blasted the fire with their high-pressure hose until the flames were replaced by white smoke and steam. With the fire contained, this was now a rescue operation, with the added complication that the ceiling was set to collapse.

Alan and Raj helped Matt to pull Turnbull out of the cellar. Visibility was still almost zero, so the crew dragged him out of the building by following their hose line along the floor. The casualty evacuation wasn't pretty. There was no place for niceties in this hostile life-limiting situation. They yanked him roughly out of the hole and then hauled him unceremoniously out of the building to safety.

As the four men left the building together, they heard the chilling sound of the ceiling collapsing behind them. As they emerged into the sunlight, their fire kit steamed as the heat from their protective clothes vaporised the moisture in the spring air. They tore their face masks off so that they could breathe normally, to reveal sweat-sodden hair and black faces glistening with dirt.

John was handed into the care of the waiting ambulance and was subsequently transported to the hospital to have his injuries assessed.

Now that the smoke had all but cleared from inside The Duke, the crews were able to re-enter to ventilate the building and improve visibility by removing some of the boards over the windows. That's when it became apparent that the cellar door hatch had been deliberately removed so it could be propped up against a wall. This was a strong indicator of arson with the malicious intent to create potentially mortal hazards for the police and firefighters.

The fire crews remained on site for another hour before finally returning to their fire station to service their kits and get the appliances ready for deployment again. Police remained at the crime scene and had boarded up and secured the building again before nightfall. CID officers interviewed the group of street drinkers, most of whom were drunk; none of them knew who started the fire or why it started. With no tangible evidence, there was no prosecution.

Turnbull suffered bad bruising to his back and legs. Nothing was broken and he had no internal injuries, so he was expected to make a full recovery within a week. As he lay in his hospital bed, he mused how he had rescued Matt from the Smoke House and now Matt had returned the favour, saving his life in the process. He was determined that when he returned to work, he would single out Matt at the first opportunity and thank him sincerely. Whatever bad blood there had been between them before was irrelevant. From that moment, they would share an unbreakable bond.

In the meantime, he had some serious business to attend to.

Chapter Thirty-Seven

Leah opened her eyes. Suspended ceiling tinged with green light. Florescent strip lights. Breathing calmly. She was lying down. In bed. Her head and upper back were propped up with pillows. Someone was sitting next to her bed. It was Dave. He looked grey and worried. He hadn't shaved for a couple of days.

'Hi.' Dave spoke in a soft whisper that she had last heard him use three years ago when his mother was in the terminal stage of cancer. He was smiling nervously.

Leah took a few breaths and then, with great effort, managed to force out the words: 'Am I dying?'

'No, you're doing great, very well.' His tone of voice didn't change. The edges of his smile curled down, betraying his fear. This was unsettling. 'You've had emergency surgery to remove the . . . tumour. The neurosurgeon says they got all of it, which is . . . the best . . . thing. Um . . . what else . . . they also drained water from your brain. Oh, it's Saturday evening now. Katie's here. She's just getting a drink . . . from the machine, but she's here.'

So many words. She couldn't keep them in her head long enough to process them properly. Was that because he was talking too slowly or too quickly?

'I'm in danger.'

'You're fine now. The doctors say that you are stable. That means you're out of danger now. You're going to be OK.'

'Dave, please . . . listen.'

'You just need to get plenty of rest.'

'David Alexander. Drug dealer . . . Basileus. Launders through Macedon Enterprises . . . bribing Charlie Price to overturn planning decisions. I found proof. Alexander is dangerous. What if one of my colleagues . . . bought by him? My computer!' She slumped her head back onto her pillow, exhausted.

'Right.' Dave breathed out slowly with a breathy whistle. 'Why didn't you tell me? What have you been doing?'

'No proof before. Looking in the wrong place—'

'Sorry to interrupt, but it's time to change your IV bag.' A tall male nurse with a flock of greasy brown hair, stood in the doorway of her room. He was holding a large transparent IV bag, that was full of fluid.

After he had sanitized his hands and studied her IV sheet, Dave and Leah watched in tense silence as he removed the new IV bag from its sterile packaging, checked the expiry date and contents and inspected for leaks. Then he turned the bag upside down and hung it on the IV pole. He closed the roller clamp on the IV line, flipped open the front of the pump module and removed the line. After unhooking the empty solution bag from the pole, he allowed the bag to drop down whilst he held the spike vertical. He gently twisted and pulled upwards to remove the IV bag and placed it in the waste bin. Then he removed the blue rubber protective cap on the new IV bag, slid the spike into its port and firmly pushed and twisted it into place. He gently squeezed the drip chamber below the bag and placed the line back into the pump module.

Leah scrutinised the nurse's face for any signs of stress, but his blank expression was oddly reassuring, indicating to her, at least, that he was following a routine that he had performed thousands of times, without deviation. He wasn't trying to kill her with air bubbles and she could read the large black text printed on the side of the bag – NaCl 0.9% Sodium Chloride – which matched the empty one. She looked at Dave, who smiled reassuringly. He didn't appear to share her paranoia.

The nurse closed the module door and then opened the roller clamp on the IV tubing. He punched some buttons to set the infusion rate and finished by sanitising his hands again.

'All done,' he said cheerily, rubbing his hands together briskly. 'Can I get you anything?'

'No . . . thank you,' said Leah. She flattened her mouth into a functional smile.

After the nurse had left the room, Leah and Dave stared at each other until they were sure he was out of earshot. Then Dave broke the silence.

'Does your PC hibernate when you leave it?'

'. . . I think so. I closed the browser but my browsing history . . . still there.'

'And you think someone in your office might work for Alexander?'

'Don't know. Can't trust anyone.'

'OK, so . . . I'm sorry but I can't take this to my superiors without your evidence. Also, I won't be allowed to work the case. Conflict of interest. Right now, you need to focus on resting and getting well. So, I think we should sit on this for a few weeks. Wait until you've been discharged.'

'No. Oh. I don't know. Dave. I'm scared. If Alexander finds out, I'm . . . sitting duck.'

'It's very unlikely that he knows anything. I wouldn't be surprised if someone in your office is in his pocket, but the chances of them deliberately searching your computer . . . Anyway, you'd probably be less safe at home. You're surrounded by staff here. It's not easy for people to just walk in off the street.'

'Easy for you to say. What about you and Katie?'

'We'll be fine. But you need to get some rest now. We'll go now and let you get some sleep, OK?'

'Please stay with me. You can stay.'

'Leah, I can't. I've got to take Katie home. We can't both sit here all night. I love you. I'll be back in the morning. Get some rest.'

Chapter Thirty-Eight

18:20 Sunday 14 April 2019

The buzz of Paul Gray's burner phone sprang him from a late afternoon dose. He reached over to the chair, which was next to his bed, but managed to knock the phone onto the floor. Cursing with panic as he fumbled in the dark, he located the charging cable and gently fished it off the floor and into his hand. He answered on the fifth ring.

'It's on. Same place. 7:15 tonight. Thirty kilos. Pick up and make safe. You know what to do.'

'This even—'

The caller hung up. Paul felt idiotic and suddenly out of his depth. Of course, it was this evening. He was always given less than an hour's notice. He felt and sounded like a rookie.

'Sort your fucking head out.' Paul bashed his palm against his forehead. 'One pick up, that's all it is. Just like all the others.' Then the doubt crept back: 'Thirty kilos. Jesus. If this goes wrong, I'm fucking dead.' His heart began to pump quickly in response to the shot of adrenaline that was now burning through his veins. He threw on his coat, slammed his front door and hurried down seven flights of piss-reeking stairs to his Fire

Service van.

He drove tediously around the city centre just as before, only this time Paul was in no hurry to reach his destination. He kept checking his watch. He had a bad feeling and, if experience had taught him anything, it was to always trust his gut instinct. He'd been out of the game for too long, but he couldn't walk away now.

It began to rain, as he inevitably reached the coast road to begin the long straight journey to the steelworks in the next town. He was five minutes early, so he parked up and walked slowly towards the waste ground in front of the old steelworks. Even from a distance, he could easily make out the huge stack of old tyres, which stood implacable and glistening wet in the light of a thin crescent moon.

As he neared the tyre stack, the churning in his stomach increased. He wanted to turn around and run away, but the need to protect his son trumped his fear. As before, there was a single tyre in front of the cage. Underneath he could see a black sports bag, barely hidden. He rolled the tyre aside and picked up the bag. It was heavy. He didn't know what the street prices were these days, but he guessed its street value was heading for £2 million.

'Hello Paul.'

Paul spun around. Ten feet away stood an eighteen-stone, pink-faced man in his early forties. His black goatee beard was flecked with grey and his forearms were covered in tattoos. The last time Paul had seen Blackout was also the last time he had seen his left hand.

'What the fuck are *you* doing here? I was told to collect.'

'Boss says I can take it from here. You've done well.'

'I was told to collect and make safe.'

'Yeah, well. It's safe now.' He held out his hand 'We don't need you anymore.'

'So, that's it? I'm done? My son . . . will be safe?'

Blackout frowned and looked momentarily confused: '. . . if that's what you agreed.'

'Right, OK. So, I don't expect to hear from . . . your boss again. Is that clear?'

'Yeah, whatever.' Blackout stepped forward and slid the bag from Paul's grasp. 'Thank you . . . good job. And er . . . I'm sorry about your hand.'

Blackout turned and walked away. Paul stood in shock. He didn't know whether to laugh, cry or vomit. Why had Alexander put him through all that for nothing? Was it a cruel test, or didn't he trust him? It was tempting to abscond with £2 million of drugs but he didn't want to spend the rest of his life on the run. He'd achieved his goal of keeping his son safe. That's all that mattered. Now all he wanted to do was to get home and go to bed.

He trudged back to his van It was still raining and he was soaking wet, but for the first time in days, he started to feel calmer.

Three seconds later he felt a vibration in his right trouser pocket. He pulled out his burner phone and stared at it with curiosity. Even as he answered the call, he made a mental note to destroy the device when he got home.

'Have you collected the inventory?'

'Yes.'

'Keep it safe for thirty-six hours. We'll contact you early on Tuesday morning.'

The caller hung up.

Chapter Thirty-Nine

Paul's son Dean was sat watching television when his phone rang.

'Dean. Pack a bag as quickly as you can and come over to my flat, right now. Do you understand?'

'Why? What's happened?'

'I'll explain when you get here. You're going to have to leave town until I can sort things out, otherwise, we're both dead. Get over here as quickly as you can.'

'What the fuck?'

'Dean, please, just do as I say. You've got one hour.'

Dean ordered an Uber and then raced around his tiny flat as fast as his crutches would allow him. He stuffed a small bag with enough clothes for three days, then buried his weed tin at the bottom. He grabbed his ear pods, toothbrush and deodorant and scanned his bedroom. A small glass heart sat on the windowsill. His mother had given it to him when he was twelve, just before she died. Etched somehow inside the glass were the words, 'Those we love don't go away, they walk beside us every day.' He scooped it into his bag, zipped it up and looked through the window. The Uber was already waiting.

'Hi mate,' said Dean as he manoeuvred himself into the back of the silver Toyota Rav4. The driver didn't respond. He continued to face forward. *Rude prick,* thought Dean. Was a nod too difficult? He gave the man his father's address and then added, 'Can you drive fast, please. I'm . . . very late.'

Once again, the driver gave no acknowledgment but within seconds, Dean was gripping the door handle for support and regretting that he had selected 'burnout mode'.

Ten minutes later, Dean was standing outside his father's flat. By some miracle, the lift had worked, so at least he hadn't had to struggle up seven flights of stairs. He knocked on the door. Nothing. He knocked again. Finally, just as Dean was starting to think this was a windup, the door sprang open and his father beckoned him urgently inside. Paul closed the door behind him and then bolted it from top and bottom.

'Dad, what's going on? Why are you being so weird?'

'Sit down, over there, away from the window. I can't explain everything right now, but we're in deep shit. I raised the money to pay your debt, right? The whole lot, and I did the drop, last week, but those fuckers wanted more. They said I could only keep you safe by doing another drugs drop for them – a big one – that's what I've just collected tonight. Thirty fucking kilos of coke. Like, easily two million quid. I was supposed to hold onto it for a few days, but this . . . guy appeared, someone who works for them . . . and he took the coke.'

'And you just gave it to him? Why?'

'Because he said they didn't need me anymore.'

'But why . . . I don't understand. Who was he? How did you know he works for them?'

'Look, Dean, I haven't got time to explain but I've been stitched up. Which means, until I can sort this shit out, both our lives are in danger. So, I need you to catch a train, right now, and go stay with your aunt in Birmingham. You'll be safe there. They won't be able to find you.'

'And what if you can't sort it out. What if they kill you?'

'I'm going to talk to the guy at the top, explain what happened.'

'Dad . . . it doesn't work like that. You can't just talk to the boss guy. It's . . . even I don't know who he is. I could get myself killed just for asking. How the fuck—'

'Trust me. I know who it is, and I know how to contact him. I'm hoping he'll be more interested in nailing that thieving bastard rather than either of us, but I'm not taking any chances with you. Either way, if I don't get those drugs back, I'm dead.'

'Dad. I'm scared. Don't lie to me. Let me help you. How did you know he worked for them? And how the fuck do you know the boss?'

'Let's just say, I've been around. I haven't been an old git all my life. You can't do shit. You've got a broken leg. And I don't want to say that this is all your fault . . . but . . . it fucking is.'

'My fault? You're the one who agreed to do another drop, You're the one who handed over 30 kilos of blow to fuck knows who.'

'I had to; they were going to grass you up to Coke Dick. I told you – I know who he is – I just need to find him and get it back. He could have easily taken it from me by force, so either way we'd be in the same shit.'

'What about Coke Dick?'

'What about him?'

'What if I tell him that there's £2 million of snow up for grabs. He might . . . help us. He's a fucking psycho, and so is Blackout. If anyone can get it back, they—'

'What did you say?'

'What?'

'You said "Blackout"?'

'Yeah, Blackout. Well, that's his nickname . . . What?'

'Huge guy, forearms covered in tats?'

'Yeah?'

'Oh, FUCK.'

'What?'

'I gave the drugs to Blackout.'

'But he works for Coke Dick.'

'Coke Dick? Are you sure?'

'Of course. He's been with him for years. That's how I know him.'

'Shit, shit, shit. This is . . . fuck! This is complicated.'

'Is it? Coke Dick stole your drop. What's complicated about that?'

'*Blackout* stole my drop.'

'Same thing—'

'No, it isn't. Blackout works . . . used to work for . . . they phoned me after the drop. They think I still have the drugs, so they don't know that he's taken them. That means . . . either he's taking orders from Coke Dick, or he could be working alone. Shit. You can't leave now. I'm going to need your help.'

'Yes! Grays don't disappear, we face our problems! That's what you said. But . . . Dad, I can't just ask Coke Dick.'

'I'm not asking you to. I just need you to set up a meeting for me.'

'What are you going to do?'

'I'm going to ask him if he's stolen my fucking merch.'

'You can't . . . he'll kill you. And if he doesn't, why should he tell you anything?

'Because I'm going to stick this in his mouth.' Paul withdrew a SIG Sauer P226 service pistol from his trouser pocket.

'Dad! What the fuck!'

'I have to get those drugs back or it's over. I'll do whatever it takes to keep you safe.'

'Where did you get—'

'OK, just shut the fuck up for a moment . . . I need to tell you some things. All these years I've tried to protect you, but now you need to know – for your own safety. Oh, God. Where do I start?'

Paul sat down and placed the gun on the table in front of him.

'Years ago, before you were born, I worked for a man called David Alexander. He's a drug dealer. Still is. He's the big boss and he's even more dangerous than Coke Dick, because as well as being a psychopath, he's a well-connected pillar of the community and he's got people everywhere. He's the guy you pissed off when your drop went to shit, and that's why they broke your leg. He's also the reason I only have one hand. I fucked up on a much bigger deal. The police took the drugs but more important, David Alexander nearly got sent down for a long stretch. They had evidence that would have put him away for years, but it disappeared and the case collapsed. But I still had to pay my dues. I had no money, so they took my hand. Your friend, Blackout did it. With a machete. That was the end of my criminal career, but I spent years wanting revenge. Eventually, I got a job as a hydrant man – disability hire – and then you came along. After your mum died, I was tempted back, but I couldn't risk getting caught and going to prison, because they'd have put you into care. So, I stayed straight and I never got even. I just got old. That's why I was so hard on you when you . . . became an addict. Maybe it's why I've . . . always been . . . withdrawn, closed down, a shitty angry father. And I'm sorry, but I couldn't bear to see you getting destroyed by the same thing that nearly got me killed. I . . . love you Dean. I'm so sorry. All this is my fault.'

'Dad . . . I love you too.'

For the first time in many years, Paul Gray hugged his son. Then they moved apart and stood awkwardly until Dean wiped away a tear with his sleeve and broke the tense silence: 'So . . . what you're saying is . . . all my life you've been lying to me . . . you're not the person I thought you were . . . it turns out . . . you're a badass!'

Chapter Forty

Coke Dick was sitting on the toilet when Dean's number appeared on his buzzing mobile phone. *What the fuck does he want?* The thought didn't stop him from answering, if only out of curiosity.

'Hello?'

Dean switched to speakerphone and took a deep breath. His hand was shaking with fear: 'Boss, I'm sorry to disturb you, but I have some important news . . .'

'. . . OK, I'm listening.'

'I'm sorry if you . . . already know this . . . in which case it's none of my business and . . . I—'

'Stop saying sorry and just tell me.'

'OK . . . um . . . so, earlier this evening, Blackout . . . intercepted . . . a drop, a rival drop.'

'Go on.'

'He's got away with two million of cocaine . . . '

There was a long silence before Coke Dick replied: 'I see.'

'With respect, Mr Choy . . . is this . . . did you—'

'No. I did not . . . know this. Thank you for bringing it to my attention.'

The line went dead.

Paul and Dean stared at each other.

'Do you think he's telling the truth?'

'Oh yeah,' replied Paul. 'He had no fucking idea. But that's bad for us. It means, if that dense prick Blackout has any sense, he should be a hundred miles away by now. He can't leave the country with 30 kilos of drugs; he's got to sell it first – God knows how – but there's no way we'll find him. So, either we both do a runner and spend the rest of our lives looking over our shoulders . . . or we pay David Alexander a visit instead. Try to explain to him what happened.'

'If he's anything like Coke Dick, he won't give a shit. Last time you lost your hand. What's changed?'

'What's changed is, this time I have a gun. I don't want to kill anyone but . . . I'll do whatever I have to . . . to stay alive.

'Surely he has bodyguards.'

'Only one when I knew him.'

'But that's still two people you might have to . . . shoot. Fuck Dad, isn't there anything else we can do? Can't we go to the police?'

'No fucking way. If they put us in prison, we're already dead. Alexander can order a hit there quicker than a delivery pizza.'

'This is so fucked up.'

'Why do you think I walked away all those years ago? Why do you think I worked so hard to get you straight?'

'I'm sorry.'

'It's OK, I don't need an apology. You're a good kid. You handled yourself well just then. Anyway, all this talk is going nowhere. We need a plan. On Tuesday morning, when Alexander and his goons find out they've been hijacked, they'll come after me, so we have to reach him before then.'

Chapter Forty-One

09:20 Monday 15 April 2019

Leah opened her eyes. Suspended ceiling tinged with green light. Florescent strip lights. Breathing calmly. She was lying down. In bed. Someone was gently calling her name.

'Leah, can you hear me? You're fine. You split a couple of stitches. You were thrashing around in your sleep. But we've stitched you up again, good as new. We're looking after you. Try to stay calm. Your colleague John is here.'

Leah's neck was sore. She gently turned her head on her pillow until she could see Turnbull, who was sitting in a black vinyl winged chair. At first, she thought she was hallucinating. He looked ill and worried.

'John? Why are you wearing pyjamas?'

John smiled. He shrugged, held his arms out to the side and looked himself up and down with mock embarrassment: 'Dead man's PJs. They're not mine. They don't even fit.'

'Why are you here?'

'Yesterday, I fell through an open cellar trap door during a shout at The Duke pub, on Wellington Road There's nothing broken but my leg's jarred and my back is sore as fuck. They kept me in overnight. Lee is bringing me some clothes soon, so I can check myself out. What about you?'

'I found the proof. It was there all the time, in plain sight. When you texted me Alexander's letter, I suddenly realised . . . I checked his company for planning reports that have been overturned by Committee. I found four without trying, which means there must be dozens. Charlie Price is his man on the inside, helping to reverse those decisions. I've told Dave everything, but he says we should sit tight for a few weeks until I'm stronger. Surely this will end Price's political career and the police can call in the auditors on Alexander and nail him for bribery and money laundering.'

'That's great, Leah. Well done.' Turnbull sounded deflated.

'What's wrong? It's OK, Dave says there's no way that Alexander knows what I've uncovered. So, I'm safe here. Aren't I?'

'Yeah, yeah. It's a bit more complicated than that. I . . . haven't been completely honest with you. Remember at your testimonial, I said that I hadn't run into Blackout for years. Well, that's not strictly true.'

'OK, but you said he works for Coke Dick now.'

'Yep. But I need to rewind. So, that kid, Daniel Lewin, the firestarter? On Thursday, he completed my three-week cadet training as a must attend – court order. I found out that he was running drug errands for Coke Dick, so three weeks ago I called up Blackout to ask a favour – to encourage Coke Dick to leave him alone. Anyway, he and I went on the lash. We hadn't seen each other for years, so we had a lot of catching up to do. After we had drunk enough to kill two small horses, he told me how much he hated working for Coke Dick as well as his former employer, David Alexander. He said he deeply regretted cutting off Paul's hand and he had felt guilty about it for years. He tried telling himself that he had just been following orders, but unlike the army, there's no honour in obeying a psycho like Alexander or Coke Dick, for that matter.

'I always wondered why he went to work for Coke Dick, but bottom line – he needed the money. He suffers from PTSD and it ate him up, what he'd done to Paul, so he quit. And now he wants to retire, but he's broke. So, he hatched a plan. Blackout discovered that Alexander was planning a big drop – 30 kilos of coke – this was his way out. He found out the time and the place – the drop was last night. Blackout planned to beat the shit out of whoever was doing the drop and disappear with the drugs but then Paul turned up.'

'How do you know this?'

'Blackout phoned me. He said he didn't want to hurt Paul, so he pretended that he was working for Alexander. Paul handed over the gear, no trouble and Blackout split, but then he realised that he had just signed Paul's death warrant. Paul mentioned something about his son, so maybe he was acting under duress. Who knows. Either way, he's a dead man once Alexander finds out.'

'Where's Paul now?'

'I don't know. But he has three choices: find Blackout and get the drugs back – he won't do that because he'll expect Blackout to be long gone and he's right – Blackout said he's in Scotland already; so, Paul could either contact Alexander and plead for his life – a suicidal idea – or go into hiding.'

'Why can't Blackout just give Paul the drugs back?'

'Well, yeah, but it's too late now.'

There is a fourth option: kill David Alexander.'

'Huh. I didn't think of that. I don't know Paul very well, but . . . he's not a cold-blooded killer.'

'What's he got to lose? What choice does he have now? Kill or be killed.'

'Maybe you're right. Blackout could—'

'John: this is crazy. An old friend you haven't seen for years decides to steal from his former employer. Why are you even involved?'

'We fought side by side in Afghanistan. He had my back and I had his. You understand and you'd do anything for your current crew, wouldn't you?'

'In the line of duty, yes but this is . . . criminal.'

'Nothing is black and white. Everything is shades of grey. We both know that. There's something else I need to tell you. You're not going to like it and you won't believe me, but I swear it's the truth. Remember I said that David Alexander should have been banged up years ago, but key evidence went missing from the police evidence room? Alexander bribed a police officer with a stack of cash. Well, that officer was Dave.'

'You're right. I don't believe you. Why are you saying this?'

'Because it's true and you might be in danger. Blackout told me and he has no reason to lie.'

'He has every reason to lie. He's a fucking drug dealer . . . he's a loser who's been a thug for hire since he left the army. And he's got you sucked right in, doing his dirty work.'

'What does he have to gain by lying about this? He's never even met you. OK, just answer me this: how did you buy your first house together?'

'I . . . saved some money while I was in the navy . . .'

'And?'

'And . . . Paul inherited £100,000 from his great aunt.'

'Yeah . . . funny that. I bet you didn't even know he had a great aunt. Let me guess . . . did she live in Australia?'

'New Zealand.'

'How convenient.'

'What was her name?'

'I can't remember.'

'I'm sorry. I'm not mocking you. I know this is horrible to hear, but you must believe me. For whatever reason, Dave accepted a bung from David Alexander in return for making critical evidence disappear. Don't ask me why. He may have had an exemplary career ever since and be the best father and husband in the world . . . but . . . he did it. It's the truth. You must accept it, for your own protection. If you want my opinion, he was young and you probably needed the money. It set you up for life. You've been able to buy a horse and a paddock for Katie—'

'Fuck off. Get out. You're the one fraternizing with criminals. Don't drag me and my husband into this. Get the fuck out of my room! Get OUT!'

'Is everything OK?' The tall male nurse was standing in the doorway. 'You shouldn't be here. She needs to rest.'

'Leah, I'm telling the truth. Please think about what I've said.'

'Come on please—'

'I'm done.' The nurse stepped sideways to narrowly avoid being shoulder-barged as John turned sharply and stormed through the doorway.

Chapter Forty-Two

Lee Stone's van pulled out of the hospital car park.

'Thanks for this, Lee.' John Turnbull stretched out his legs in the passenger seat and winced with pain.

'You sure you're OK?'

'I'll be fine. But I can't stay in there. They didn't want to let me go, but I'm an adult with full capacity, so that's the end of it. If you turn right here, then second left, it's quicker.'

'I know John, I drive a fire truck, remember?'

'Sorry. Just want to get home.'

They travelled in silence for several minutes.

'The police think the pub fire yesterday was arson,' said Lee.

'No shit.'

'Kids from the estate.'

'I know who it is. It's that Daniel Lewin kid. I'm going to pay him a visit this morning and then turn the little fucker in. He's way out of control.'

'Don't get involved. Just tell the police.'

'Oh. I don't know. He's just completed my cadet training. I thought I'd connected with him on some level, but I'm sure he's still at it, the little shit.

'Be careful though. Remember, he's a minor.'

'I'm not going to lay a finger on him. This is me, on

the left. You can turn around over there. Thanks again, Lee.'

'No problem. Take it easy.'

John watched as Lee drove away, but he didn't enter his house. Instead, he eased his bruised body into his car and started hunting for Daniel. It didn't take long. He only drove past McDonald's to rule it out, but there was Daniel, sitting in the window, filling his face with nourishing brain food. He turned the corner and parked on double yellow lines in almost the same place as before, although there was no sign of Daniel's off-roader.

Fifteen minutes passed and then Daniel appeared. As before, Turnbull placed his arm paternally around Daniel's shoulder and guided him towards his car. 'Hi Daniel. I think congratulations are in order. You aced the cadet's course. Jump in, I want to have a little word.'

Turnbull was well prepared for Daniel to resist, like he had the last time, but he obeyed without making a fuss.

'Sure. Where are we going, boss?' There was something different about him. He was more self-assured, less twitchy. For possibly the first time ever, Daniel looked Turnbull in the eye and held his gaze. He even smiled.

'Somewhere quiet, where we can talk, man to man.'

'Mint.'

If Daniel was experimenting with a new persona, it was working. His shoulders were pulled back and his customary slouch was conspicuously absent.

Turnbull felt only marginally less angry than he had been the last time and he had been hiding it better, but Daniel's attitude was disarming. Turnbull started the engine and pulled out carefully but didn't feel the same urgency as before. Daniel settled into his seat with an open posture: one hand in his pocket, the other resting on his lap.

'What happened to you, boss?'

'What do you mean?'

'You was limping and your face is bruised.'

'I got injured on a shout, yesterday. The Duke pub, on Wellington Road. Lucky for you, there's nothing broken but, yeah, I'm a bit sore.'

'What do you mean?'

'You started it, didn't you?'

'No.'

'Were you on your own or did one of your little stoner mates help you?'

'Don't know what you're talking about.'

'Well, it doesn't matter what you tell me, but the police won't be so easy-going.'

'Nah, you won't. We have a deal.'

'I'm driving you to the police station, right now. And you can say goodbye to any deal. You blew it. I told you. No buildings, just bins.'

'I wouldn't do that if I was you.'

'I don't see that you have any choice.'

'I'll tell them that you've been paying me to start fires.'

Turnbull snorted. 'Try it. See who they believe.'

Daniel took his phone out of his pocket, scrolled with his finger and then held it away from Turnbull. His VoiceMemos app started to play:

'So, you want me to start twenty fires?'

'No, I want you to start a hundred fires. I'll pay you £20 for each one. That means there's another £1,600

coming your way this year if you're smart and you don't get caught.'

'How can I start a hundred fires without getting caught?'

'I dunno. That's your problem. Use your imagination. Dream big.'

Daniel stopped the recording. 'If you destroy or steal my phone, it's backed up on the cloud and I emailed the MP3 to myself. I've got multiple copies.'

Turnbull was silent. He was furious with himself but at that moment, he wanted to swing his left arm repeatedly into Daniel's face. Smash his nose and wipe that smirk off his face. The car slowed as they reached the outskirts of the town and the same derelict building on waste ground. Once again, Turnbull parked behind the building so that they were out of sight. They were completely alone. He turned off the engine.

'What do you want?' asked Turnbull.

'I light fires, you keep paying me. Not £20 but £50.'

'I can do that. But you've got to stop torching buildings. Stick to bin fires and no one gets hurt.'

'I'll do what I laik and you can't stop me, innit.'

Turnbull grabbed Daniel by the throat, 'What's to stop me breaking your neck, right now? Huh? You little prick.' He pressed hard against Daniel's windpipe; his jaws clenched in a rictus of pure hate. Daniel flailed but Turnbull was several orders of magnitude stronger. Daniel's face started to darken, then just as Turnbull's conscience started to churn in his stomach, he heard a gunshot, and something whizzed past his ear into the car roof.

For a moment, this new information was impossible to

compute, even for a former soldier. It was the distinctive crack of a small caliber weapon. Turnbull looked down. He glimpsed a black pistol in the youth's left hand. In a fraction of a second, everything came into sharp focus: Daniel was pointing a 9mm Glock at his forehead.

'What the FUCK—'

'Get off me.' Daniel screamed with terror. 'I'll kill you.'

They both scrambled away from each other. Turnbull grabbed the door handle and fell sideways onto the ground, breaking his fall with his right hand. Daniel kicked at him and now holding the gun with both hands, shot again, shattering the driver-side window. Then it was his turn to fall out of the car. He yanked the door handle and crawled away from the vehicle on his hands and knees.

Turnbull was livid with himself. During his army training, he had disarmed numerous opponents, but just then, his muscle memory had failed him and, instead of knocking Daniel's arm sideways he had instinctively leapt backward and fallen out of the car like a clueless civvy. There was blood on his hands, from embedded gravel and as he breathed, his already damaged ribs generated waves of sharp pain. He lay on his belly and peered underneath the car to locate Daniel, who was pushing his hands against the ground and getting to his feet.

This time, Turnbull knew he had to act decisively. He had to catch and disarm Daniel before he could either fire another shot or start sprinting away. He leaped to his feet and ran around the car directly towards Daniel, who was already steadying himself to shoot again. When Turnbull was ten feet away, Daniel aimed at his head and took his third shot. That was his mistake. He should have aimed lower, at the torso. The bullet missed its target because Turnbull was already flying low through the air towards Daniel's legs.

He hit Daniel hard with his right shoulder and the youth crumpled as Turnbull landed on him with his full body weight. Daniel dropped the gun as his head slammed against the ground. Turnbull raised his arm to hammer-fist Daniel hard in the face, then stopped himself just in time as he realised that he was already heavily dazed.

Turnbull grabbed the gun and stood over Daniel, breathing heavily. Daniel slowly tried to sit up, but he was too dizzy.

'Stay the fuck down. Stay down.' Turnbull was deeply shocked at the casual way this kid had just tried to murder him. He had fired three shots, two in anger and the third in self-defence.

'You stupid, stupid cunt. What were you thinking? And what the fuck do we do now, huh?' Turnbull pointed the gun at Daniel's head, to scare him.

'Give me your phone.'

Daniel reached into his pocket and slid the phone towards him.

'You've got copies. Yeah, but I could kill you right now, and I don't miss. So, I think we're even, don't you? I let you walk away from here with your life and I'll keep your gun. If you rat me out to the police, I'll post bail and I will fucking track you down and fuck you up. Understood?'

Daniel nodded.

Turnbull started to limp back to the car. 'You'll have

to walk home. See you around.'

'That's not mine,' said Daniel. 'Coke Dick paid me to look after it. He'll kill me.'

'Not my problem.'

'Please. I have to give it back to him.'

'Well, you should have . . .' Turnbull hesitated. He sounded like a petty admonishing parent. He stared down at Daniel. He looked completely lost and suddenly much younger than his years. He could see the ten-year-old child hiding in the gawky body of a cocky teenager. He hated to admit it, but he could see a lot of himself in Daniel. He just needed several second chances.

'I can't give you the bullets.' Turnbull removed the magazine and emptied the contents into his pocket, then he removed the bullet that was already in the chamber and replaced the now empty magazine. He tossed it onto the floor, next to Daniel.

'You've got a second chance at life kid. If you'd killed me, that's your life fucked forever. Three years in juvey and another eight years in prison. Locked up until your late twenties. You're a good lad. Grow up. Join the army. Become a firefighter. Whatever, just . . . make better choices. Also, I'm taking the cost of my window out of your wages.'

Turnbull's feet crunched on the scattered pieces of tempered glass as he climbed into his car. He covered his hand with his shirt sleeve and bashed out the remaining glass, then he looked down as he guided the key into the ignition barrel. When he looked up again, Daniel was standing in front of the car, legs wide and head cocked to the side. He quickly extended his right arm until the gun was pointing directly at Turnbull's head. Daniel's face was twisted with hatred and the desire for revenge.

Turnbull didn't even have time to sigh with exasperation; he couldn't know that Daniel had brought a second magazine. Without hesitation, he fired three shots, on target this time. The first bullet hit Turnbull in the forehead, sending his head backward so that the second shot entered his cheekbone and exited through the top of his skull; the third bullet struck his neck, severing his spinal cord. Even if he had, by some miracle, survived the first two shots, he would have spent the rest of his life as a quadriplegic.

Mercifully, Turnbull lost consciousness within seconds and within less than a minute, his heart stopped beating.

Unfazed by his own clinical brutality, Daniel calmly walked towards the car with the intention of rescuing some bullets from Turnbull's pockets, but there was too much blood and he didn't want to risk leaving any more forensic evidence inside the car. He paused, thinking quickly, then fished out a cigarette lighter from his back pocket and set light to Turnbull's clothing. Then he turned and fled the scene before the black smoke that was already beginning to curl skyward could reach above the roof level to alert passers-by.

Chapter Forty-Three

Chelsea and her husband were in the supermarket, with their two small children.

'Mummy, we need this don't we?'

Chelsea stared patiently at the tin in her daughter's hand. 'No love, I don't think we need those. Put them back, please.'

'But I *want* them.'

'We don't need prunes, love. Put them back, there's a good girl.'

'Can I have some sweeties?'

'And me!'

'Yes, you can both have some sweeties in a minute. Go on, put it back.'

Chelsea's pocket started buzzing.

'Sorry hun, I've got a shout. Can your mum pick you up? I need the car. See you later. Sorry. Love you.'

Chelsea kissed her husband on his cheek and then ran to the exit, where her path was blocked by a wiry security guard with leathery skin and a pencil moustache.

'Excuse me, madam—'

'I'm a firefighter, on call. Can't stop.' She thrust her alerter towards his face as she breezed past.'

The hapless security guard looked utterly bewildered, then the penny dropped. He nodded briskly as his right arm jerked upwards and pointed outside, by which time Chelsea had already reached her car.

At 11:25 hrs the teleprinter at the retained fire station printed out the fire call message. Ten people who had been going about their civilian lives, tending to their daily business, were now either waiting on an appliance or in the locker room changing into their uniforms. Each of them had been interrupted by their alerter and had automatically sprung into action. Since Leah and Turnbull were in hospital, they were two crew members down.

Lee collected the printed incident report and shouted to the crews: 'Report of black smoke, possible bin or tyre fire. Both pumps required.' It was a routine call. They were all amped up with adrenaline and ready to face whatever danger awaited, but none of them were prepared for the sight that they were about to witness, which would change all their lives.

The blue light drive took just over six minutes. Drivers Lee and Chelsea spotted the smoke as they approached, but they had to drive off-road and onto waste ground to see the source of the fire, which was hidden behind a large derelict red-brick building. Both vehicles turned the corner of the building simultaneously and the crews caught their first glimpse of the fire. It was a motor vehicle with what appeared to be an inert person in the driver's seat.

Both teams were busy getting under air and setting out the high-pressure hoses, when the first bullet exploded. Then a second. And a third. Everyone dived for cover as shrapnel scattered in all directions. Trapped behind the appliances, none of the crew were able to perform any of their duties safely so long as the explosions continued. Lee sent a radio message to the control room: 'Sierra Whiskey 01, I can confirm at least one casualty in the burning vehicle as well as live ammunition, which is exploding.'

'If we back the appliances around the corner of the building,' called Chelsea, 'we can set up the hoses and apply whoosh water safely.'

'Yes!' replied Lee. 'Use the corner of the building as protection.'

Two police cars arrived.

'You'll have to set up a cordon,' shouted Alan. 'There's live ammunition in the car.' One of the police officers said, 'We'll run a check on the number plate.'

Lee and Chelsea jumped into their respective cabs and backed up their appliances, then they set up the hoses so that Raj, Ricky, Jordan and Steve, could send two thirty-metre-long arcs of water towards the flames, whilst taking cover. As they worked, the bullets continued to explode intermittently.

Eventually, they managed to extinguish the flames before the petrol tank exploded, by which time the roof was missing and the body in the driver seat was a misshapen black mass, though still visibly human. The charred body was still smoking; the putrid fragrance of human flesh polluted the air, silently imprinting a lifetime of trauma on anyone unfortunate enough to smell it. The body was stiff. The carbonised hands still gripped the steering wheel.

The firefighters couldn't risk approaching the burned-out car in case there were more live bullets, so they began to pack away their equipment whilst the car and corpse were cooling down.

'We've run the plates,' said a police officer as she reached Lee. 'The car is registered to a Mr John Turnbull. We'll have to take DNA but it's a good start. How long before we can approach the vehicle?'

'It can't be. I picked John up from the hospital less than two hours ago. What's the address?'

The police officer showed him her phone. Lee peered at it, then backed away, shaking his head in shock. 'It can't be John, I don't believe it.'

'Do you know him?'

'He's our . . . guvnor.'

'And you say you were with him this morning?'

Lee nodded.

'What's going on Lee?' Seeing the shock on Lee's face, Raj knew something was seriously wrong. 'What's happened?'

As the news spread amongst the crew, everyone was in disbelief that the burnt human remains inside the car was JT. How could this possibly happen to one of their crew in this small town of Stockwood on Sea?

'Lee, we'll have to take a statement from you,' said the police officer. 'Did Mr Turnbull say anything?'

'Yeah. He said he was going to meet up with a kid called Daniel. I can't remember his surname. He said he'd caused the fire at The Duke pub, on Wellington Road yesterday afternoon. He was going to confront him – talk to him – he knew the kid from cadet training and then he was going to tell the police.'

'You think that's what he did?'

'I don't know,' replied Lee. 'I dropped him off at his house, about quarter to eleven. That was the last time I saw him.'

'We need to find this Daniel. Do you know anything else?'

'Yeah, he's the kid who did the arson attack on those puppies a few weeks ago. You'll have him on file. Lewin! Daniel Lewin – that's his name. He's on your system. He just completed a three-week fire cadet course at the station. I can't see him doing anything like this though. *What the fuck happened?*'

'Well, that's what we need to find out. Thank you. If you can give me your name and address, can you come down the station this afternoon to give a full statement?'

'Sure, whatever. As soon as we get back to our station, I'll get cleaned up and come right over.'

After Lee had updated the fire control room, they all headed back to the station in silence. Then, without speaking, they prepared the appliances ready for the next shout.

Chapter Forty-Four

Leah opened her eyes. She was sitting up. In bed. Someone was gently calling her name.

'Hi, Mum.' Katie was standing next to her bed, smiling nervously. Leah's mothering radar immediately told her that her daughter was working very hard to conceal her fear.

'Hello, darling. It's so good to see you. Come and give me a big hug. It's OK, I won't break!'

'You gonna be OK?'

'Yes, I . . . I think so. But shouldn't you be at school?'

'INSET day,' said Katie.

'We can't stay long.' Dave's stern, inscrutable face loomed into view, behind Katie's shoulder.

'Is everything all right? Dave?'

'Yep. Fine. There's um . . . some stuff kicking off at work . . . I can't really go into detail. But it means I've got to get back soon. We just wanted to see you and . . . you know . . .'

'Dave . . . I need to ask you a question. And I want you to answer it.'

'OK?'

'Your great aunt. The one who left you all that money.'

'From New Zealand, yeah?'

'What was her name?'

'Um . . . her name . . . her name was Mary. Why are you—'

'On your mother or father's side?'

'Um . . . mother's, I think.'

'So why didn't she leave the money to your mother?'

'I don't know. The will . . .'

'She died intestate and the lawyer said they were lucky to track you down.'

'Well, yeah.'

'Your mum was the next of kin. The money should have gone to her. I thought it was strange at the time.'

'Oh, well maybe it was my father's side then.'

'But he was alive too. He died just before Katie was born.'

'OK . . . then maybe there was a will. I can't remember, it was such a long time ago. Why are you—'

'Nothing. It doesn't matter.' Leah's heart began to pump faster. *He's lying. John was telling the truth. My husband is a bent cop who has been bought by David Alexander and I've told him everything.*

'Hadn't you better go, then?' said Leah. 'If you're busy at work. You'd better go. Katie can stay though, can't she? You can pick her up later.'

Dave's phone buzzed. He looked at the screen and frowned. Leah sensed he was reading a text message. 'Sorry, I have . . . got to go. Yes . . . Katie can you stay here with Mum and I'll come to collect you later, OK? Love you.' Urgently tapping a reply as he rounded the threshold, he looked up, blew a kiss and disappeared.

Leah's head was fizzing. Everything she thought she knew about her husband was a lie. Dave was working for David Alexander. So that's why he was so keen to sit on the evidence that she had uncovered, on the pretext of waiting until she was out of hospital. What was it he had said? '... *can't take this to my superiors without your evidence ... won't be allowed to work the case. Conflict of interest ... you need to focus on resting ... we should sit on this for a few weeks.*'

How far did his loyalty extend? Was she in danger from him? Would Dave hurt her rather than allow her to destroy Alexander and Charlie Price? But there was something that Dave didn't know. John Turnbull knew everything as well as the fact that Dave was crooked. John could get the story out. He could search the internet, just as she had done, and then go above Dave's head and take the evidence to senior police officers. He could also tell them that Dave had taken a bribe. Did she want to go that far?

'Katie. Do you have your phone with you?'

'Of course!'

'Can I borrow it for a second? I need to call someone.'

'OK. Hold on, I'll just unlock it.' She handed the phone to her mother.

Shit. I don't know his number. Shit shit shit. Come on, think. Suddenly she remembered. A few months earlier, she had been on a shout and her phone had died, so she had called Katie from Lee's mobile to tell her to catch the bus home from school. Lee's number would still be in Katie's call log. She could even remember the date – Valentine's Day – because Katie had been embarrassed because an anonymous admirer at school had left a huge bunch of flowers next to her locker which she had to carry home on the bus.

Leah started to scroll through the call log.

'Hey, what are you doing?'

'Sorry, chick, I'm just looking for a colleague's phone number . . . it's in your call log. . . Ah, here it is.' She tapped the number. Lee's avatar appeared on her screen as the phone rang.

'Hello?'

'Hi, Lee? It's Leah. Walsh.'

'Oh . . . hi.'

'Can you do me a favour? I need to get hold of John Turnbull, urgently. Do you have his number?'

'John? Um . . . no, I . . . I do have his number but . . . um . . . he's . . . Leah, I'm sorry but . . . he's dead. We've just been to a shout and he was found dead in his car . . . this morning.'

Leah slumped back against her pillows.

'. . . hello? Are you still there?'

'Yes,' replied Leah. 'What happened?'

'The police say he'd been shot. At least twice . . . and then . . . his car was set on fire.'

'Oh, fuck no!'

'I'm at the police station now, giving a statement.'

'You're at the police station. OK . . . . I need to talk to a senior police officer. Right now. I've got some important information.'

At that moment, two plain-clothed police officers ran into her room. One of them snatched the phone from her hand; the other one closed the door.

'What are you doing?'

'Sorry, Mrs Walsh. We're here to protect you.'

'What do you mean? Who sent you?'

'Your husband. DCI Walsh. We have instructions not to allow you to leave your room or to contact the outside

245

world. For your own safety.'

'Oh, I see. For *my* safety?' she said sarcastically.

'That's my phone,' said Katie, holding out her hand. 'Mum. What's happening?'

'I'm sorry, but I'm going to have to keep hold of this, for the moment. You can have it back . . . when all this is . . . over. DCI Walsh wanted me to give you this message: he said, to please trust him and that he would explain everything in due course.'

'In due course . . . sounds exactly like . . . something Dave *wouldn't* say. And where is DCI Walsh? Where is he?

'I'm not authorised to give you that information.'

'Je–sus.'

'Mum, what's going on?'

'I don't know. But it's OK. These officers are here to . . . keep us nice and quiet. Safe even.'

John is dead. Shot dead. Did Alexander put a hit on him? Am I next? Is Dave really trying to protect us?

'Can I ask, how long you are going to be here?' Leah's tone was softer now, less hostile.

'I don't know, madam, but we *are* here to protect you.'

'Thank you . . .'

One police officer remained in the room; the other one stood guard from the other side of the closed door. Leah couldn't think of anything else to say, so for the next few minutes, silence prevailed.

Chapter Forty-Five

'Charles. Thank you for changing your schedule and coming all the way over here to meet me at such short notice.' David Alexander stood up and held out his hand.

'It's my pleasure, David.' Charlie Price began to make his way across the highly polished marble floor towards Alexander. It was a long walk. The room was huge, much longer than it was wide, with light grey walls. Each concrete brick was easily three metres long. Charlie estimated that the ceiling was more than eight metres high. An expensive grey modular sofa ran along the entire wall to his left and a strip of low reddish-brown wooden drawers ran along the other. The understated opulence and brutalist style managed to be both coldly corporate and warmly inviting. It intimidated as it welcomed. This was, Price mused, the perfect expression of the complex sadistic personality of its owner.

'Dalbergia,' announced Alexander, with a broad smile.

'Pardon?' said Price.

'The wood. It's Dalbergia. *Dalbergia retusa* to use its proper name. From Central America. Commonly called *Cocobolo*.

The two men shook hands. Firmly.

'It has a Janka Hardness of nearly 3,000 pounds-force and a crushing strength of nearly 12,000pf per square inch.'

'Oh . . . is that . . . good?'

'You tell me . . .' Alexander said quizzically and then smiled again.

Alexander's entire opening gambit was intended to throw the other man off-balance, and it worked. Price was suddenly on the back foot, even though on the surface, their exchange had been nothing but warm and friendly.

'Um . . . I don't know much about . . . erm wood . . .' His sentence tailed off abruptly. Price had dropped the conversational ball. He tried to regain his composure, but he was already out of his depth. 'But you have a really . . . nice home here. Very . . . the walls . . . and the floor! How do you p-polish—'

'Relax, Charles. Please take a seat.' Alexander waved his arm magnanimously in the direction of the nearest sofa module.

'Thank you.' Charlie sat upright on the edge of his seat. He knew that if he were to sit further back with his spine against the wall cushion, his feet would dangle. He hated himself for allowing Alexander to dominate him like this, every time they met. It was subtle but tangible and deliberate.

It was at moments like this that Charlie was forced to confront the reality that, although he owed much of his success to Alexander, he was sick of being his lackey, jumping every time he was called, laundering hundreds of thousands of pounds each month and taking the lion's share of the risk.

He doubted that Alexander had the first clue about the

fragility of his company accounts. He always dreaded the prospect of an ad hoc audit by HMRC. His company had never been properly structured to legitimize the sheer volume of dirty cash that Alexander kept shovelling in his direction. Charlie's complicit accountant submitted meticulous company accounts every year, but there was no way that they would stand up to forensic scrutiny. For this reason, he had spent what should have been the best years of his corporate life worrying that it could all be taken away in an instant. Then there were the numerous planning applications that he had overturned in Alexander's favour. Once again, illicit activity, only this time, barely hidden and easily available in the public domain to anyone who bothered to join the dots.

Charlie appeared to the world as a contented self-made multi-millionaire. He had achieved more material success in his life than he could have possibly imagined, when he was growing up in a council house in Longsight, but at what cost? He was always waiting for that knock on the door. He had pictured the moment a thousand times: two police officers asking politely if they could come in to discuss some 'financial discrepancies.'

For this reason, Charlie had accepted Alexander's invitation, but that morning he had sworn to himself that today he would finally find the courage to tell Alexander that he wanted out.

'Can I get you anything? A cigar? Glass of whisky? Coffee?'

'No, I'm fine thank you.'

'Do you mind if I smoke?'

'No, of course . . . please . . .'

Alexander opened the nearest Cocobolo drawer and

removed a large wooden box, lifted the lid and withdrew a single cigar. As he busied himself unwrapping, cutting and lighting it, he launched another salvo of small talk that made Charlie feel even more uncomfortable. 'Arturo Fuente. Seven years ago, a very dear business associate in the Dominican Republic presented me with this centenary box. Four generations of the same family have been making these cigars since 1912. Imagine that. I don't know about you, but that passion, loyalty and craftsmanship doesn't appear overnight. It takes decades to refine and develop. Wouldn't you agree?'

'Yes.' Charlie knew he was alluding to their own longstanding business arrangement, but he couldn't think of anything else to say. He just wasn't feeling it. So, he nodded sombrely for added sincerity.

'I've always surrounded myself with people whom I can trust and so far, it's been an effective strategy. Property development and . . . procurement . . . are dangerous and risky businesses. Some people . . . don't make it. But when there's trust and mutual respect on both sides . . . you can achieve anything.'

'I agree, David, wholeheartedly. And for that, I am very grateful. We both know that I wouldn't be where I am today without your unstinting support.'

'I'm glad to hear it. Charles. But over the last few months, it hasn't escaped my notice that your focus has begun to shift. Am I right? I hope we can be candid.'

'Well, since you've brought it up, I can't deny it. I appreciate our business dealings have for many years been . . . closely linked . . . but now I'm starting to feel it's time to focus on developing my political career. And unfortunately, that means—'

'Divestment. Yes, I understand.'

'Well, I wouldn't put it as strongly as that.'

'Ah. Wouldn't you? So, tell me what you want, Charles.'

'Well, I think it's . . . time to take a small . . . step back . . . from our long-standing arrangement, so that I can start with a clean slate, so to speak. We've done a lot of . . . business together and I feel that after all these years I've . . . paid my dues. I've more than . . . paid you back for your financial support and generosity. I hope you understand. We've had a good run together, for which I will always be in your . . . grateful, but I think it's time for me to . . . move on.' Charlie stared at the floor.

'Hmm.' Alexander took a deep draw on his cigar and then sat back in his chair, with his arms outstretched along the top of the cushions as he blew a huge cloud of smoke into the air. 'That's disappointing. I'd go so far as to say that it's a problem. A big problem. Aren't you wondering why I asked you to come here this afternoon?'

'Well . . . yes—'

'Two million. The shipment arrives tomorrow morning and I need you to process half of that. Just half.'

'Tomorrow! That's impossible. I . . . I can't . . . I need more notice than—'

'Let's call it your platinum handshake. One final project. I'll pay double your usual percentage.'

'But David . . . it's way too much, I can't. If you'd given me several weeks' notice—'

'I've never been able to give you that, Charles. You know how we work. This is a fast-moving industry. I keep as few people in the loop as possible on a just-in-time basis. It's safer for all of us.'

'Yes, I appreciate that but . . . '

'Then we're agreed? You will process one million pounds.'

'NO!' Charlie had not meant to raise his voice, but years of anxiety and frustration had led to this moment.

Two seconds later, a stocky young man with ginger hair stepped briskly through the door at the other end of the room. 'Everything OK, boss?'

'Everything is fine. Charles is just getting a bit hot under the collar.' I'll call if I need you. Thank you, Duncan.'

Duncan nodded and left the room, closing the door quietly behind him.

'Let's not fall out over this, Charles. I'm sure we can reach a compromise.' Alexander continued to nurse his cigar and blow the smoke towards Charlie.

'I'm sorry David, but now that it's out in the open . . . that is my . . . firm position. I haven't made this decision lightly. I've been feeling this way for some time now, as you've noticed.' Charlie's shoulders began to relax. *That wasn't so bad, was it, after all? We're both adults. Businessmen. I just had to stick up for myself.*

The door at the far end of the room opened again. It was Duncan.

'I'm sorry to disturb you again, boss, but there's a gentleman – Mr Kwang Lin Choy – he wants to speak with you. He says it's urgent. I've scanned him. He's clean.'

'Really?' Alexander shrugged. 'Please, show him in.'

Duncan nodded and then ushered in a short pot-bellied Chinese man with brown eyes and overplucked eyebrows. Coke Dick looked completely unfazed, despite his sudden uninvited arrival at the personal residence of his biggest potential enemy.

'Good afternoon, Mr Alexander.' Coke Dick started walking towards the two men. 'Forgive me for this unprecedented . . . visit. But I have some important information which I need to tell you, face to face. In return, I hope you will reciprocate the courtesy that I am showing to you.'

'Welcome, Mr Choy. Please take a seat.'

'Thank you, but I'd rather stand.'

'Fine, well um . . . please go ahead.'

'Thank you. To be very brief: yesterday afternoon, one of my employees, without my knowledge . . . intercepted a . . . large consignment belonging to you. I don't know where he is, so I have come here – at the earliest opportunity – to respectfully assure you that he is acting alone and to offer you all my available resources to help track him down. He used to work for you. His name is Mark Payne but everyone calls him Blackout.'

Before Alexander was able to respond, there was a sharp scraping sound outside. Then, the door at the other end of the room opened slowly and Duncan walked stiffly forwards, closely followed by an outstretched arm holding a semi-automatic service pistol. The three men at the other end of the room could see that the arm was shaking visibly. Two more steps and any curiosity they might have briefly mustered about its owner were swiftly satisfied. It was a man with one hand and he appeared to be highly agitated.

'That's it,' said Paul, 'Keep moving. Forward. Don't try anything clever or I'll blow your fucking head off.' Duncan had no choice but to obey. Paul had already forced him to surrender his own weapon, which Paul had then kicked hard, sending it scuttering across the floor, causing the scraping sound outside that the three men had heard.

'Right, you get over there with the others. Go on.' Paul attempted to kick Duncan in the small of the back, but Duncan had already stepped forward, causing Paul's foot to miss its target and land heavily on the floor, comically overextending his leg. He nearly dropped the gun. He hopped his back leg forward to close the gap and then barked another order, to try to reassert his authority (although at this precise moment, he was the only one in possession of a gun, so, he held everyone's attention).

'Sit there.' Then he waved his gun at the short potbellied man who was standing a few feet away. 'And you. Now, put your hands on your heads where I can see them.'

The four men obeyed.

'That's it. Good.' Paul turned to face David Alexander.

'Mr Alexander. I'm sorry to have to do this . . . in your own home . . . but you have left me no choice. A few weeks ago, my son was supposed to do a job for . . . you . . . but the police seized £25,000 of the drop. My son couldn't pay it back so one of your . . . goons . . . broke his leg. I raised the money myself and gave it to this man here.' Paul nodded at Duncan. 'But that wasn't enough. He told me that I had to do one more drop. So last night, that's what I did. But then Blackout turned up and took the gear from me. I assumed that big lug was still working for you, so I handed it over and put up no resistance. But I was wrong. He works for another drug dealer, called Coke Dick.'

Coke Dick raised his head indignantly at the mention of his reviled nickname. Paul glanced at him, startled by his sudden movement. Then he realised with prickly horror the identity of the curious little man with overplucked eyebrows, who now knew – because Paul had stupidly blurted it out – that his son, Dean, had betrayed him.

'It's you!' He pointed the gun at Coke Dick, who was already imagining the varied and sadistic methods he would use to punish the back-stabbing traitor.

'What's going on here?' Paul looked at David Alexander and then back at Coke Dick. 'I said, what's going on?'

David Alexander cleared his throat. 'Paul, isn't it?' Paul flicked his head back in a half-nod. 'May I speak?' Paul nodded again.

'This gentleman' he looked at Coke Dick, 'came here this afternoon to assure me that Blackout has gone behind his back and that he intercepted you without his knowledge. He has even offered to help track him down. That is the sole reason he is here.'

'Well . . . yeah,' said Paul, 'that's what he told me . . . or rather, my son, over the phone.'

'So . . . I think we can all agree that the real . . . enemy here . . . is Blackout. We would all like to know where he is.'

'No, that's not enough. I need you to promise that when I leave, you won't have me or my son . . . killed . . . or whatever . . . because of this.'

'Well . . . you have made your views abundantly clear. You said you believed that Blackout was working for me, so you handed over the merchandise. I have no reason to disbelieve you. As far as I'm concerned that is the end of the matter.'

'Yeah but, I'm holding a gun. How do I know you won't put a hit on me the moment I walk out of that door?'

'You haven't really thought this through, have you, Paul? I could easily put a hit on you . . . and your son. But considering the circumstances and since you have been so persuasive, all I can do right now is to give you my word.'

'I need money. You must have a safe around here. I want a shit load of money so that my son and I can leave the country.'

'So now you're saying that you want to steal from me? I thought you simply wanted to give your side of the story. I believe you. I won't seek revenge. But when you hold me at gunpoint and steal my money. Well, that's a different situation, isn't it?'

'I don't want to steal from you, but it's my only chance of . . . of starting again. I could shoot you dead right now . . . but I'm not a killer.'

'I'm glad to hear it. Neither am I, Paul. Neither am I. At the moment, you are the only person in this room waving a gun around and threatening to kill people. I think you have watched too much television. I am a pragmatic businessman and a man of my word. I do not want any trouble and I certainly don't want to kill anyone.'

'Don't pretend you're innocent. I lost my hand because of YOU. You commanded it. Blackout cut off my hand because you gave him the order and he obeyed. So, give me one reason why I should believe a single word that's coming out of your mouth right now? If I wasn't pointing a gun at your head . . .'

'OK, Paul. You leave me no option. I do have a safe.

There is one in this room, in fact. It contains approximately £350,000. Would that be enough to . . . encourage you to leave?'

For a moment, Paul didn't know how to respond. 'Show me.'

'OK then. I am going to stand up now. I will keep my hands on my head. The safe is over there, in the wall behind the large painting. Not a very original hiding place, but there you are.'

Alexander stood up and started walking slowly towards a monumental square canvas hanging on the far wall. It was an expensive copy of 'The Apotheosis of Athanasios Diakos' by Greek artist, Konstantinos Parthenis and it took up more than 14 square metres of wall space. If Paul had been thinking clearly, he would have questioned the impracticality of having to remove a large and heavy painting to use the safe. He might even have suspected that Alexander was lying to set him up in an ambush. But he was so focused on corralling four potentially dangerous men, that none of these thoughts occurred to him.

'Incidentally, I don't know whether you've noticed, but I can't lift this painting on my own. It usually takes at least three people.'

Paul frowned. He was beginning to realise that Alexander was right – he really hadn't thought any of this through. He had naively imagined that he could, against all the odds, calmly explain his predicament to David Alexander, who would appreciate his directness and honesty and show him clemency. Had he really believed that a man as ruthless as Alexander would be gracious about losing £2 million of cocaine? Also, he had quickly discovered the impossibility of being polite whilst threatening someone with a gun. He'd seen it done in countless films, but he had failed to be either polite or intimidating.

He stared forlornly at the stump where his hand had been, as if willing himself to become a channel for hatred and revenge. He was starting to rationalise that killing Alexander and making off with a huge pile of cash was the only way to save his own skin. Paul didn't know if he could pull the trigger, even though he was certain that if Alexander had a gun, he would already be dead.

'I said, I can't lift this painting on my own. It usually takes at least three people.'

'I heard you,' said Paul. He lied, realising with horror that he had been lost in his own thoughts.

'You two,' Paul called to the men who were still seated at the other end of the room, 'come and help . . . David . . . remove this painting . . . please.' *You've done it again. No need for politeness, you idiot.*

Coke Dick, Duncan and Charlie stared at each other with uncertainty.

'MOVE, NOW!' Paul turned around and realised his mistake. 'Coke Dick and ginger . . . man come here. You, other one . . . I don't know your name—'

'Charlie,' said Charlie.

'I don't need to know . . . just stay there. You other two come over here. NOW!'

Coke Dick and Duncan leapt off the modular sofa and walked quickly towards Paul, who responded by taking several sidesteps to maintain some distance in case they tried to jump him.

'OK, slow down! Easy!' By now, Paul had his back

against the side wall and was facing the door. Alexander stood facing the wall at the bottom left corner of the painting, with his right hand underneath and his left hand held above his head, gripping the side. Duncan was on the opposite corner.

'Duncan,' said Alexander, 'if you mirror me, it's quite heavy and you'll need to support it with both hands and then lift up and then down.' He had his back to Paul, so he used the opportunity to make eye contact with Duncan. Then he widened his eyes and moved his pupils quickly to the right to signal that this was their opportunity to knock Paul over with the painting. Duncan looked confused.

Being the shortest, Coke Dick slotted himself in the middle, gripping the base of the frame with both hands.

'On a count of three, then,' said Alexander. 'Lift up and then down. One, two, three!'

The painting came easily off the wall to reveal the safe. Thinking Duncan was working in tandem with him, Alexander expected him to pivot the painting ninety degrees and then slam it into the wall where Paul was leaning, but things didn't go to plan, mainly because that plan was solely in Alexander's head. Duncan had no idea that this was his moment to save the day. The result was that Alexander and Duncan wrestled the painting in opposite directions so that it remained parallel to the end wall with the bottom of the frame at waist height. Then Paul realised that the painting would rest nicely against the wall where he was standing, so he moved quickly out of the way, foiling Alexander's solipsistic ambush.

'You can put it over here.' The men obeyed. Alexander glared at Duncan, who responded by contorting his freckled face in even greater confusion. However, Paul hadn't anticipated that Coke Dick would make a move.

While the other two men took the weight of the painting and were leaning it against the wall, Coke Dick saw his one and only opportunity and took a running dive at Paul's legs. It was an impressive rugby tackle that floored Paul like a corner flag. As he fell backward, he hit his head on the low wooden drawers which ran along the wall and dropped the gun, which spun and clattered along the marble floor towards Charlie, who immediately sprang off the sofa and grabbed it.

Unfortunately for Charlie, he was the only person in the room who had never even held a gun before, let alone fired one. He stood with his legs wide apart and pointed the gun at Paul.

'Shoot him!' yelled David Alexander.

'Coke Dick scrambled away from Paul. As soon as he was out of the line of fire, he too shouted: 'Shoot him!'

'CHARLES! Fucking SHOOT him!'

To his credit, Charlie may have been a money launderer, petty criminal and wannabe politician, but he was no murderer: 'I can't!'

'Give me the gun!' Charlie stepped backwards and fired a warning shot into the ceiling. Alexander responded by kicking him hard between the legs; he snatched the gun as Charlie crumpled to the floor. Then Alexander strode over to Paul, who was sitting on the floor, feeling nauseous and mildly concussed and pointed the gun at his head.

'I thought you were a man of your word,' said Paul angrily. 'You said Blackout was the real enemy.'

'I am and he is' replied Alexander, 'but I also warned you that when you hold me at gunpoint and steal my money, that changes everything. Have you got anything to say before I end you?'

Paul looked momentarily terrified, then his face relaxed. He looked up at Alexander and said, quietly: 'What if I told you where Blackout is?'

Alexander laughed. 'How could you possibly know where that stupid ape is?'

'I can give you his exact location . . . he's standing over there, right behind you.'

Alexander darted his eyes to the right and back, expecting Paul to attempt a leg sweep while he was distracted. But Paul remained motionless, staring at the door. Standing in the doorway was the unmistakable monolithic figure of Blackout. He was wearing a grey funnel neck wool overcoat and carrying a black sports bag. His goatee beard jutted from his chin like a ship's prow.

'Hello David,' said Blackout. 'It's been a long time.'

'What . . . wh . . .?' For the first time in his adult life, David Alexander was lost for words.

'I hope that Paul has told you everything that happened. That it wasn't his fault. That I took the drugs and he thought I was still working for you. A very human mistake. But look at you. Reacting just how I knew you would. No compassion. No flexibility. You're a cruel man, David. But also, a cliché.'

'I . . . I . . . he came here with a gun and tried to rob me—'

'Whatever. I'm just saying what I see.'

'I wasn't going to kill him.'

'Whatever. That's why I came back. I couldn't let Paul suffer anymore. He's been through enough already.'

'Are the drugs in there?' Alexander nodded at the black sports bag.

'Oh yeah. You can have them. But in return, Paul and I walk out of here unharmed.'

'That sounds like a fair swap,' replied Alexander.

Blackout tossed the bag so that it landed with a heavy thud at Alexander's feet. Alexander unzipped it with his left hand and looked inside.

'There's only half here. There's half missing.'

'Oh yeah, I forgot to say. I didn't bring a gun, so the other half is somewhere safe. You can have it tomorrow morning if you let us both go.'

'Huh,' said Alexander, 'you didn't bring a gun?'

'That's correct.'

'And there's at least a million's worth in this bag?'

'Correct again.'

'Well, I think I'll cut my losses and cash in my chips. Thank you very much!' He aimed the gun at Blackout's head.

There was a loud crack as a gun discharged. Looking aghast, Alexander staggered backwards clutching his throat as blood started to flow from the flesh wound in his neck. Blackout pulled his hand from his overcoat pocket and fired a second shot into Alexander's hand, causing him to drop his gun. Paul scooped it up.

'I said I didn't *bring* a gun. I didn't say I didn't *have* one. I found this on the floor outside. You'll survive. You can keep your half. We'll keep ours. We're leaving now.'

Coke Dick, Duncan, Charlie Price and David Alexander put up no resistance as Paul and Blackout exited the building and walked to safety.

As Duncan busied himself tending to David Alexander's superficial bullet wounds, and Charlie Price sat nursing his testicles, Coke Dick began to feel that he had outstayed his welcome.

'Right, well I think our business is concluded.' He started to edge towards the door.

'Where are you going?' barked Alexander? 'I haven't finished with you.'

Duncan moved quickly to the door to block his escape.

Coke Dick sighed. 'Really?'

'Blackout is still one of *your* men' said Alexander, 'And I'm down £1 million.'

Coke Dick glanced at his wristwatch. 'Look,' he said, with a newfound confidence, 'do you really think I would come here without support? If I don't walk out of this building unharmed within the next five minutes . . .'

Coke Dick's swaggering speech was interrupted by the sound of breaking glass as a Molotov cocktail crashed through a window and landed on the huge Persian carpet in the neighbouring room.

'Oh' said Coke Dick, 'he's early.'

A second Molotov cocktail quickly followed. It landed on an expensive Kerstin Hörlin-Holmquist armchair. Despite its intensive fireproofing, it was no match for a litre of petrol. The third cocktail missed its target completely. Daniel hurled it with such enthusiasm that it landed on the roof of Alexander's three-storey mansion. It was the black smoke from this third incendiary that alerted his nearest neighbours, even though they were several hundred yards away. It was they who called the emergency services.

Daniel's soul lit up at the chaos he had created. He almost skipped into the burning building, where he quickly ran into Duncan. He fired two warning shots and Duncan dived for cover. Daniel was high on cannabis, he felt superhuman. He loved the euphoric feeling he had created with carnage everywhere in the luxury mansion. Then he spotted Coke Dick.

'Let's get out of here,' yelled Coke Dick to Daniel. 'I'm taking this!' He was carrying the sports bag. They hurried past the burning carpet in the direction of the exit, but before they could leave, a megaphone crackled into life outside.

'Armed police. You are surrounded. Surrender your weapons and leave the building with your hands up. DO IT NOW!'

Chapter Forty-Six

At 14:36 hrs the teleprinter at the retained fire station printed out the fire call message and ten alerters were activated, commanding the now ten on-call firefighters to attend the fire station.

Lee was the first person to arrive at the station. His alerter had buzzed while he was giving his statement to the police. This was the second shout of the day. Lee's nine colleagues already looked exhausted and they had barely had a few hours in which to begin to process the trauma of John Turnbull's murder. But every one of them had raced to the station to fulfil their obligation.

Lee collected the printed incident report and relayed instructions to both crews: 'House fire at 5, Treetop Heights – aka millionaire's row – persons and gunshots reported. Police and medical crews have been alerted.'

The two engines roared around the outskirts to an exclusive raised area of the town overlooking the sea about a mile and a half from the station. They raced up Kings Road towards the Heights, passing a large private school and its several tennis courts and playing fields. This was the exclusive area of Stockwood on Sea that they rarely visited. Lee parked his appliance and sent a radio message to the control room to inform them they were in attendance and that fire was in progress and that police and paramedics were already on the scene.

A plainclothes policeman approached Lee: 'My name is DCI David Walsh and I'm in charge of this operation. We've arrested four individuals who evacuated the building. One person, a teenage youth has escaped to the top floor and has now climbed onto the roof. Two armed officers are stationed on the third floor in case he tries to escape back through the house. The youth is armed and he's wanted for questioning in connection with the homicide and vehicle fire you attended this morning. We don't believe there are any persons trapped downstairs.'

'So, it's the same kid who killed John?' asked Lee.

'At the moment, he's our only suspect, so it's vital that we get him off the roof safely,' said Dave.

Both crews spilled out of their appliances and got to work. Matt, Alan, Mike and Sandi donned their breathing apparatus and Lee slotted their ID tags onto the BA board.

'Gauge check,' shouted Matt. They all checked their gauges and then the two couples ran into the building, as two yellow and black hoses unfurled behind them and immediately started to apply whoosh water to the burning carpet and multiple sofas and curtains. The concrete structure of the building was undamaged as David Alexander's taste in minimalism meant there was very little for the fire crews to extinguish. The fire had spread to the oak railings and banister of the grand staircase in the foyer; the crews quickly extinguished all the flames and were able to establish that there were no casualties.

Both crews went outside and examined the building: its highest point was a pitched roof with two dormer windows. It was ten metres from the ground, so they could easily reach it using their 13.5-metre ladder.

Daniel had climbed out of one of the dormer windows and was sitting astride its small, pitched roof. He had nowhere to go. There was no escape. Paramedics were on standby in case he jumped or fell. The police had three snipers stationed at various locations around the building, but Daniel could potentially stay up there for hours. The last thing anybody wanted was a long stand-off.

'I'm going in,' declared DCI Walsh. Two minutes later, both armed officers who had been upstairs with Daniel, exited the building, leaving DCI Walsh and Daniel alone. It soon became clear to the onlookers on the ground that DCI Walsh was attempting to initiate a dialogue with Daniel, although it was impossible to hear what they were saying. To everyone's amazement, Daniel suddenly raised the gun above his head before gently tossing it underarm onto the roof. It slid down with enough momentum to sail over the gutter and fall to the ground three storeys below.

Moments later, they both walked out of the front door to a chorus of clapping, whistles and cheers. DCI Walsh handed Daniel into the custody of two uniformed police officers, who guided him into the back of their patrol car. Then DCI Dave Walsh strolled over to Lee.

You guys take yourselves off now, you've had a hell of a day.'

'We will,' replied Lee. 'I have to say, that was amazing what you did there. What did you say to him?'

'Oh, you know, the usual,' replied Dave. 'Textbook stuff really. Active listening, establish a rapport, validate his feelings, demonstrate an understanding of where he's coming from . . . so we could move forward together to a resolution.'

'Right,' said Lee, scratching his head. 'So, what now?'

'Well, my team will recover whatever additional evidence they can from inside the house and ideally we'll get this lot banged up without bail.'

'You're Leah's husband, aren't you?'

'Yeah, yeah. I am.' A flash of panic crossed DCI Walsh's face. He looked like a man who had just remembered something very important that had slipped his mind.

'I thought I recognised you. How is she?'

'She's er . . . probably going bat-shit crazy at this precise moment, but she's making a good recovery.'

'Great, well tell her I said hello and that we're all thinking of her.'

'Will do. On second thoughts, I'm going to split now – got to take these reprobates down the nick – catch you later.'

DCI Walsh jumped into his unmarked car and screeched his tyres across the Cotswold stone chippings like a man who had left the gas on as well as several baths running.

Chapter Forty-Seven

The police officer opened the door to Leah's hospital room and Dr Srinivasan shuffled in looking bemused. He was wearing the same navy blue and silver striped tie and turquoise shirt as the day when he had given her the diagnosis and she had run away!

Leah guessed why he was here, but if she'd been superstitious, she wouldn't have known whether to interpret this sartorial coincidence as a good or bad omen.

'Good evening, Mrs Walsh—'

'Please called me Leah.'

'Very well. Leah . . . um . . . is everything OK?

'Oh yes, I'm not under house arrest, although it looks like that doesn't it? More for my protection. It's a long story. I'm hoping my husband will come back and explain . . . soon. He certainly has some explaining to do. This is my daughter, Katie.'

Katie smiled sweetly and fluttered her hand in a pseudo wave.

'Hello Katie. Um, well . . . Leah, I won't keep you . . . I just wanted to let you know that we have completed your biopsy. I'm sorry it's taken so long but the weekend got in the way. Anyhow, I'm pleased to say that the tumour is benign.'

'No cancer?'

'We found no cancer. There's a very small possibility that the tumour might grow back, but we believe we have removed all of it. This is a very good result for you.'

Katie burst into tears and hugged her mother.

'Thank you, Doctor. That's incredible.'

'Now you just need to rest and heal. If everything goes well, we'll be able to send you home quite soon.'

'Thank you.' Leah exhaled with a baneful mixture of relief and anxiety: the day that she got her life back, she had lost her husband.

'I'll see you in a few days' time. Goodbye for now.'

As soon as the doctor had gone, Leah confronted the other police officer: 'Look, my daughter can't stay here all night. You can't hold her against her will unless you arrest her. Also, we have a puppy at home alone who needs feeding and some human company. So, what the fuck happens now?' The relief of her prognosis was fuelling her rising anger.

Right on cue, Dave popped his head around the door. Leah immediately bristled. She could already sense that he was going to attempt to be jaunty.

'Where the fuck have you been?'

'I'm sorry, I've been . . . we've nicked David Alexander. We've got him. Nailed him. And Charlie Price and another big drug dealer called Coke Dick and we've caught the kid who we think killed John. We finally did it! It's huge.' Dave was beaming with spontaneous and genuine excitement.

'Katie needs to go home. The puppy's been on her own for hours. Can you take her?'

'My colleagues can take her. And while they're doing

that, I can explain everything. Thanks guys. You can knock off now, but can you drop my daughter home? Katie, have you got your key?'

Katie nodded, sulkily.

'Are you sure?'

'Yeah, I just said.'

'Well, you nodded. OK. See you at home later . . . love you.'

'There's some macaroni cheese left, which you could heat up. If you don't want that, there's burgers and curly fries in the freezer, OK?' said Leah. 'Dad will be home soon.'

They were finally alone. Silence. Leah sat in bed with her arms crossed, staring at her husband.

'I took the money,' said Dave. 'Alexander paid me £100,000 in exchange for making a crucial piece of evidence disappear. It was a portable hard drive. But it was inadmissible evidence, or at least, it would have been if we'd gone to court.'

'How convenient.'

'It was unlawfully gathered by a rookie colleague who didn't know what he was doing. If we'd gone to trial, Alexander's lawyer would have torn it apart and the case would have collapsed anyway, making us all look incompetent and potentially criminal. I only found this out at the last minute, so I struck a deal with Alexander to protect my colleague.'

'So, you took his money.'

'I had to. That way he thought he'd bought me, don't you see? It meant that I could spend all these years trying to nail the bastard, whilst all the time letting him think that I was bent.'

'You took his money. You broke the law.'

'You remember when our house got broken into?'

'Yes. But how's that—'

'Twice in two months. Smashed the place up both times but didn't steal anything.'

'Yeah?'

'That was Alexander warning me to stay out of his business. So, I took his money and let him think he'd bought me. The attacks stopped. It's kept us safe ever since.'

'Drug money though. Dirty money.'

'There's no such thing as clean money, Leah. OK, I admit, I broke the law. If my superiors found out, I'd lose my badge and I'd be sent to prison. Which was why I brought in those two police officers, to stop you from ruining everything. Now that we've nailed Alexander, you can do whatever you think is right, but I know I have a clear conscience. I took that money for the right reasons. And now that bastard is going to rot in prison for a long time.'

'Won't Alexander tell the police anyway?'

'It's my word against his. He has no proof. It was all cash.'

'You didn't have to spend it though, did you?'

'No, I didn't. But it would have been riskier to stash a hundred grand under the bed than spend it on my family. It's not like I bought a Ferrari. Although I suppose it did help to pay for Katie's horse and riding lessons.'

'Oh, God. This is a lot for me to take in. I feel so . . . You lied to me all these years.'

'Sometimes you have to fight fire with fire.'

'Ha!' Leah exploded with laughter. For the first time

since she could remember, she started laughing uncontrollably, tears flowing down her cheeks. 'You do *know* what I do for a living? Ha ha ha. I feel like I'm going to pop my stitches again! Ha hah!' At first, Dave was puzzled, then he too started laughing at the absurdity of his earnest remark.

When they both finally stopped laughing, the tension between them had dissipated.

'It's not cancer. The consultant just gave me the biopsy result. The tumour was benign.'

'Oh, thank God.' Dave started to cry. They hugged. Then Leah said, 'So, am I married to a future detective superintendent? What happened today?'

'Well, it's not just today. I've been working on this for years, but our big break came about twelve months ago, when we managed to turn a notorious hard man and drug dealer to work for us. His name is Blackout and he used to—'

'—work for David Alexander and then for Coke Dick,' said Leah.

'How do you know—'

'John Turnbull told me. They were in the army together. Blackout told John that he wanted to quit and that he'd been trying to bring down his current boss, Coke Dick, then found out that Alexander was planning a big drop – 30 kilos of coke – this was his way out.'

'That's right, but we put him in there, although initially, we didn't know where or when. Then two weeks ago we got a breakthrough. Coke Dick bought a gun on the black market. He showed it to Blackout, who recognised that it belonged to Paul the water guy, because they had worked together years ago for Alexander. If Paul was selling his gun, that meant he needed to raise a large amount of cash quickly. Which probably meant he was in trouble. Paul's son, Dean had recently had his leg broken, so Blackout made the connection. He confronted Dean, who confessed that he had gone behind Coke Dick's back to do a job for Alexander, which had gone wrong, landing him twenty-five grand in debt. So, we put surveillance on Dean and Paul and waited for one of them to make the drop, which Paul did, later that week. We followed him to a tyre dump on waste ground in front of the old steelworks.

'Next, we stopped tracking Paul and instead watched that drop site night and day for the whole of the next week, hoping that they'd use it again for the big 30-kilo drop. But last Thursday, my boss pulled the plug and told us it was a waste of resources. That was the very same day that you found out all that juicy shit about Alexander and his dodgy planning reversals with Charlie Price, but then you collapsed, so you didn't tell me until Saturday evening. That's why I rushed off with Katie, even though you begged me to stay, remember? I took Katie home and then I used your evidence to convince the boss to give us another three days of surveillance. I couldn't have done it without your discovery.

'The very next evening – last night – the big drop was made in the tyres. We couldn't believe our luck – although, it wasn't luck because we'd been watching the site for ten days, with Blackout on standby. Paul arrived and Blackout took the drugs from him. We knew then for sure that Paul was being coerced because he said something to Blackout about his son's safety. We also knew that taking the drugs was going to drop Paul in the shit, but we guessed that so long as we kept Blackout out of sight, Paul would try to approach Alexander to plead for his life.

'So we went back to the boss, who was very happy to let us stake out David Alexander's gaffe with armed police, because we'd been right about the drop. There were several things we hadn't expected. We didn't know Paul was going to show up with a fucking gun and when Blackout heard a gunshot and ran in unarmed to rescue him, we didn't expect him to pick up a gun from the floor of the foyer, although it's lucky that he did because it saved both their lives.

'We didn't foresee the bonus of being able to arrest Coke Dick and Charlie Price at Alexander's house. That's the end of both their careers. But we also didn't anticipate the arrival of one-delinquent army, Daniel-fucking-Lewin.

'What's going to happen to him?' asked Leah.

'It depends on what we can get to stick. There's no usable DNA at the scene to link him to the murder. If we do get a confession, he will most likely claim self-defence. John confided in Blackout that he'd been paying Daniel to start bin fires, to increase the shout rate of the station. Stupid bastard. This morning, John told Lee Stones that he was going to pay Daniel a visit because he was convinced that he started the pub fire. So, we've got lots of leads to follow.'

'What happens to the station now?' asked Leah.

'The station is safe. We'll question everyone involved, starting with Graeme Dollins – Charlie Price has already started squealing. By this time next week, we'll have a full confession from him and we'll be able to arrest anyone who has been corruptly involved in its attempted closure.'

'Did you know that Blackout told John that you accepted money from Alexander? John told me. Why would he do that and jeopardise everything if he was working for you?'

'Maybe he didn't trust me completely and confiding in his old friend John was a smart act of self-preservation, to give himself some blackmail leverage in case I double-crossed him. But he didn't know that you and John knew each other. He wouldn't have realised that he was undermining everything. Shit, if I hadn't stopped you from phoning my boss, things would be very different right now.'

'Yeah, OK, I get it. For the greater good . . . blah blah blah.'

'For the lesser of two evils, you mean. Daniel must be about fifteen years old. He's progressed from bin fires to homicide in a few short weeks. If he goes to prison, he'll remain a violent criminal for the rest of his life. No chance of redemption. I had to talk him down from the roof. He was threatening to shoot someone or jump. He was a mess. But I'm proud to say that I gently talked some sense into him.'

'What did you say?'

Dave grinned. 'Oh, sorry – it's classified.'

'Go on, tell me.'

'Well, it was basic male psychology. I gave him a choice: I promised that if he surrendered, I would buy him a McDonalds Chocolate McFlurry.'

'And if he didn't?'

'If he didn't . . . then, I would have had no choice but to shoot him in the balls.'

ABOUT THE AUTHORS

LES JONES got involved in firefighting in 1980 at 20 years old, and worked at a large chemical company. Due to its risk and hazards, the company had its own internal fire service. This continued into another chemical industrial role until 1996. He attended external training courses including attending the Fire Service College in Gloucestershire.

He became a member of the IFE (Institute of Fire Engineers) and sat their examination at Crewe Fire Station in 1994. He became assistant team leader of the eight-person crew on his shift and focused on training and fire drill events.

In 1996 he became a police officer and found himself torn between Policing and the Fire Service as he had opportunities with both organisations. He spent 20 years in both uniform and plain clothes duties.

MIKE POWELL is a former RADA-trained professional actor, musical director and managing editor in book publishing. For the last 20+ years he has been an author, with 150+ books, including many bestsellers, published by a wide range of industry leaders on topics as varied as world history, virulent diseases, international etiquette, serial killers, puzzles and brain training to popular culture, humour and the performing arts. He lives in Cardiff with his wife, their two grown-up children and a golden retriever called Douglas.

STEVE EGGLESTON is a law school Valedictorian, former law professor, author, lecturer, and colourful trial lawyer. In his renaissance life, he has launched a hip-hop start-up, produced feature films, helmed a rock 'n roll magazine, booked 1000+ live shows worldwide, and managed Grammy-winning artists. As an international bestselling author, he is published in fiction and non-fiction and lives with his family in Somerset, England, where he draws and paints in his free time. Steve's business can be found on steveegglestonwrites.com.

ALSO BY LES JONES

BELLS THE FIRE DOG

One orphaned puppy. One red ball. One brave heart.

"Bells whimpered out loud. There was a strange horrible smell that burned her nostrils and stung her eyes. She couldn't breathe. She couldn't see a thing for all the swirling, thick, smoky stuff. And it was getting so hot. There was a frightening roaring noise and something huge, orange and wild was dancing closer and closer..."

When Bells the Cocker Spaniel puppy is left all alone in the world after losing her family in a terrible fire, she believes she will never be happy again. Then, just when she thinks her favourite red ball and her new girl, Katie, are helping to heal her heart, Bells' life changes forever when she is sent to London to train as a fire investigator dog. London is a big and noisy, and Turnout the trainer dog is fierce and scary.

And how will Bells ever become a brave Fire Dog is she is terrified of fire? And if she fails to earn her badge will she end up being sent to the dreaded Dog's Home?

BELLS THE FIRE DOG

LES JONES & STEVE EGGLESTON

FROM THE WRITERS OF 12 DOORS

Printed in Great Britain
by Amazon